When Kingdom Comes

When Kingdom Comes

Ashea S. Goldson

www.urbanchristianonline.com

Urban Books, LLC
97 N18th Street
Wyandanch, NY 11798

ISBN 13: 978-1-60162-666-0
ISBN 10: 1-60162-666-5

First Trade Paperback Printing August 2014
Printed in the United States of America

10 9 8 7 6 5 4 3 2 1

*This is a work of fiction. Any references or similarities
to actual events, real people, living or dead, or to real
locales are intended to give the novel a sense of reality.
Any similarity in other names, characters, places, and
incidents is entirely coincidental.*

Distributed by Kensington Corp.
Submit Wholesale Orders to:
Kensington Publishing Corp.
C/O Penguin Group (USA) Inc.
Attention: Order Processing
405 Murray Hill Parkway
East Rutherford, NJ 07073-2316
Phone: 1-800-526-0275
Fax: 1-800-227-9604

When Kingdom Comes

by

Ashea S. Goldson

Dedication

To anyone who has ever feared that God's Kingdom
would not come to pass on earth, or who has ever
doubted that they would see God's goodness in the land
of the living: May this story restore your faith and give
you hope.

Dedication

Acknowledgments

To my eternal and loving Father, for once again blessing me to do what I do. It is an honor and a privilege to bring these words to life. Thank you for giving me an awesome job to do for your Kingdom.

To my immediate family, Donovan, Anais, Safiya, Jamal, Syriah, Jamian, Symari, and Aria for taking this awesome life journey with me. What would my life be without you all to share it with?

To Mommy, for your love, continual support, and encouragement. What would I do without our Sunday evening chats?

To Grandma Ruthell, for always having a *sharp* word in due season.

To Tamicka McCloud, my sister-friend for life, thank you for sixteen years of love and adventure.

To my godchildren Emmanuel, Hannah, and Faith, thanks for keeping me young at heart.

To Pastor Frank Salters and First Lady Merriam Salters of Word of Faith Light of Joy Church, for always bringing forth the Word with honesty and integrity.

To The Parable Players Drama Ministry at LOJ, and most especially Leslie Daniels, whose passion for life and ministry inspires me.

To LOJ choir, my fellow worshippers, for allowing my love of singing to be used for God's glory.

To my old friends since childhood: Bernadette Page (best friend since fifth grade), Sherri Holmes-Knight,

Acknowledgments

Hope Raymond, Joy Jones-Garrett, and Pastor Alfonso Jackson, thanks for still believing in me, even after twenty-five years.

To Elva Branson-Lee, my writing partner and friend, thank you for your listening ears, for your creative feedback, and for hot-java time.

To LaToya Forrest-Heard, my spiritual daughter, for always being a blessing to me and to the body of Christ!

To my editor, Joylynn Ross, thank you for always demanding the best from me even as you lead by example.

To my literary agent, Sha-Shana Crichton, of Crichton & Associates, thank you for keeping my business in order!

To the Kingdom writers of the WordThirst Writers group. You can do all things through Christ who strengthens you.

To my writer-sisters, Rhonda McKnight, Veronica Johnson, Shawneda Marks, Dwan Abrams, Tia McCollors, Kendra Norman-Bellamy, Sherri Lewis, Roishina Henderson, Rhonda Irby, and Denise (Chicki) for encouraging me since the beginning.

To my students everywhere, thank you for cheering me on as I run this race. You are the future!

To all the Christian fiction authors, trailblazers, my fellow writers, bloggers, social media organizers, book clubs, reviewers, and radio hosts: Thank you for promoting, tweeting, hosting, or encouraging me in some way. To all of those who helped make this book a reality or a success, thank you for all of your support.

To anyone who has not specifically been named—and most especially my readers and fans—thank you for whatever part you have played in my life, big or small. I appreciate you all!

Chapter 1

The moment the prison guards released me and the miracle of daylight hit my sun-deprived skin, my eyelids released a tear, my soul leaped, and my lungs began to ache for the taste of a cigarette. Believe it or not, I'd never smoked before I went to prison, but a group of very persuasive, big-boned women turned me onto it. They were not the kind of women who cared about health or moral responsibility. No, they were all convicts of the worst kind: dangerous and yet defenseless. They spent their free time puffing out rings of cigarette smoke in a quest to soothe their wounded soul, as if any external thing could actually reconcile their crimes. I wasn't exactly like them, yet despite my resolve, I was one of them. I was lonely and seeking solace within the confines of the Louisiana Correctional Institution.

Desperate, drained, and feeling like the life had been sucked out of me, I figured I might as well fill up on something. So what if it was nicotine and smoke? So what if my lungs ended up exploding into a dark black mass? I'd seen the public-service announcements on television but I didn't care about that, either. And why should I have? Up until a few days ago I thought my life was over, anyway. There's nothing like a six-year stint on death row to put things into perspective.

I was released on the first Monday in April. Flowers were blooming everywhere and yet my spirit had already withered and died. I looked back one last time to take in the enormity of the prison compound, all seventy-five acres of it. Unlike similar facilities I'd heard about, there were no searchlights, capped towers, or barbed-wire fences. Truly, with its meticulously landscaped lawns, a fully equipped playground, and a prison courtyard with flowing fountains, it looked more like a college campus than a prison. But just like everything you could see, looks were deceiving. Built in 1970, it was merely a glorified holding pen with a capacity of 1,084 women, buried deep in the swamps of southern Louisiana. It was a place I'd spent what seemed like a lifetime diminishing in spirit each day as the calendar and the judges marked my time.

My first day back on the streets was nothing short of surreal. I closed my eyes and I could see the visions again, purple and red-like dusk at first, then even softer images appeared until I saw my son Justin's face. Once again, I didn't know what the visions meant. I tried to blink them away until my sight was blurred, but I only ended up with a headache. I gently rubbed the sides of my temples to ease the pain, then closed and opened my eyes again. This time I saw nothing, but still the vision bothered me. I just knew I had to get home to Justin and figure out what was wrong.

Mama had taken me to the eye doctor the first time I complained about *seeing* things. Believing that I needed glasses, she spent an hour and a half going off about how blind I was. As it turned out, my eyesight was twenty-twenty.

As I walked toward the bus stop, I realized there was no one there to meet me, to put their arms around me and tell me everything was going to be okay; not my mother, not my son. Not even my sweetheart, Smooth.

I'd been pining away for Mr. Smooth McGee the whole time I was locked up, full of sorrowful memories and deep regrets. He wrote me letters from time to time and even visited me once. That's when I told him not to come back again. My heart couldn't stand seeing the ones I loved, knowing I couldn't ever join them on the outside. By my fifth year Smooth and I lost touch altogether. One of my letters was marked *return to sender—address unknown.* It broke my heart to know he'd slipped away from me, but at that time, I felt like I was slipping away from him. Now that I was surprisingly free, who could I depend on to help me through the healing process? Was there really healing after death row? Perhaps that was wishful thinking.

I trembled with anticipation as I stepped aboard the public bus, placed my coins into the fare box, and rode as far away from St. Gabriel as I could. It was a trip I once thought I'd never take again. I squeezed into a seat beside a muscular young man with a shiny bald head. He had tattoos all over his arms and neck. Looking down at his muscular thigh, I realized it was twice the size of mine and I was no small woman. He sat up high, with biceps piled upon triceps, looking straight ahead, and I wondered if he spent every hour of his probably twenty-plus years working out in the gym. I smiled as he stretched out his bulging arms, almost touching me.

Despite my attempt not to stare at his dark, chiseled face and sculpted body, I soon found it necessary to fan myself with a piece of cardboard I'd picked up along the way. I quickly realized I'd been locked up with women for too long.

The bus driver took LA-74, then made the first left onto LA-30. I looked out of the huge bus windows, admiring the cars passing by as we rolled down the street. I hadn't seen cars since I was put in prison and many of them looked different now. SUVs and pickup trucks seemed to be even larger than they were before, but cars seemed to be smaller and many were more turtle-shaped. Some even had funny-shaped lights.

Finally, the bus driver made a right onto Government Street. I could hardly believe I was experiencing the outside world again. Lately, my attorney had been trying to prepare me for my departure, but my head was full of so much noise, I couldn't really hear him. I'd dreamed of this day for so long; freedom never seemed possible. Once I remembered dreaming that I'd escaped and hopped on a public bus until a swarm of police cars caught up to me. In the dream, I swallowed my spit and looked around as an army of uniformed officers opened fire on me. Thankfully, it was just a lucid dream. Maybe this bus ride was all a dream too. Maybe I was really still asleep in my cell with the smell of death just days away.

Then I opened my eyes just in time to recognize the bus pulling into my stop. I stood up and hurried toward the door, wiping the sweat from my forehead.

"Have a nice day, now," the bus driver said as I climbed down the stairs carefully. I looked back, not knowing what to say or how to answer. Years of confinement had stolen my sense of courtesy. Awkwardly, I forced a smile, something I hadn't done in a long time. When I got off of the bus, I sniffed in the fresh, dew-covered grass that tickled my nose. This was the closest I'd come to freedom since the public defender told me I'd be released. I'd been so isolated for so long, locked away in what seemed like my destiny. After all I'd been through I was just grateful to be free of what we'd affectionately called "the death house." I took a deep breath and although I was sure I'd taken in more than my fair share of hot, mosquito-ridden air, I was home. After six years, God help me, I was finally back in Baton Rouge.

After getting off the bus at the little depot, I hitched a ride with a local truck driver the rest of the way. He had a long, grayish-red beard and he smelled like burned popcorn.

"Thanks," I said as I stepped off of the bread truck in Baton Rouge.

"No problem," the truck driver said as his big stomach lapped over the steering wheel. "See ya around."

I let my eyes smile but didn't answer. I didn't want to be too friendly. Mama always said I was too friendly, especially to menfolks.

I took a long look around and realized that not much had changed. As I walked toward the dilapidated little shack I used to call home, apprehension filled me where the cigarettes had left space. I stepped onto the rickety staircase that led up to the front porch, taking another deep breath. I laid my head against the door before knocking, hoping to hear any sign of life or happiness, so much so that the strands of hair from my unkempt ponytail became tangled in the splinters of wood. I carefully peeled myself loose and stood upright. Was Mama the same way? I hadn't seen or talked to her in over two years. By the end of the fourth year Mama claimed to be too sick to make the trip down to the prison. Had she changed at all? When I touched it, the door was still warm. My heart beat with a familiar intensity. I was home. I knocked, then waited. Finally, the screen door swung open and there was Uncle Charlie.

"Gal," he said, taking a step back and adjusting his glasses. "You out?"

"Yes, Uncle Charlie," I answered. "I'm home."

Uncle Charlie's front teeth were missing. "You ain't on the run, is you? 'Cause . . ."

"No, I'm officially free." I wrapped my arms around Uncle Charlie's frail body and he squeezed me back. I braced myself. "Where is Justin?"

With my eyes, I frantically searched the room for my son.

"He's in school down the road, you know. I reckon he'll be home on the bus soon."

My heart began to beat faster with anticipation. "Soon?" I looked at my watch. I'd forgotten that it was a school day.

I couldn't wait to see my son, knowing he could've been neatly tucked away in foster homes for the past six years since Mama didn't like taking care of him. Mama never liked children, period, said she never should've even had me, my sister, or my no-good brother. Secretly, I'd hoped Mama had at least learned to love him. Would Justin even remember me? I'd been taken away when he was three. He was nine now.

Uncle Charlie turned toward Mama's room. "Rosalee, Trinity is here."

There it was, *Trinity*. I hated the sound of my name because it was everything I wasn't: beautiful and whole.

Long before I was even born, Nana named me Trinity. I was told that Nana would anoint my mother's belly with olive oil and pray over me. Despite Mama's belligerent protests, Nana decided her son's first child, her first grandchild, should be branded with the Father, the Son, and the Holy Ghost. And since that first day, I'd been called Trinity. Nana prayed that God's spirit would follow me.

I must say that God has been with me all of my life, saving me from my wretched environment and more importantly, saving me from myself. Not that I've ever been *saved*, sanctified, or filled with the Holy Ghost. In fact, the truth was far from that. I knew I was a heathen. Still, I also knew God was real and I was too afraid to play with Him. I truly believed that if a person claimed Him at all, then they should do right by Him.

Suddenly, Mama appeared in the doorway of her bedroom, looking older than she did the last time I'd seen her. Her body appeared soft and lumpy all over, kind of like an uncooked biscuit. Her long, silky silver hair, pinned underneath a scarf, framed her peach-colored face and dull gray eyes. I moved toward her with caution. She didn't move. I imagined that she was stunned. I'd been released without warning. Not that I hadn't tried to call her, but apparently the phone had been disconnected for the past few days. I guess Mama was still having problems with paying her bills, despite her and Uncle's combined retirement benefits. Social Security sure wasn't all that it was made out to be. So nothing could've prepared her for this, her baby girl coming home from death row.

I imagined I must've looked like a ghost to my mother, since I had only been weeks from my official expiration date. I imagined that she'd already reconciled my death in her mind. It had certainly been reconciled in my own mind. Yet, here I was, standing before her, thinking, walking, and breathing in new air. Yes, I was still alive. The system that prosecuted me and sentenced me to death, hadn't killed me. Despite all of my suffering, I was still here. God must've had a purpose for my life, although I didn't have a clue what it was.

Mama squinted her eyes. "Gal, you home?"

"I'm home, Mama." I moved toward her awkwardly. "I tried to call a few days ago."

Mama didn't move, just stared at me. "Oh, bill collectors kept calling, so I had to change the number."

I wrapped my arms around her and squeezed, trying to feel her love, trying to fill that hole in my heart. Mama didn't squeeze back. Maybe she was disappointed that I didn't die.

Mama broke out of our embrace and headed toward her recliner. "Sho' am glad to see ya, gal."

I followed her to her chair and kneeled down beside her. "I'm glad to see you too."

Uncle Charlie sat on the cloth couch with the faded stripes.

Mama leaned forward. "How did you get out of there?"

"They let me go," I whispered, still unable to fully comprehend what had happened.

"Let you go?" Mama's eyes danced with excitement.

"Yes, the court reversed my conviction." I slapped my hands together. "And let me walk out free and clear."

"That's real nice, but what happened?" Mama continued. "Why would they do something like that?"

"The real killer confessed, Mama," I explained. "It should be in the newspapers."

"You know I don't read no newspapers." Mama sucked on her tongue, something she did when she didn't have her teeth in.

Uncle Charlie cleared his throat. "Confessed?"

My eyes welled up with tears. "The real woman who murdered those people, the Hartfords , finally confessed. She told them she wanted to clear her conscience after all these years, that she wanted to wipe her slate clean."

Mama raised her eyebrows. "Wipe her slate clean? What kind of cow dung is that?"

"Well, as it turns out, she's very sick and they don't think she'll even make it to trial." I didn't like having to explain. Weeks after finding out, the truth still made me cringe.

Mama frowned up her face. "A woman, eh? But she had you rottin' away in prison all these years?"

"Yes, but she wanted to say something before I was executed." It was still hard to tell the story.

Mama swallowed hard. "A fine time for that, don't you think?" Then she lifted herself up and began to pace the floor.

I knew it was time for Mama's nerve medicine. I could see it in her twitching eyes.

"I'm not bitter, though. I'm just grateful she came forward before it was too late." My eyes darted back and forth between Mama and Uncle Charlie.

For years I wondered, Why would anyone come into that diner, go mad, and shoot all those people? More importantly or at least of equal importance, I wondered why had a stranger said it was me? It was one of those freak things I'd never be able to figure out. Now, after having some answers, I just wondered what my life would have been like if I hadn't gone to prison. Before I went away, I'd been saving money to go to beauty school so I could do something worthwhile with my life.

I sank down into the old sofa. "How is Alyssa?"

"Alyssa, she's all right, I guess." Mama still moved about. "She don't come by here much."

I could certainly understand that. My sister and I had never been very close to our mother. In fact, when we were teenagers we used to make bets on who would leave home the fastest.

My sister, Alyssa, who was only one year my junior, was a lawyer—not a criminal lawyer, but the kind who looks after corporate accounts and stuff. She'd done really well for herself and had practically renounced me when I went away to prison. Since she felt that my criminal record would taint her public image, she carefully separated herself from me; not all at once, but like peeling away the layers of an onion. It didn't bother me much though, because we were never that close either. Oil and water is what my mother affectionately called us, although she never cared much for either of us, to tell you the truth.

My brother, James, just two years younger than me, was the one I'd been the closest to. Unfortunately, he'd been killed in a round of gang violence when he was just fifteen. His death shocked us all. It must've hurt Mama too, but we never saw her cry. Not one tear. Instead, she had him buried quickly, then had all of his things removed from the house in the middle of the night.

Since Mama happily proclaimed, throughout the years, that she never wanted kids, my sister and I believed her. Sadly, when our dad left, so did the dream of possibly having a normal family. When I got older I wondered if Mama even knew what a real family was. I watched her slowly shuffle around the small living room and I felt sorry for her.

Then suddenly, I heard a creaking of the floorboards coming from the front door and I held my breath. My heart began to beat fast as I waited in anticipation.

Chapter 2

I stood up just in time to see Justin coming in, swinging his backpack beside him. I lunged forward, looking into his dark eyes. He was the spitting image of his father: tall and slender, but strong-looking. Carefully, I pulled his body toward mine, holding him close. I could feel his heartbeat against my chest. He was the son I hadn't seen in six years, the son I'd lived for, and the one I'd die for.

All of the memories came rushing back. Me, holding him after he was born, the fuzzy-headed baby boy who was so dark around the ears. His father had been standing over us, grinning with pride. Life was good back then, for a little while at least. I remembered Justin learning to walk in our little apartment off Bourbon Street. He'd wobble across the linoleum floors and land in one of our arms with a giggle. Later, we'd collapse into bed with all of the love and admiration for each other and for our child. Those were such easy times. I guessed that's why New Orleans was called the Big Easy. Why couldn't things have stayed like that? Maybe if things had been different, maybe the police wouldn't have gotten me *that* night. Maybe if my husband and I had still been together, he would've fought for me and not let them take me. But unfortunately, they had.

My mind returned to the present and to the child I still held in my arms. Tears spread across my face now as I took in his scent, all boy. My boy. He had the smell of the streets and I worried about what he'd been into while I was away for so long. I ran my hand across his uneven Afro. He badly needed a haircut.

"I missed you," I finally found the courage to say.

"I missed you too." Justin was crying also.

I loosed him. "Do you know who I am?"

Justin stared into my eyes. "Of course I do. How could I forget my own mom?"

After all I'd been through, his words were like magic to my ears and heart. I hugged him again and again, just like I'd imagined it for the past few days.

Although I'd been stuck on death row, no threat of le-thal-injection poisons flowing through my veins could've kept me from my baby. And I knew God had ordained for me to be here. I didn't know why I had to ever go to prison in the first place, but I knew why I was standing there. It was something Nana called *grace and mercy*. I wasn't sure which one applied to this particular situation or even what the difference between them was. But I knew I was blessed to be there. Tears began to roll down from the corners of my cheeks. Nana always said my high cheekbones favored the American Indian. Mama said I was just black and ugly like my daddy, with no Indian features at all.

Either way, at that moment, standing free in front of my son, I knew I was special. Somewhere deep on the inside, I knew that God loved me. Me and my son were destined to be together after so many years of being kept apart. I closed my eyes for a moment and a million memories ran through my mind: my baby shower, the night he was born, his first day of preschool. Then I opened my eyes, only to stare into my son's bright ones. His large eyes were one of the only signs that he was mine and that his father had not just spat him out. And when he smiled, I saw *my* dimple, the last physical link to me. He was such a product of his father's strong genes.

"Don't know how in the world anyone could be so stupid." The sound of Mama's shrill voice was like a rock to my soul, dragging me back to reality.

Reluctantly, I let Justin go and ran out to the kitchen to find Mama leaned over a knife and bleeding.

I eyed her curiously. "What's the matter, Mama?"

Mama squawked, "Somebody left this darn thing out."

She grasped her wound with her other hand, her body a mass of peculiarity.

"It's a knife, Mama," I snapped.

"Ya think I don't know what it is?" Mama threw the knife into the sink. "It cut me. That's what it did."

"Let me look at it." I reached for her hand just as she pulled it away.

Mama eyed her wound without looking up at me. "Naw, I don't want you to touch it."

"Why not? I've always been good with things like that."

Mama snickered. "Gal, go on with yo' foolishness. You might've picked up one of them jail diseases from that filthy place. Only God knows what . . ."

I swallowed my spit, unable to believe what Mama had just said. "You're right. Only God knows." I backed away from her, feeling a distance between us like never before. It was one different than the space of a generation, but one of a mother who had devoured her child.

I couldn't feel Mama's love. I could hardly feel anything. How could she say such a thing, without knowing the pain I'd suffered and the insecurity I felt? What kind of monster would remind me of the darkest years of my life?

I remembered the day my life changed like it was yesterday. It was a normal evening, with the sun setting like any other. I'd been serving tables all day and I was just about to go into a double shift to make up for the child-support check that was late again. I'd been sauntering between tables, flashing my pretty white teeth, insuring that I'd get all the tips I deserved when an argument broke out between two customers. I remember that it happened so fast I hardly knew where the noise was coming from. Everyone was confused. Then there was a gunshot and the next thing I knew, people were running and screaming. The sound reverberated in my ears. Then there were more shots, one, two, then three. Somehow I landed under a table, but I didn't remember ducking there. Maybe I was pushed.

When I opened my eyes, my boss, his wife, his fourteen- and fifteen-year-old daughters and three other staff members were dead: a total of seven white people. I must've been knocked down and trampled on in the crowd, because the next thing I knew, I was being lifted up from the floor by the police. Blood covered my hands, my face, and my chest. It was everywhere. Surprisingly, I had a gun in my hands. One of the customers, an older white lady I had never seen before, told the police that a colored girl had shot my boss and his wife. Hmph. *A colored girl*? I knew, without even looking at her, that she had to be really old. So I turned around to look at her.

She was small, wrinkled, and hunchbacked. She wore her thin gray hair up in a bun and she wore what looked like bifocals on her speckled face. I took a deep breath and waited to hear what she would say about the perpetrators, about the argument. Then she looked past the policeman, pointed her bony little finger toward me, looked into my eyes with her bright blue ones, and said, "She did it. She shot all those people." That's when everything went black.

Finally, my thoughts returned to the present and after a couple of awkward hours of helping in the kitchen, I settled down with my son.

I sat across from him in one of Mama's corduroy-covered armchairs. "So you're in the fourth grade now, then?"

Justin nodded as he grinned with pride. "Yes, ma'am."

"How are your grades?" I reached over to touch his hand. "I hope you got your brains from your father."

"Sho' know he wouldn't get the brains from you, that's for sure," Mama said, trotting out of the kitchen.

I'd never done well in school. The lessons always seemed like one big puzzle I couldn't figure out. Mama just called me stupid all the time. I knew I could learn, but not in the way I was being taught. It was amazing that I'd graduated at all. But with the help of a few friends and my sister, I was able to accomplish the bare minimum, and escape the Louisiana public school system. I now had a diploma that said I successfully completed high school and I didn't know how true the *successfully* part was, but I was able to put that phase behind me.

Justin reached down to pick up a football. "School's okay, but I like football a lot better."

"Football." I remembered my vision. "That's a little dangerous for someone your size, isn't it?"

"Naw, I'm pretty good." Justin chuckled. "Coach says in a few years, I'll be much bigger and even better."

I grabbed both of his arms. "Well, that's probably true, but what about you getting hurt now?" I couldn't help it; my fears were running away with me.

Justin hunched his shoulders. "I'm really strong, even though I'm small. I'm sure I can handle it."

I felt a warmth in my heart for him like never before. He looked so much like his father and yet he was so much like me—determined. "It's been a long day. How about we turn in, now?"

"Sounds good. I'm kind of tired too," Justin agreed. "I'll go take my shower first."

I remained sitting on the couch until it was my turn to use the bathroom. When I came out, Uncle Charlie stopped me before I made it to the bedroom.

"Here are some more clean towels fer ya." He smiled. "Good night, child."

"Good night, Uncle Charlie." I smiled back at him. "Good night, Mama." I leaned my head against her bedroom door.

Mama just yelled back, "Gal, it's hot, so don't run that fan all night and run up my electric bill."

"Don't worry. I won't." I walked into the room that once belonged to me. It had been Justin's room for the past six years and I looked forward to spending more time with my son. Justin was already asleep in his own twin bed in the corner of the room, the same one I'd purchased for him before I went away. Did he usually go to sleep this early?

I stopped in front of the dresser mirror and took a look at my reflection. I took down my hair from its ponytail and let my long, curly locks fall down to my shoulders. I was clearly a mix between my mother's creole-mulatto pale skin and straight, waist-length hair and my father's jet-black Mandingo-warrior complexion with tight, coarse curls.

I scoffed at my burnt-sienna skin with mid-length curls. At its best, my hair was wavy when wet, and at its worst, it was a kinky, curly disaster. Either way, it was nowhere near being straight like Mama liked. And my eyes were big enough to see right to heaven, as Nana used to say. Mama said my eyes always saw too much and that if I ever told her business outside of the house, she'd poke them both out. My full lips and teeth were okay, but when I went beyond my shoulders, that's where I had to draw the line. I didn't really like my fully curvaceous body, although men seemed to. It had caused me too much drama over the years and all I wanted was to cover it up and pretend that it didn't exist.

I had hips that were too wide, in my opinion, enough buttocks to squash anyone flat, and a bust line that made fitting into the average bras a terror. Mama said I used my body to entice men, which was one of the reasons why I had so much bad luck. Maybe Mama was right. I was only twenty-nine and yet I did have my share of short-lived relationships, often brought on by a common bout of lust. I shook my head at the thought of my mistakes, deciding to give up on me and go to bed. *What a mess.*

Just sleeping in my own bed was like a luxury to me. Soft comforter, pillows, and paisley sheets. Mama always loved paisley. Nothing like that in prison, I thought as I remembered the iron cot I used to lie on, staring helplessly at the ceiling. I turned off the lamp and waited for sleep to come. When it did, I slept in my bed greedily, hoping I could somehow drift away into another world. I wanted to escape to a world where there was no disappointment and no pain. No matter how hard I slept, I was stuck in this one.

In my dreams I kept hearing the doors of the prison slamming shut. I kept seeing the faces of the cruel guards who liked to spit in my face and put their hands on me. After that last incident, when a guard busted my jaw because of my smart remark, I'd promised myself and God I wouldn't let another soul put his or her hands on me, male or female.

It didn't even bother me anymore that I'd been locked up for something I didn't even do. In fact, I was numb to the fact that I'd never laid a hand on any of the Hartfords and never even said one bad thing about them. And it wasn't because I liked them or anything, either, but they weren't bad employers as far as employers go. I'd had worse, much worse. Like my job at the butcher shop, where I had blood squirting out everywhere or Sheila's Barbecue Shack, where Sheila's daughter—who couldn't count worth anything—kept messing up the register and blaming it on me. Then there was that two-month assignment at the car-rental company, where the manager kept eyeing me and finding reasons to touch me like I was his dessert.

No, working for the Hartfords was nothing like that. They'd always been pretty fair to me, at least as much as I could tell. They always paid me on time, let me get some days off every now and then, and they didn't mind if I came in a minute or two late once in a while when my car broke down. They weren't bad people and anybody in their right mind would know I had no reason to want to kill them.

But seeing them dead that day did something to me on the inside. Even before the police arrested me, I was sick. Seeing their bloody bodies, piled up on one another like that: Mr. Hartford and then Mrs. Hartford, and their daughters, dead together, shot in the head and torso. Seeing them shot to death—or as my paternal grandmother would've said, "shot to thy kingdom come"—did something to me. I was never the same again. How could I have been?

Indicted in April and convicted and sent to death row by mid-September, I boarded the bus and was taken twelve miles south of Baton Rouge to St. Gabriel's. Surrounded by other inmates, hardened and repeat offenders who were in for the selling of narcotics, burglary, fraud, or homicide, I learned to survive. During my time there, one judge would sign a death warrant, then I'd wait for a stay of execution. On the basis of all kinds of inconsistencies during my original trial, including the specifics of the police investigation and the prosecution's conduct, I had my public defender file all kinds of appeals from the state to the federal level. I'd been caught up in litigation for so long, trying to appeal. I'd proclaimed my innocence to anyone who would listen. Yet the system left me frustrated and imprisoned. Time after time I was led away in handcuffs and ankle chains back to my rugged cell. By the time I had appealed to habeas corpus, my chances were done. There would be no court-appointed attorney after the completion of this process and I knew that my family couldn't afford an attorney of our own. Would my potential freedom depend on what was in my bank account? I wondered where my justice was. Where was the fairness and kindness I was promised in the American dream?

The sunlight pierced my eyes and I rolled over to look at the clock. It was 7:40 and when I looked over at Justin's empty bed, I realized he was already gone. Sitting up, I peered at the worn flowered wallpaper, the raggedy old dresser, the polyester panels that hung over the small window. Then I noticed the sharp ray of sun that shone through the same window I used to wake up to every morning. It had been so many years since I'd seen it coming from this window, or since I'd seen direct sunlight at all. Six years to be exact. I smiled and thought about how good God was. Then I swung my legs over the side of the bed.

I wanted to see Justin off to school so I slumped over to the closet and searched it furiously. After all these years, many of my things were packed away in boxes. I looked behind a few of Justin's clothes that were hanging, which were mainly jeans and polo-style shirts. To my surprise, I found a few of my old outfits still piled up at the back. I realized that Mama must've put them away for me, probably around the same time that she sold my banged-up Ford Escort to pay bills. I thumbed through my old frocks, feeling the fabrics as if they were silks and satins. Most of them smelled like mothballs but I didn't mind. Anything was better than prison orange.

Shoving my big hips into a pair of old sweatpants, I pulled a pink T-shirt over my head and stepped into a pair of dirty sneakers. I panicked at the thought that Justin had left without saying good-bye, until I heard his voice. Justin was talking to Uncle Charlie in the kitchen.

I heard Uncle Charlie's raspy voice, "Boy, you know I don't have no lunch money fer ya."

I was headed to the kitchen to greet them but just as I walked out of the bedroom, they were walking into the living room too.

"That's okay, Unc. I'm carrying a bologna sandwich for lunch." Justin held up a brown paper bag.

I crept up behind him and put my hand on his shoulder. "Good morning."

Uncle Charlie flashed a toothless grin. "Morning."

"Hi, Mom." Justin gathered his backpack. "I've gotta go."

I grabbed his arm before he went through the door. "Wait, have you had anything to eat?"

"Yeah, I ate cereal, like I always do." He loosed himself from my grasp and continued walking through the door.

I followed him outside. "Wait, aren't you gonna kiss your mom good-bye?"

"Naw, " Justin turned around to face me, with eyes as cold as the wind.

I furrowed my eyebrows. "Why not?"

"I don't know. It just don't feel right." Justin looked away and kept walking. "I'm just too old for that."

I realized that I was treading on the edge. Maybe I wanted too much, too soon, from him. I decided to step back and not push so hard.

As he approached the gate at the end of the front yard, he stumbled over a rock, then kicked it. I watched him walk all the way down the street until he caught the school bus. Reality set in. I had missed such a big piece of his life, that although he probably had some vague recollection of me, he didn't know me. And I didn't know him, at least not as the bright, strong, independent boy he was today. I knew him as my baby, the precious child I carried and nurtured for three years before I was ripped away from him. I would never see those days again. Clearly, I'd been robbed of our relationship and I wondered if the past could ever be reconciled.

Ironically, a new attorney stepped into my life as soon as the confession and my overturned conviction hit the news. Maybe I couldn't get back the time, but he'd make sure I'd get back some money. Millions of dollars had never been my motivation, but at this time in my life, a little spare cash would certainly help with restoration.

Still, I went back inside and glanced around the room. My second day had already started off wrong. Everything felt strange around me. Mama emerged from her cocoon, complete with her head wrapped in a head scarf and a bathrobe that had so many holes, it was only fit for the lining of a garbage can as far as I was concerned. It was clear that life had not been so kind to her.

Mama yawned. "Y'all up so early?"

"Yes, Justin had to leave for school." I wondered what life was like for him while I was gone.

Mama put her hands on her sagging hips. "Justin has been leaving for school on his own all this time. What makes today so special?"

I looked her square in the eyes and faked a smile. "Well, today Justin's mother is home. That makes today really special."

"Hmph." Mama cast her eyes downward. "I guess I'll make us something to eat, then, seeing as how we're all here together like this, 'cept for Justin, of course. He'll have to catch it this evening."

Mama didn't smile, but she served us bacon, eggs, and cheese grits, which was once my favorite. Even the food had a different taste in my mouth now. I was so used to prison mush.

Uncle Charlie looked across the table at me. "What you goin' to do now that you're out?"

I hunched my shoulders. "I thought maybe I'd go back to waitin' tables."

Mama slammed her fork onto her plate. "Oh no. Not that again."

"Just until I can save enough money to go to beauty school." The truth was I wasn't even sure if there was any beauty in the world anymore.

"You always did talk about that beauty-school stuff. What's the use in it?" Mama threw her head back and cackled. "Those that are pretty, stay that way. And those that are ugly—well, there ain't no real help for 'em anyway."

"I think I'm pretty good at it." I remembered the special way styling someone's hair made me feel. Back then I could bump a curl like nobody's business. Now everything had changed.

"Always has been good at that hair stuff, Rosalee." Uncle Charlie nodded.

"I used to do Alyssa's hair and all my friends at school." I twirled a strand of my own hair around my finger. "Don't know why I didn't go to beauty school right after high school."

Mama swirled her tongue around in her mouth and I could tell she was adjusting her false teeth. "I'll tell ya why, 'cause you was too busy running yo' fast tail after that wild man of yours, Smooth." His name rolled off of her tongue like it was poison.

I bit my lip to keep the peace. "He was my husband, Mama."

"Now, that was the problem," Mama snapped.

"Well, he's not my problem anymore," I said, pouting.

"That's what all his women say, I'm sure." Mama rolled her eyes. "But I don't believe it, though."

I pushed my chair away from the table."What do you mean, you don't believe it?"

Mama squinted her eyes. "Ya know what I think?"

I was hoping Mama wouldn't go there, but she always did. "What?"

Mama nodded."I think that if that no-good man showed up and snapped his fingers, you'd run off with him all over again."

I sighed."Well, you're wrong about that. I'm not the stupid girl I used to be."

"Hmph," she spat out. "Could've fooled me."

Her cruelty bounced off me like usual, although I refused to let it penetrate any deeper than it had in the past. Being able to meditate for six years, I'd learned that life was short. It was funny, but now that Mama had mentioned Smooth, now that she'd reminded me of how strong our love was, the ache started all over again. And somewhere deep inside I knew I had to find him. I knew I had to find the rest of my family.

Chapter 3

Rosalee sat in her favorite chair facing the television, but she wasn't interested in what was on the screen. Her oldest daughter was back in town and thanks to her, Rosalee had bigger problems. Problems big enough to make an old lady like her cry like a baby. She sometimes wondered if she was meant to be a mother, because she'd waited forty-three years to become one and because it brought her so much pain. She looked down in her lap at her hands, speckled with age spots, and remembered when they were soft and young. Her weariness was the result of toiling long and hard for her family for so many years. Now Trinity was back with her youthful drama, disturbing her rest.

"Come and sit by me, Justin," Trinity popped another chocolate-chip cookie into her mouth.

"Okay, Mom." Justin sat down next to his mother and she put her arm around him.

Rosalee watched them from the corner of her eye. She wasn't jealous or anything like that. She just didn't quite know what to make of her daughter, Trinity. She was so different than her and so hard to understand. She looked different, like her good-for-nothing daddy and she sure did act like him. Stubborn child. In fact, Rosalie couldn't believe that the hardheaded girl still wanted that no-good, tar-black man of hers. She could see it in her daughter's eyes. Yes, she wanted him back in the same way she used to want Trinity's father. It was that same raw lust in her daughter's eyes. She could see it and it frightened her. She'd learned through the years that once a man had a woman under his spell, he could make her do anything; that she'd never be free. Hadn't six years in prison been enough torture for her or did she have to have fresh heartache to go alongside of it? "Women have got to just wake up," Rosalee mumbled.

Uncle Charlie shook his head as he entered the room. "What are you fussing about now, Rosalee?"

"I'm just talking. Not fussing." Rosalee fanned him away. "And it don't make no kind of sense."

Trinity sat up straight on the couch. "Is something wrong, Mama?"

"Nothing, nothing at all. You just make sure you're doing all you can for yourself and that boy of yours." Rosalee pushed her hair from her face as she spoke.

Without even looking at her mother, Trinity asked, "What are you talking about? Exactly what else should I be doing?"

Rosalee put a crooked smile on her face. "Well, for one thing, he should be doing his homework instead of watching television right now."

"I figured it would be okay to take a little break so I can spend some time with him, that's all." Trinity rolled her eyes when Rosalee wasn't looking. "He'll get back to it soon."

Rosalee leaned over toward Trinity. "Oh really? I wonder if his teachers would agree with that."

"Has anyone seen the remote?" Uncle Charlie settled in on the couch next to Trinity and Justin. "I want to see what else is on."

"It's no big deal." Trinity handed over the remote.

Rosalee didn't take her eyes off of Trinity. "Nothing is a big deal to you. But when you were gone, I had Justin doing his homework assignments first. Every day."

"Thank you for being such a role model," Trinity said, smirking.

Rosalee pounded her fist against the wall. "Don't get smart with me, gal. A boy needs a good education."

Trinity continued, "I'm sorry, but don't you think I know that? I live in this world too."

Rosalee walked back and forth, fussing. "Sometimes I think you don't. Sometimes I think your head isn't on straight."

"The way I see it, considering I was almost given a lethal injection on death row, I'm lucky to have any head at all." Trinity tapped the top of her head and smiled.

"You've got jokes." Rosalee nodded. "I used to think like you too. In fact, I used to be you."

"I doubt that very much," Trinity said.

"Why? Do you think you're better than me? Why? Because you're young and strong?" Rosalee raised her voice as she spoke. "All of that fades away and if you're not careful you're left with nothing."

Uncle Charlie interrupted: "I thought you said you wasn't fussing, but it sounds like fussing to me."

"Hush, old man." Rosalee fanned him away again.

Trinity turned to face her mother. "Okay, so what do you want from me?"

Rosalee pointed one finger up to her head. "I want you to think."

She shrugged my shoulders. "Think about what?"

"I want you to think about what you want and about what you're going to do, whether or not it's the best thing for you or the boy." Rosalee pounded her fist in the palm of her other hand.

"I'm lost, Mama, so until you stop talking in riddles, pardon me if I continue to watch television," Trinity mocked.

Rosalee had married Trinity's father right after she had Alyssa. Formerly a forty-two-year-old cocktail waitress, she thought she'd finally gotten her life together when she met this seemingly hardworking man from the loading docks. She thought she'd actually found happiness when they bought a little house in New Orleans, until one day, when Trinity was about seven. It was then that Rosalee realized her husband had skipped town with the mortgage money, leaving her stranded with three young kids. She knew it was that gambling streak of his that ran through his veins, but she never did forgive him. Nor did she ever take him back, even though he eventually came back "begging and sniffing around," as she would say. She was glad to be rid of him, with his endless gambling debts and his nagging, holier-than-thou mother. He'd already ruined Rosalee's life by saddling her with three children and there was no turning back from that. However, marriage to a deadbeat was optional.

Shortly afterward, Rosalee observed Trinity reading the newspaper. "I hope you're looking for a job, gal," she yelled.

Trinity didn't even look up from her reading. Never even said a word.

Rosalee wondered how much more she could take. She'd suffered as much as anyone else, looking after Trinity's boy and worrying about her daughter's life on death row. Knowing her child had gotten herself entangled with such a mess almost killed her. Not that Rosalee ever believed Trinity was capable of murder, but she sure believed Trinity was always following the wrong people. She was always trusting everyone, Rosalee thought. Maybe, just maybe she had followed the wrong people into a trap. That was Rosalee's theory of what happened the night Trinity was arrested. She went on believing that her daughter was framed until Trinity showed up on her doorstep two days ago.

Now that she was back, Trinity hadn't even seemed grateful for all she had done. Why couldn't her daughter realize the pain she'd been forced to endure while she was gone? No mother in her right mind wanted to see her child put to death by the state prison system, even if the child was hateful and hardheaded. No mother wanted her own child to suffer. Not even Rosalee.

No. All she wanted was for Trinity to listen to her for once, to let her dark man and her dark powers go before she destroyed them all.

Chapter 4

It was my third day in Baton Rouge and I'd spent most of it looking for jobs. Unfortunately, a news reporter caught me as I was walking down a main street. She had her cameraman zoom in for a close-up and she spoke boldly into her microphone. "How does it feel to finally be off of death row, Ms. Crawford?"

The reporter shoved the microphone into my face. "It feels great," I responded. "I'm glad to be alive. I'm glad to be free."

"Now that the perpetrator has confessed, and you've been released, do you feel vindicated or are there plans for legal justice?" The reporter pushed the microphone right up to my mouth again.

"I am not looking for money, if that's what you're asking." I gently guided the microphone a few inches away from my lips. "I'm glad the killer finally did the right thing, even if it took six years to do it."

The reporter sneered, "Is that so? So you sound like you sympathize with the person who had you put behind bars?"

How was I supposed to answer that? I took a deep breath. "She didn't have me put behind bars. The judge and a jury of my peers did that, so now if you'll excuse me, I've got to get back to my job hunt."

The cameras followed me until I disappeared down the street. My feet were killing me from the hours of walking in tight leather pumps. My hair was wet with perspiration and my head throbbed. No one seemed to be excited about hiring an ex-con, even if I had been wrongly accused.

A couple of hours later, discouraged, I walked toward the front porch, looking up at the overcast sky. The clouds were dark and full, threatening to pour at any moment. I unlocked the door with my key and found Uncle Charlie sitting on the couch, watching television.

"Hey, I'm back." I went over and stood next to the couch, glancing around the room. "Where's Justin?"

Uncle Charlie scratched his white beard. "He went to a friend's birthday party."

I wasn't familiar with Justin's life. "A friend? What friend?"

"Just a friend that lives down the road there." Uncle Charlie never looked away from the television screen. "He should be walking back soon."

I began to pace around the living room. "Walking? Are you sure?"

"Of course I'm sure." Uncle Charlie chuckled. "Don't worry, he's a big boy."

I looked around. "Where's Mama?"

Uncle Charlie maneuvered the remote. "She's in there," he pointed toward the kitchen.

So I took off the pumps and stepped barefoot into the kitchen with my last bit of strength.

Mama turned and rolled her eyes when she saw me. "You trying to sneak up on me, gal?"

I'd only been home for three days, but already I knew I had to move out. Staying with Mama and Uncle Charlie was no longer an option. Like I said before, Mama and me never could get along. It was always, "get out of my face, gal" this, or "move your big behind" that. Sooner or later I'd get tired of it and unfortunately, this time it came much sooner than later.

Mama stood over the sink, holding a pot in her hand. "Where are you coming from, all dressed up?"

"Job hunting." I felt accomplished when I said it. "Remember?"

Mama sneered, "Still thinking about waiting tables?"

"Maybe. Just temporarily." I didn't like Mama questioning me before I had things figured out. "There was a help-wanted sign down at the gas station too."

Mama snickered again. "What are you gonna do, pump gas?"

"Maybe, if I have to," I spat out.

Mama kept washing the dishes without looking back. "It would've been nice if you had turned out like your sister."

"Maybe that would've been nice for you, but not for me. I'm not some fancy lawyer. I'm just me." I sighed. "Not her."

"Well, things are real tight around here in this town and you don't have much to offer, so I don't know how you're gonna get a job, any job." Mama wiped her hands in her apron.

"I'm just going to try my best." I began drying the plates with the dish towel.

"And what's that supposed to mean?" Mama put her hands on her lumpy hips. "Are we supposed to be satisfied because you say you're doing your best? I think it's hogwash."

I quickly thought of how I'd answer her. "I ran into a news reporter today and I managed to get away without extra drama. That's my best."

Mama stared at me with her light gray eyes that seemed to flicker in the light. "Your best has never been good enough before, why would it be good enough now?"

Normally, a statement like that would've made me wither, but I'd seen and heard worse than that in the past few years. A part of me had toughened while sitting in the bowels of the state penitentiary. So I decided to taunt Mama a little. I leaned forward and with a little smile on my face, said, " Maybe I'll just put the word out on the street, then sit back and wait for it to come back to me."

Mama immediately turned around to face me. "What did you say?"

I knew what to say to get to her. "I'm gonna do like Aunt Ruby always says, put the word out."

"No, I heard what you said, gal, but I just can't believe you're saying it." Mama paused.

"How dare you mention that woman's name to me. And in my own house."

"But she's *your* sister." I spoke matter-of-factly. "Besides, she's always been good to me."

"Half sister. Remember that," Mama snapped.

I knew that was Mama's sore spot, good ol' Aunt Ruby. She was only Mama's half sister because Grandma Jean never acknowledged Grandpa Jim as Aunt Ruby's father. Not after he left her to raise three kids on her own, that is. Grandma Jean liked to say Aunt Ruby was another man's child, a man whose identity she refused to disclose. No matter how Grandpa Jim cursed and called her names, she held her ground. Since Grandma was a fireball, Grandpa's anger just seemed to get her even more fired up, and she kept the paternity a secret even to his and her deathbed. That's probably why Mama was so messed up. They did say the apple didn't fall far from the tree. Well, in my case, a whole heap of apples were rotten.

"I love Aunt Ruby." I circled her, then went in for the kill. "She's my special aunt. She's so smart and sassy."

"Well, maybe you need to go live with her then," Mama mumbled. "She's special, all right."

I thought about how detached Aunt Ruby was from the family. I didn't even have her number to let her know I had been released. Maybe she'd seen it on television.

Maybe not. No matter how anyone tried to bring the family together, it seemed like everything just consistently fell apart. Mama, Aunt Ruby, and Uncle Charlie were an odd bunch, truly products of the late Grandma Jean's multifaceted, dysfunctional parenting.

I opened the refrigerator and took out an apple. "Actually, I'll be looking for a place of my own real soon."

Mama squinted her eyes. "Still high and mighty, aren't you, gal?"

I took a bite of the apple and watched Mama. "No, ma'am. Just want things to get back to normal, that's all."

Mama took off her apron and threw it down to the floor."I hope *normal* don't mean you're going to be running off to you-know-where with you-know-who."

I finished chewing before answering her. "Mama, please."

"Uh-uh. Don't *Mama, please* me. You were always the hardheaded one for sure," Mama snapped.

I stooped down to pick up Mama's apron, then handed it to her. "Well, I'm sorry I didn't turn out better, that I'm not a bigger success like Alyssa."

Mama snatched the apron from my hands."Maybe it's 'cause she left that wicked place alone. You know I swore I'd never set my foot back there."

I turned to face Mama directly. "You swore, Mama. Not me."

Mama raised her hand and I grabbed it before it hit my face. I did swear when I was in prison that I'd never let anyone hit me again. We stared at each other for a moment before she yanked her hand away from mine and walked away from me.

I remembered that Nana always taught us that violence wasn't the way, but it sure did seem like it was the way of the world, especially as I was growing up. Nana would talk about peaceful things and sit around, telling us about how much Jesus loved us. Then I'd go home and Mama would tell us how much we looked like our father and how ugly we were. Thankfully, Nana told us we were her little princesses and that we were the most beautiful girls in the world.

I guess you could say I missed Nana the most.

Nana was my paternal grandmother and although I didn't remember much about my dad, I had impeccable memories of her. She was a beautiful woman with thick, curly, dark hair, high cheekbones, and smooth chocolate skin like mine. It was hard to believe she was even a grandmother, except for a few silver streaks that lined her hair. I remembered she wore pearls and other fine jewelry, that she spoke in quiet sentences and that she smelled of vanilla. She'd always come to take my sister, my brother, and me to church when we were young, against my mother's will, of course.

Mama was totally against the church and so was Grandma Jean. My maternal grandmother was nothing like Nana. In fact, she was everything like Mama: pale, stone-faced, and gray-eyed. Mama and Grandma Jean used to say that church was just a waste of time. They also said that even though they believed in God, people didn't have any business judging their relationship with Him. It didn't look like they had any relationship with Him at all, if anyone asked me.

As an adult, I guess I could understand their sentiment, but still I wondered what was so bad about sitting in a Sunday service and coming home happy. Not that I liked going all the time, but I always felt closer to God when I got around other church folks. Never did know why that was, though. Sometimes my sister, my brother, and I wanted to stay home and play instead.

But Nana kept us focused, coming by like clockwork, insisting that my mother have our clothes already pressed and shoes already shined, and drag us by the hand, off to

Sunday school first and then church every week, rain or shine. In fact, she did this faithfully, up until the day she brought the three of us to the altar. She'd prayed over us, then had us baptized.

When Mama found out what she had done that day, she threw a fit and we were never allowed to go with Nana again. I never knew that a ten-year-old being dipped into a shallow pool was such a big deal. Why had Mama gone ballistic and threatened to fight Nana? Why had Nana started speaking in tongues and put up her hands to rebuke Mama? My sister, brother and, I were led out of the room by Uncle Charlie as the argument continued. Had they all lost their minds? Needless to say, there was a rift in the family and the next thing I knew I was witnessing my dad—the tall, dark mystery man—defending Nana, yelling at Mama. All I remember is that the police came and I never saw my father or Nana again. That was nineteen years ago.

Mama followed me out to the living room. "You don't have no business worrying with that sneaky Ruby Jean or that boy's sorry daddy. Going back to the past is nothing but trouble."

I threw my hands up in exasperation. "I'm not going back to the past. I'm looking for my future."

"Well, you're looking in the wrong place," Mama sneered.

Despite Mama's protests, I knew it was time to find my man, and by *man* I meant my ex-husband, Smooth. We'd divorced each other two years after my son was born, but despite my best efforts, I still had feelings for him. Besides, I hadn't laid eyes on him in almost two years and that was an awfully long time to be away from someone you love. I knew he didn't feel about me the way I felt about him. Probably never had. I guess you could say he'd been some sort of savior for me at one time, rescuing me from my destructive self, all the while making me fall in love with him. He was a smooth brother, a musician, and I did appreciate the music we made together. He could play a mean saxophone anytime, anywhere.

Although he probably wasn't the best-looking man by most people's standards, that was because he was a deep, dark brown, rough-bearded, and with a broad African nose, and a voice that could draw in any woman. He'd drawn me in the same way the first night I'd heard him sing at a supper club on Bourbon Street. From that moment on I knew it was him I wanted. Even when he left me to run around the country with his mistress—music—I loved him.

So naturally, when I'd heard he was back in New Orleans from Vegas, six and a half years ago, I couldn't help but bring myself right back to him. I'd packed my things, left my son with a friend, and went after him, although Mama cussed me the whole time. She told me not to ever go back to New Orleans, that she'd barely escaped herself, that the place had broken up my marriage in the first place. Mama called me the hardheaded one and said I should be like my sister, who swore she'd never marry nor set foot back in New Orleans. I ignored Mama and ran off, just to find Smooth shacked up with some other woman.

I'd went off in all different directions at the sight of that. That was another reason the authorities thought I'd shot those people, because they'd arrested me for making a public disturbance the night before. Of course, I wasn't really the fighting type, but when I saw that skinny woman with her arms around my man, I snapped. Started swinging, scratching, and pulling her weave every which way. Police had to pull me off of her and calm me down. I guess the handcuffs did it. My ex-husband bailed me out, though, only for me to be arrested for a mass murder the next day. I guess things were funny like that sometimes.

Anyway, that was the last time I'd seen him, except once behind bars, and I had to make up for lost time.

"Don't worry, Mama, before I do anything I've got to get myself together, get a job and a car so I can take care of my son. More importantly, I've got to get used to being on the outside again and get some peace in my soul. Then I'll figure out how to find Mr. Smooth McGee."

Mama fanned me away with her hand, something she often did when she was disgusted.

"Why don't you leave the girl alone, Rosalee?" Uncle Charlie protested.

Mama shot him a glance. "Why don't you mind your own business?"

The bickering had begun. The house brought back so many old memories, good and bad.

Three days and I was already worn out.

"I love you, Uncle Charlie." I kissed him on his wrinkled cheek.

"Love you too, Trinity." Uncle Charlie finally looked up from his television show.

There it was again. That name. I didn't know why it bothered me so much to be called that, but it did.

It had begun to rain and it hit the roof like a waterfall. I went to my bedroom and snuggled under my blanket, trying to wait until the storm passed. I never did like storms. Finally, I felt comfortable enough to close my eyes for a little while.

When I opened my eyes I saw a vision of Justin. He was wearing a hospital gown and I was crying. Then he floated up to the sky and disappeared while I was left alone in a hospital room, still crying. I blinked and waited for the image to clear out of my mind, but it never did. I blinked again. A cold feeling ran through my body, stifling me.

Panicked, I jumped up and ran into the kitchen. Mama was there. "Where is Justin?"

Mama pushed out her bottom lip. "You know he went over to that party. What's wrong with you, gal? And why are you asking?"

I stepped back. "What do you mean, What's wrong with me? Can't I ask about my own son?"

"You can ask all you want, but it's the way you're looking right now that scares me."

Mama pointed her bony finger at me. "You had a vision, didn't you?"

I shook my head. "Why would you say that?"

Mama came closer. "You didn't answer my question."

"I'm not going to." I tried to hide my fear.

Mama pointed her finger in my face again. "Then you did see something?"

"Mama, please." I let out a deep breath.

Mama kept coming closer, step by step. "Don't you *Mama, please* me. Gal, if you know something you've got to tell it."

"No, Mama." I stepped back further and further.

"Trinity, you're as stubborn as your father ever was." Mama stopped walking. "You saw something. I know you did."

My back was against the refrigerator. "No. I just want to see my son."

"Nobody's stopping you from seeing him. He'll be coming home soon, I reckon. You can try to find him, but when you do, you've got to tell us all what you saw." Mama leaned close to me.

I turned away from her and covered my ears. "Why won't you stop?"

"'Cause I know you. I know that wild look in your eyes. Same look you always had whenever you saw something. Ever since you were little, you had that evil look in your eyes.

Means you done seen something evil." Mama pointed her shaky finger in my face. "Didn't you? Didn't you?"

"No, I haven't." I squeezed away from her.

"I blame that no-good father of yours. If he hadn't brought that woman into my house, rubbing my belly with all her evil, you wouldn't have what you have on you now." Mama spun around to face me. "Nothing but witchcraft, I tell you."

"There's nothing evil on me, Mama. And I'm not a witch." I paused. "Nana was a good woman."

"What do you know about it? You were just a little girl when she brought that mess into this house. You haven't been right since." Mama paced around the kitchen, throwing her long stringy ponytail back and forth.

Unable to hear another word, I grabbed an umbrella and ran outside to look for Justin.

The rain had slowed down to a drizzle. I asked for him around the neighborhood, but no one had seen him. So I sat on the front porch with my head in my hands, watching the sky clear up and waiting for Justin to come home.

Before long, Mama yelled out to me, "Gal, aren't you gonna help me with this dinner?"

Reluctantly, I went inside to help her in the kitchen, setting the chicken in the batter so Mama could fry it. Then I put the last batch of biscuits in the oven. Just as I had taken off the oven mitts, I heard a loud knock at the front door. It was then that I glanced at the wall clock, remembering that Justin was still not home.

"I'll get it." I threw down the oven mitts.

Mama pushed past me. "No, I'll get it. It's my door."

Taking a step back, I let Mama go ahead of me. I peeked out from the kitchen.

Mama pulled the door open. "Good evening, sir." Then she looked at Justin. "Boy, what have you done?"

"Nothing, Grandma," Justin spoke quietly.

"Ma'am, I chose to bring your boy home." The man helped Justin to come inside as if he could hardly walk. He was tall, dark, and dressed like a soldier.

I ran out into the living room and grabbed Justin into my arms. "What happened?"

The man said, "Ma'am, we found your boy laid out by the side of the road down by the creek."

"Thank goodness, he's all right," I helped him to the couch and sat down beside him. "Thank you, sir."

Mama stared at the man. "Uh-uh, don't thank him just yet. Now who did you say you were again?"

The man smiled. "I'm Private Malachia Rembrant."

"That's a strange name for folk around these parts." Uncle Charlie leaned forward in his armchair.

"Well, I'm not from around here, sir," Malachia said.

Mama squinted her eyes. "Is that so?"

Malachia turned toward Mama. "I'm from Pittsburgh, actually. Just visiting."

"Pittsburgh, huh? I see." Mama studied him.

"Thank you so much, Mr. Rembrant. Me and my son are so grateful." I stroked Justin's head, which was soaked with sweat. "Can we get you something to drink or eat?"

"No, thanks. I'm just glad I was able to help." The man turned and opened the door.

"Take it easy there, little man."

"Thanks a lot, sir." Justin lifted his head slightly.

Malachia looked at me. "If I were you, I'd have him checked out by a doctor. Good-bye."

Mama followed him to the door.

"Good-bye and thanks again." I stood up and walked behind Mama, peeping my head out from behind her.

Mama closed the door behind him without another word. "Well, what's wrong with him?"

"I don't know." I went over to Justin to see if he had a fever. "How do you feel?"

Justin gently moved my hand off of his forehead. "Wet, but I'm okay."

His words were cold and firm. I cringed at the emptiness of them. "You passed out on the side of the road, so obviously you're not okay."

Justin sat up straight. "I'm just a little dizzy, that's all."

"You're cold and wet, probably hungry too." I ran into the bedroom, grabbed some dry clothes, returned to the living room, and handed them to him. "We're gonna get you dry, then feed you."

"Okay, thanks." Justin stood up and made his way toward the bathroom.

"I wonder what happened to him?" Uncle Charlie switched the channel on the TV.

"Well, I don't want to upset him, so I'll wait until he has eaten before I ask him more questions." I sat on the arm of the couch for a moment.

"Upset him? He's just a child. Don't matter 'bout whether or not you upset him. Just get the truth out of him." Mama leaned in close to me and Uncle Charlie. "You don't suppose he's taken up with them bad boys and is on them drugs, do you?"

"I doubt that, Mama." Disgusted, I stood up and walked into the kitchen, with Mama on my heels. "Justin seems like a really good boy."

"Hmph. Seems like." Mama nodded.

I folded my arms against my chest. "Have you had any problems with him while I was away?"

Mama's eyes looked scarier than usual. "Every day you was away was a problem with him. I didn't sign up to raise no more kids, you know?"

"I know." I wondered why Mama was telling me this when she knew I was in prison through no fault of my own.

Justin came out of the bathroom wearing the T-shirt and shorts I had handed him.

"Let's go, boy. Come on in this kitchen to eat," Mama said, standing in the doorway.

"I'm coming, Grandma." Justin put his hand up to his head.

Mama shook her head. "You're so skinny that it's a wonder you haven't dropped down sooner."

"Mama." I looked over at Justin.

"It's the truth, anyhow." Mama rolled her eyes. "What do you think is wrong with him?"

I touched Justin's shoulder. "Mama, please."

Mama put her hands on her sagging hips. "Gal, what is it?"

"Nothing. Would you please let your grandson eat his dinner?" I sat down at the table next to Justin. "If he's not feeling any better soon, I'm taking him to the emergency room."

Justin ate his food quietly, coughing mildly every now and then. I ate my food beside him, but focused on him the whole time. What had caused him to fall by the side of the road?

Why did he look so pale and weak? And why couldn't I get that vision of him in a hospital gown out of my mind?

Although I hadn't had a vision for quite a while, I used to have them all the time.

Mama thought my visions were evil, though. In fact, I grew up believing just that until Nana told me differently.

"Those visions you have are a gift and one day God is going to use you in a special way," Nana had said.

I wasn't sure of exactly what she meant, but I certainly liked the idea of being used by God. I missed my grandmother and wondered where she was now. Why had she forgotten about me? Maybe, when I finally got settled, I'd look for her. Maybe I'd even look for my dad.

"Thanks for dinner, Grandma and Mom." Justin grinned. "It was really good."

"You're welcome, son." I was so grateful to hear him call me *Mom*.

Mama walked right up to him and asked, "How do you feel now that you're full?"

"I feel okay, I guess." Justin yawned, then stretched.

I asked, "Are you sure?"

Justin nodded, then pushed away from the table. "Yeah, I'm sure. I'm good."

As soon as Justin left the room, I spoke up. "I guess he's all right, then." But something didn't feel right.

Mama hunched her shoulders. "If you say so. He's your burden."

"No, he's not my burden." I smiled as tears filled my eyes. " He's my joy."

Mama rolled her eyes.

I gathered up the dinner plates as Mama started to put away the food.

Uncle Charlie rubbed his potbelly and steadied his walking cane as he stumbled into the living room. "Good dinner, y'all."

"Be careful, Uncle," I reminded him. Uncle Charlie was five years older than my mother and neither his hip nor his legs were in good shape.

"Go on, you ol' fool." Mama chuckled.

Within seconds, we heard a loud sound in the living room and we ran in to see if Uncle Charlie had fallen. Instead, we saw Justin on the floor with his eyes closed, not moving.

"Oh, my goodness," Uncle Charlie shouted, shaking his head.

"Mama, call nine-one-one." I leaped to Justin's side. "Hurry."

Chapter 5

I was so scared that my heart almost pounded outside of my chest. The paramedics had resuscitated him. He gasped for air, then fell limp again, so they gave him oxygen. I sat in the back of the speeding ambulance and stroked his hand. Then Justin's eyes began to roll upwards and he began to tremble. His hand was so cold. His chest heaved. He was flatlining. I knew enough about medical procedures from years of watching hospital programs to know that my son was dying.

"Do something," I shouted as I looked at my son.

One, two, three, *zap*. I shivered as the paramedics revived him. Why was the heart of a nine-year-old boy stopping in the first place? What in the world was wrong with him? Was this why I kept seeing him in a hospital gown? What did those visions really mean? All I knew was that we needed to get to the hospital as quickly as possible. If only the ambulance could have gone a little faster.

I shivered as they performed their procedures on him. My own heart beat like the sound of a train coming into a station. Tears ran down my face as I didn't want to imagine losing my child. Then I remembered Nana's voice: "Whenever things seem hopeless, child, just pray. Pray like your life depends on it." I hadn't heard her voice in nineteen years, yet the memory of it calmed me.

Without hesitation, I closed my eyes and spoke to God, "Lord, please help my son." I wondered if He remembered me since I hadn't talked to Him much since I was a little girl. "Lord, have mercy on me."

The next thing I knew my son's gurney was being unloaded into a crowded emergency room, wheeled away to a curtained-off area, and then he was connected to all kinds of machines.

Justin was examined by a tall nurse first, then by the head pediatrician. I stood by, shaking.

An older nurse tapped me on the shoulder. "Are you okay, dear?"

A medical technician came in with an IV pole with a hanging bag of fluid.

"He's stable now, but very weak," the doctor explained. "His liver seems enlarged. We'll order X-rays and an ultrasound."

I nodded as they proceeded to run their tests one by one, sticking Justin with needles of all sizes.

The sound of the equipment beeping sent off signals of panic in my brain. I hadn't liked hospitals since I had my tonsillectomy at six years old.

"The results will be back in a little while, ma'am." The nurse smiled.

I wondered what there was to smile about.

"Thanks." I nervously rubbed my hands together.

Then I grabbed my son's hand. "Justin, Mommy is right here and you're going to be all right."

Justin nodded, unable to speak because of the oxygen mask over his face.

It was so hard seeing him like this. It was so hard waiting.

An hour later the doctor and nurse came into the room. The nurse moved the IV pole and began hooking up two other bags of fluid.

I jumped out of my chair. "What is it, Doctor?"

The doctor put his hand on his graying beard. "Justin, have you been feeling weak or tired lately?"

Justin answered, "I guess so."

The doctor looked down at Justin's chart. "Have you been feeling any pain in your bones or joints, like maybe your knees?"

"I don't know, maybe." Justin shrugged his shoulders.

The doctor scribbled a few notes on Justin's chart. "We're putting Justin on antibiotics just to be sure."

I looked from the nurse to the doctor. "Just to be sure of what?"

The doctor spoke calmly. "Why don't we step out into the hall while Nurse Molly checks his vitals."

"Yes, sir." I followed the doctor. I turned back to Justin before exiting the room.

"Mommy will be right back."

The doctor closed the door behind us.

I didn't waste any time. "What is it ? Does he have some kind of infection?"

"Maybe, but it's highly unlikely. We found that Justin has decreased red cells, decreased platelets, a low number of normal white blood cells, and increased lymphocytes." The doctor shook his head. "His whole immune system is shut down."

I sat down to brace myself for the worst. "Shut down? What exactly are you saying, Doctor? Tell me."

"I'm saying that it looks like your son has AML, acute myeloid leukemia, a fast-growing form of leukemia that's rare in children."

I put my hand over my mouth. "Leukemia?"

"Yes, I'm sorry." His deep blue eyes seemed to sparkle under the fluorescent lights. "It's the most common cause of death for young children in the U.S. than any other malignant disease."

"But that doesn't make any sense. Check those test results again. I want a second opinion." I began to breathe heavily.

"You are welcome to get as many opinions as you like. But with the exception of an infection, which in this case doesn't really fit the symptoms, the diagnosis is firm." The doctor barely blinked. "It's a fast-growing disease, so as soon as you're ready, we'll discuss your options."

I put one hand on my head. "Options. What do you mean, options? You don't understand. I've been gone for six years—six long years—and the only thing that kept me alive was thinking of my son. I had to fight so I could come back to him. Now you're telling me that I could lose him." I buried my face in my hands. "No, no, no."

"Ms. Crawford, there are treatments for leukemia." The doctor patted me on the shoulder.

I couldn't believe what I was hearing. "But it's cancer, isn't it?"

He nodded. "Yes, it's cancer."

I stood up, then began to pace. "I'm so scared, Doctor. How can I tell him this? He's so young."

"If you need help telling him, we can help," the doctor said.

I closed my eyes. "No, I've got to do it myself."

The doctor started. "Perhaps his father can—"

I shook my head. "No, not at all."

"Ms. Crawford, this is so serious that you'll still have to notify his father about his condition." The doctor leaned against the wall.

I thought about my ex-husband for a moment and wondered where he was. Was he sitting in a jazz club somewhere smoking and drinking his problems away? Or was he running the streets with some hussy as usual?

The doctor continued. "What about Justin's grandmother? Maybe she can help to tell him."

I thought of my harsh-mouthed mother. "Definitely not. I'm afraid that I'm alone on this one, doc."

The doctor closed the chart. "Well, we're going to run a few more tests and the results will be in the next couple of days. Until then, we're going to have to admit him."

I was stunned. "Admit him so soon?"

"Yes, but first he'll be put on room isolation for forty-eight hours. He must stay in his room just in case he's coming down with a cold or flu. This protects the other patients."

I stopped pacing for a moment. "What about visitors?"

The doctor's face looked old but confident, as if he had explained this prognosis many times before. "There is no restriction on that, although you will have to wear a mask and gloves."

"This is a nightmare." The enormity of the situation was beginning to sink in.

"I'm sorry, Ms. Crawford. I'll keep you posted and if you have any other questions, please feel free to call me." The doctor turned on his heels and sped away.

"Thank you, Doctor." Those were the only words I could manage to get out.

Poor Justin was only nine years old. I sighed, then watched the doctor disappear down the corridor before I covered my face with my hands. I had to go back inside the room and tell him, to shadow his dreams with nightmares of cancer. I looked toward the tiled ceiling, and for whatever it was worth, threw my weary hands up and said, "God, help me."

By Friday the blood and bone-marrow tests results came back positive.

"Hello, I'm Dr. McClendon, the oncologist," Dr. McClendon was a tall, middle-aged man with fluffy dark brown hair and light brown eyes.

"Pleased to meet you." I offered him my hand before sitting down in the vinyl guest chair.

Dr. McClendon shook my hand briefly. "I'll get right to the point. Your son has a rare form of leukemia that is called undifferential acute myeloblastic, or acute myelogenous leukemia: AML.

"Okay." I took slow breaths.

Dr. McClendon pushed his square-shaped glasses up on his nose, flipped a page on the chart he was holding, then looked at me. "I'm afraid that Justin may need a bone-marrow transplant."

I tried to process the information as quickly as possible. "Okay, a bone-marrow transplant?"

"Yes, a transplant in order to replace the damaged bone marrow with healthy bone-marrow stem cells." Dr. McClendon smiled. "For me, it's a fairly common procedure."

I wiped away the tears that had started to fill my eyes. "But it's not your baby having to go through it."

Dr. McClendon continued: "The first step is induction chemotherapy for one week with three weeks of recovery. If it's not in remission, then the second phase of chemo consolidation chemo is to destroy remaining cells."

Anxiety began to creep in. "And what if that doesn't work?"

"Well, that's where the transplant comes in. Potential donors will take a histocompatibility antigen test to determine his or her blood-tissue traits," Dr. McClendon said.

I took a tissue out of my pocket. "It sounds complicated."

Dr. McClendon nodded."No, it's just a quick blood test, actually."

My heart skipped a beat. "A blood test?"

"Since tissue types are inherited, like hair or eye color are, usually the most successful matches are siblings. Does Justin have any brothers or sisters?"

"No. He's an only child." I remembered the day I had my miscarriage. There had been a million wrong things going on in my life at the time, but the pregnancy had been a right one.

Then one day when Smooth was out of town with the band and I was home alone with baby Justin, my dream of happiness was washed away and dispensed into the bathtub. At only two months of pregnancy, I never told another living soul, nor did I ever try again.

Dr. McClendon shook his head. "I see. Well, you can try his family members, including yourself, and if all else fails, then there is a national donor registry database we can search. I'll tell you also that the chances of a minority patient finding a registry match are lower than the chances of a Caucasian patient."

I looked Dr. McClendon right in the eye. "What happens if I find a donor?"

"If you find a donor, his or her tissue will have the same genetic type as your son. You see, bone marrow produces stem cells. The stem cells eventually develop into blood cells. In any case, the donor will be checked into the hospital for a few days while he or she receives medicine, then when the blood is ready, we will collect the stem cells with a needle. Meanwhile, Justin will have had high doses of chemo to clean out any old traces of bone marrow to make room for the new."

I looked Dr. McClendon right in the eye. "What happens if I don't find a donor, period?"

Dr. McClendon looked over his glasses. "If he doesn't respond to the initial rounds of chemo and you cannot find a donor, family or otherwise, I'm afraid that Justin will die."

That's when I lost it. I couldn't hold in the tears any longer. There was so much on my newly released shoulders. I blanked out at some point, knowing I needed help, that the state health insurance my son had wouldn't be enough, knowing that I had to round up potential blood donors for the procedure that could save his life. Just days ago I had walked away from death row, only to be stalked by an uglier threat of death.

I thanked the doctor as I walked away in a daze-like stupor, wiping my eyes with a torn piece of tissue.

I went into Justin's room and kissed his forehead as he slept. He appeared to be so weak.

I needed to find Nana, because I remembered that she was a woman who knew how to pray. She used to bring the whole house down with her prayers and everybody around her knew that everything would be all right. That was what I really needed now—prayer. Besides, she could help to lead me to my father. I also needed to find my Aunt Ruby, who was very resourceful and could usually set any situation straight once she set her mind to it. But mostly, I needed to find Justin's father, Smooth McGee. He had been estranged from Justin's life for so long, I wasn't sure what to do to find him.

I closed my eyes and saw a vision of a glamorous casino by the docks of what appeared to be the Mississippi River. Suddenly, I knew exactly where I had to start my search.

Chapter 6

To say that the bus ride to New Orleans from Baton Rouge was uncomfortable would be an understatement. It was an hour-and-a-half bus ride, although the two cities were less than an hour away from each other's borders. Nonetheless, I'd arrived in the city that held so much promise and yet so much pain for me. It was the first week of May and it had now been a month since Justin had been diagnosed.

As described, there had been one week of induction chemotherapy and three weeks awaiting recovery. After Justin's cancer failed to go into remission, I took the money I'd earned working at the local gas station for the past three weeks, bought a bus ticket, and left town. The only clue I had to help me was a slip of paper with Aunt Ruby's address on it. She'd written me many times when I was in prison, but she'd changed her number since then. It seemed that after years of hard work and struggle, Aunt Ruby had managed to start a business of her own.

I walked through the streets, looking around, enjoying the balmy air, and noticing some of the devastation caused by Hurricane Katrina. Although for the most part, things were back to business as usual, I could see the signs of a slow economic recovery. As painful as it was, I could see the struggle in the eyes of the people and in the now abandoned properties that lined some of the streets. Still, most of what I saw made me smile. There was such a natural and distinct beauty here in the Big Easy.

I followed the numbers on the buildings as I walked up the winding street: 2201, 2202. . . . Finally, I came upon 2203 and saw the sign on the building that read RUBY'S RED HOUSE. With confidence, I walked inside.

A tall, heavyset woman wearing a long dress and long blond weave stopped me at the door. "Welcome to Ruby's Red house. How may I help you, honey?"

"I'm looking for Ruby," I took off my shades to get a better look at the place.

"Girl, now that you've taken those shades off, I'd recognize you anywhere," the woman said. "Imagine those bright eyes."

I looked around me. "You would?"

The woman stepped back. "Of course. You're Ruby Jean's niece, aren't you?"

I squinted my eyes to get a better look at her. "Yes, I am. How do you know who I am?"

The woman laughed so hard that the rolls in her flesh jiggled. "Last time I saw you, you were just a little one. Girl, don't you remember me?"

I shook my head. "No, I'm sorry, ma'am, I don't."

"Don't worry about it, honey, but I'd remember those big eyes and long, pretty hair anywhere. Always did have a different look about you." The lady laughed heartily. "I'm Magnolia, your Aunt Ruby Jean's BFF for the past forty-five years."

"Oh, okay." I couldn't believe that she was such a larger-than-life character and yet I didn't remember her at all.

"Anyway, welcome to Ruby's Red House, the best bed-and-breakfast in all of New Orleans." Magnolia laughed so heartily that her double chin shook. "Ruby went out to run some errands, so you're welcome to wait down here in the lounge or I can give you a room, if you like."

I looked around at the beautiful paintings, diamond-shaped wall mirrors, French-style furniture, and Mardi Gras masks on the wall. "I think I'll wait for her right here. Thanks." Magnolia smiled. "Well, can I get you something to eat or drink while you wait?"

"No, thanks." I held up a bottled water I had in my purse. "I already ate and I have this, so I'm okay for now."

"Whatever you want, darling." Magnolia put her thick arms around me and squeezed. "It's so good to see you again, child."

"Same here." I watched her walk away. "Thanks again."

I sat at a table for two, quietly waiting for Aunt Ruby, wondering what she would be like after all of these years. Then I thought of Justin, all alone in the hospital back in Baton Rouge, hooked up to tubes and machines. I knew Mama would visit him, but she wouldn't be happy about it, not one bit. As I was leaving she told me she'd sue me for abandonment, that I had no business leaving my only child to run down a man. Clearly, she didn't understand my explanation for leaving. There was more at stake than me getting together with my ex. Justin's life hung in the balance and I was determined not to stand by and do nothing about it.

Within minutes Aunt Ruby walked in with her jazzy short hair cut, dyed half red, and a dress so tight you'd almost doubt it wasn't skin.

Aunt Ruby too recognized me immediately. "Gal, Trinity, is that you?"

I stood up and ran into her arms. "Yes, Auntie."

"You're such a sweet thing." Aunt Ruby wrapped herself around me and squeezed. "It's so good to see you."

"It's good to see you too." I hung onto her a little longer than necessary before sitting down.

"I read about you being released in the paper. What a terrible, terrible mistake they made keeping you locked up like that." Aunt Ruby shook her head as she sat down. "Broke my natural heart."

"Yeah. " I really didn't know what else to say.

Aunt Ruby leaned forward in her chair. "At least the real killer finally confessed. That was good luck, wasn't it?"

"I guess so." I looked down at my hands and noticed how rough they looked.

Aunt Ruby put her soft hand on top of mine. "Why did you refuse to see me when I came to visit you that time?"

I looked up slowly. "I don't know. I was feeling so low. I just didn't want anyone to see me like that."

Aunt Ruby's dark eyes softened. "Like what, honey?"

"Broken." I cast my eyes downward.

For a moment I remembered the prosecutor asking the jurors to murder me. And from that day forward I was treated like an animal. Every time I was allowed to leave my cage to go anywhere, I was handcuffed or chained. I remembered the frequent prison brawls, the lack of human interaction, and the corruption. So, in time, despite my best efforts, I began to feel like an animal, like there was not one drop of humanity left in me.

"I can only imagine what you must've went through. It broke my heart that you didn't want to see me, though." Aunt Ruby pressed her hand to her heart.

"I'm sorry." I turned away from her and began to reflect on that time in my life. "I don't know what was going on with me. I guess I'd given up on life. It was terrible in there, on death row."

"I know it was. I kept hoping something would turn up and turn things around for you. I wanted to call that old, foolish mama of yours, but you know how she is." Aunt Ruby frowned up her plump face.

I swallowed hard as I thought about my mother's crudeness. "Yeah, I do know how she is."

Aunt Ruby turned sideways in her chair and looked at me from the corner of her eye. "You still staying with your mama and your Uncle Charlie in Baton Rouge?"

"Yes, for now, but what I really need right now is a room here in New Orleans." The clock was ticking so I didn't have time to play games.

"Well, my dear, you've come to the right place." Aunt Ruby faced me again and smiled. "Ruby's will be the most fun you'll have in a long time."

"No, you don't understand. I'm here on a mission for my son." I held back my tears.

Aunt Ruby looked deeply into my eyes. "How is Justin?"

I met her gaze with my own. "Not good at all, Aunt Ruby. He's sick."

"Sick? Oh no." Aunt Ruby put two hands over her mouth.

I sighed before starting to explain. "He has a real aggressive form of cancer. He has had chemotherapy and three weeks of recovery, but he still has the cancer. Now, if I don't round up all of his family and find a suitable blood donor for him, he could die."

"Oh my goodness. No." Aunt Ruby raised her arched eyebrows.

"Yes. Seems like everything in my life is always critical," I added.

Aunt Ruby shook her head. "Yeah. Looks like you've been dealt another bad hand, child."

I hunched my shoulders.

Aunt Ruby put her plump arm around my shoulders. "Well, you're here at Ruby's Red House now and I'm telling you, little girl, it's the absolute best place you could be."

I nodded, then smiled a weak smile. "I'm sure it is."

Aunt Ruby stood up, then pushed her chair under the table. "Come on and let me show you around while you fill me in on what's going on with Justin."

She took me on a quick tour of her establishment, which was decorated with French furniture and pale orange walls. As we walked, I explained Justin's prognosis and every time we stopped she'd introduce me to another one of her employees.

"This is what I'm going to do for you. I'm gonna put you in one of my best rooms upstairs for as long as you need it. I'm sure you don't have the best insurance. So I'm going to have Justin transferred to a hospital here in New Orleans, probably Mercy. Don't worry about the money. I've got plenty of that." Aunt Ruby pointed her two-toned fingernails.

"Thank you so much, Aunt Ruby." I hugged her. "What would I do without you? "

"Don't thank me, child. You and Justin are the only family I've got." Aunt Ruby smiled.

"Now, how about something to eat? I've got a big ol' pot of crawfish and some red beans and rice cooking."

Aunt Ruby dropped down into one of the lounge armchairs. Sweating profusely, she reached for a box of tissues on a side table, then handed it to me.

"I'm not hungry right now." I sat down also, took a handful of tissue, then passed the box back to Aunt Ruby.

"Worried about your boy? I know it's rough. I'll make some calls and we'll start the procedure of getting him down here." Aunt Ruby took out her smart phone and began dialing.

I nodded my head as tears began to well up in my eyes. "That's a nice phone you've got." I wiped my face with one of the tissues.

"You're right and you need one just like it." Aunt Ruby examined her phone.

I shook my head. "No, Aunt Ruby, I didn't mean for you to—"

"Of course you didn't, but I want to. " Aunt Ruby smiled. " You probably don't know this, since you've been away for so long, but things have changed. Everybody needs a good cell phone these days. No more pay phones around, you know?"

I shook my head. "Yeah, I kind of noticed, but I can't let you do that."

"Nonsense." Aunt Ruby patted me on the knee before she stood up. "As far as I'm concerned, it's already done."

Aunt Ruby stopped walking and stood back just to look at me again. "So glad you're home, child. Can't believe you're finally out."

"Neither can I," I said.

The mention of being *out* reminded me of what it was like to be *in*. I remembered being led away in ankle chains and handcuffs by big, burly female guards, coming out of my cell block only three times a week, and being locked down for twenty-four hours a day. Or sleeping on the concrete floor at night sometimes because it was cooler than sleeping in my bed. It was nothing I wanted to discuss with anyone, but the reality of it still haunted me.

Aunt Ruby leaned her painted face into mine. "So after we have Justin situated, what's next for you, honey?"

"Aunt Ruby, as soon as Justin is transferred to a hospital here and settled, I'm going to start my search." I hoped she could feel my determination. "I'm going to find his family, find out where they've been all this time, and in the process, get my son a donor."

"Just be careful. Sometimes folks are hidden 'cause they don't want to be found. Same thing with the truth, baby." Aunt Ruby clapped her hands together two times. "Same thing with the truth."

Chapter 7

Passing by Bourbon Street, I was reminded of me and Smooth's rocky past together, dancing in smoky jazz clubs until all hours of the night, roaming through downtown New Orleans until the sun came up, or arguing about his scandalous groupies. I leaned against a lamppost and let the memories wash over me for a moment. There were so many interesting people, one of which was a young woman with a blond Mohawk and an earring in her nose, playing a guitar right in front of a grocery store. I started to walk again, taking in all of the local sights, the parks, plantations, and the bayou.

I had a list of those who I needed to find and Smooth McGee was the first person on it.

I set out on foot early that morning, void of direction. Yet, I'd hoped I'd be able to find him in some of his old hangouts. Back in the day he practically owned the streets of New Orleans.

Finally, I decided to stop by Ray's Coffee Shop because Smooth always loved himself some rich coffee with just a little bit of vanilla in it. That man drank so much coffee, I think it balanced off the alcohol he loved to consume. Surprisingly, he seldom appeared drunk even when I knew he was.

As soon as I entered and took a look around, I realized that a lot had changed. Maybe new management was responsible for the changes. There were bright green vinyl booths now instead of just tables. There was central air-conditioning instead of the flowered ceiling fan that used to run. And the entire look of the place was more modern, ecclectic even. There were a few abstract paintings displayed along, with framed poetry. There was a small stage with a microphone, which was never there before. Quite a few people sat around sipping their coffees and talking. I peeped into several corners and booths, but no one even vaguely resembled Smooth. So I slipped onto a stool at the coffee bar and ordered a double mocha latte. I'd missed having these when I was incarcerated and I couldn't wait to taste the sweet confection on my tongue. Then, as I casually glanced beside me, I saw what seemed like a familiar face sitting a few stools down.

I slid off the stool, stood up, and walked up behind him. "Bingo?"

He turned around and hopped up. "Is that you, Puddin'?" He lifted me up high in the air.

"Well, I don't go by *Puddin'* anymore. It's Trinity." I chuckled as he put me down.

"Good, 'cause I don't go by Bingo either." He chuckled too. "It's Tyrone."

I eyed him curiously. "Is that right?"

Tyrone stood back and looked into my eyes. "How have you been?"

"Well, I'm sure you heard what happened to me." I twisted my lips.

Tyrone cast his eyes down. "I'm afraid I did."

"My case was overturned," I explained.

"Yeah, I heard about that on the news. It's a good thing that lady confessed. I felt so sorry for you." Tyrone looked so serious. "I prayed for you, you know?"

I smiled. "Thanks, but how did you know I was innocent?'

"Oh, come on, I knew you couldn't hurt anyone like that, not murder all those people."

Tyrone shook his head. "Not a killing bone in your body. Those of us that know you, knew that."

I nodded. "I'm just glad to have that behind me."

Tyrone sat down and signaled for me to sit also. "So you're here in New Orleans for good? "

"No, actually I'm here on a mission." I faced him on my stool.

Tyrone looked into my eyes. "What kind of mission is it?"

"My son is ill, so I'm here to find his family, including Mr. Smooth."

Tyrone grinned as if memories of the old days soothed him. "Oh yes, my man, Smooth."

"I was hoping you'd know where he was." My smile disappeared behind my fear.

"I haven't seen or heard from him in a while. We stopped playing together a few years back." Tyrone looked as if his mind was far away.

I tilted my head to the side. "Really?"

"I still play sax, but I don't run with the wild crowd anymore." Tyrone ran his hand over his short haircut.

I pushed my neck back. "You don't?

Tyrone smiled. "Nope. Not since I found Jesus, I haven't."

I burst out in laughter. "Wow, you found Jesus on Bourbon Street?"

Tyrone stopped smiling and became very serious. "Actually, he found me on Bourbon Street. No, really; I've turned my life around. I'm a new man."

I stopped laughing, then punched his arm. "I believe you. I was just teasing."

"Same old Puddin'." He looked me up and down, chuckling.

Now I was serious. "It's Trinity now, remember?"

Tyrone laughed again. "That's right, Miss Trinity. I'm sorry."

"It's okay." I batted my thick eyelashes. "I know old habits are hard to break."

"It is still *miss*, isn't it?" Tyrone squinted his eyes. "I mean, you haven't gone off and remarried, have you?"

"No way. Not a chance." I waved my hands back and forth to signal my answer. "Never."

Tyrone showed all of his pearly-white teeth. "Pretty woman like you should never say never."

I could feel myself blushing beneath my brown skin. "Is that so?"

"That's so," Tyrone confirmed.

Tyrone pushed his almost empty cup to the side. "Look, I'm finishing up here. Why don't I take you somewhere, buy you some *real* lunch and we can catch up?"

I gave a quick nod. "Sure, why not? That sounds cool."

It was good to see an old friend. Tyrone and Smooth used to play in a band together for many years. They used to be as close as brothers at one time. We were all friends, the whole band and I, until Smooth started to get jealous whenever the band members were around me.

They used to call me *Puddin'* because that's what Smooth would call me. The next thing I knew he made an embarrassing scene in front of his entire group, then banned me from coming down to the club to see his shows. He should've known better than that. That made me more determined than ever to attend and to keep an eye on him.

Tyrone and I left the coffee shop together and went to the deli two doors down. A waitress came over to take our orders, then disappeared behind the counter.

Tyrone fumbled with his mustache. "So when was the last time you saw him?"

"The last time I saw Smooth was during one of my contact visits. He'd been writing me for a while, then he had showed up against my wishes, and the guards brought me down to see him. I wasn't in a good place at that time. I didn't want to see anyone." I played with the napkin in front of me.

"Last time I saw him he was playing a gig down at Essie's over on Front Street. I'd been coming from a Bible study with a few friends of mine and there he was, standing on the corner with that sax in his hand," Tyrone said.

I twisted my lips. "Typical."

"Said he was waiting on somebody. We talked for a few minutes. I told him what I was up to, how good God had been to me. He told me about how much music and money he'd been making." Tyrone hunched his shoulders. "I gave him my contact information. Said we needed to stay in touch. He agreed, but never gave me his information. We shook hands. Then I left."

I looked up as the waitress set down our food. "Did he say where he was staying or anything?"

"Naw, and that was a while back anyway." Tyrone snapped his fingers. "I hope he's still in the area."

I smiled. "Smooth can travel all over the world, but I don't think he'll ever leave New Orleans. It's too much a part of him."

Tyrone nodded in agreement. "You could just be right, little lady."

"Nobody calls me little except my aunt." I took several bites of my sandwich.

"Well, you are to me." Tyrone was about six feet two and built like a tank.

I laughed. "That's just because you're so tall and ... uh ..."

"And you're still li'l Puddin' too as far as I'm concerned," Tyrone continued, laughing.

"Just teasing. How did you get that name Trinity anyway? It's beautiful."

"Thanks. My grandmother gave it to me," I explained as I crunched on a pickle.

Tyrone pushed a strand of my wild hair out of my eyes. "She must've been a woman of God to give you a name like that."

"From what I can remember, yes, she was." I hesitated. "Can I ask you something?"

"Sure." Tyrone gave me his complete attention.

I looked straight into his eyes. "How did you get mixed up in the church?"

Tyrone put up his two hands. "Well, first of all, I'm not mixed up."

"I'm sorry, but you know what I mean." I hunched my shoulders. "How do you go from the life you used to live to the one you *say* you're living now?"

"God has His own way of cleaning you up and turning you around. I was on a downward spiral going straight to hell. My life was empty, but nobody knew it but me. I was thinking about suicide, to tell you the truth."

I bit my bottom lip. "You're kidding?"

"Nope. I didn't want to live anymore. Then one day I was flipping the channels and I ran across this ministry. They were asking people to call in if they needed prayer. First I ignored it, but I kept watching the program. The people at the church all seemed so happy, smiling, singing and shouting; just happy. The next thing I knew, I'd called in. One of the prayer counselors prayed with me and I felt the power of God coming over me so strong. It was like a miracle. He led me to the Lord right there on the phone in my little motel room, and I haven't been the same since." Tyrone smiled. "Now I've got a really nice apartment about fifteen minutes from here. My church is in the area too. But most of all, I'm happy, really happy."

"Wow, that's quite a story." I continued to chew and covered my mouth with my hand as I spoke.

"Not a story, Trinity." Tyrone put his fist up to my chin. "It's my testimony."

I wiped my mouth with the paper napkin. "Sorry."

"No, it's okay. It's so good to see you." Tyrone put a forkful of fries into his mouth. "I don't really see any of the old crew anymore. It's kind of sad, really, how we all grew apart, but it happens."

"Yeah, I guess." I shook my head as I thought about some of the old drama: band members not getting along, sometimes fighting, and sometimes quitting.

Tyrone wiped his mouth with a napkin, then smoothed his moustache with his fingers. "Everyone in your life is not a part of your future. Too bad I had to learn that the hard way."

I saw how serious he was. "That's true."

"Funny how my life is going a whole other direction now." Tyrone bit into his sandwich again. "Yours too."

I stared at him. "What do you mean?"

"Well, just days ago your life was on the line. You were being led to the slaughter for a crime you didn't commit. Then you were snatched from harm's way just in time. I would say that's a miracle." Tyrone snapped his fingers. "I mean, the murderer confessed and look at you. Now you're here, sitting in front of me, looking great as ever, ready to face the world."

Tyrone pretended to frame me with his hands.

I shook my head. "I don't know if I'm ready for all of that."

Tyrone reached across the table to pat my hand. "But I can tell that you are. Being on death row has matured you. I can see something in you that wasn't quite there before."

"Are you sure that isn't fatigue? My years in prison made me tired, tired of fighting people and systems," I said, smirking.

"Maybe tired is just where God wants you to be." Tyrone smiled.

"Well, that's definitely where I am. Six years, only to come out and have to fight for my son's life." I let out a sigh.

"Maybe you don't have to fight this time. There's a better way." Tyrone balled up his napkin and set it down on the table.

I squinted my eyes at him, doubting him. "And you have all of the answers?"

"Not at all, but I do know someone who does." Tyrone paused. "What exactly is wrong with your son? Tell me about him."

"Justin is a great kid. Best thing that's ever happened to me was having him. But he was just diagnosed with an aggressive form of cancer and like I said before, I need his father to be notified. I also need him to test to see if he can be a bone-marrow donor," I explained.

Tyrone looked up at me in between bites. "Wow, I sure am sorry to hear that. Must be hard dealing with all of that alone."

"It's not easy, that's for sure, but my aunt has been very supportive." I drank the last of my raspberry iced tea, but kept my eye on him. He was definitely interesting.

"Well, if I can do anything to help, just call me." Tyrone slipped me his number. "I'd really like to help if I can."

I forced a fake smile. "The only way you can help right now is by helping me to find Smooth. He's first on my list."

Chapter 8

I opened the blinds in Justin's room so that the midday sunlight could flow through.

Thankfully, Aunt Ruby had Justin transferred to Mercy Hospital in New Orleans right away so I could be close to him. I opened the box of action figures and DVDs I'd purchased for him and set them on the table in the corner to add character to the room. I'd originally wanted to bring a few of his toys from home, but I was warned about bringing in germs that could potentially contaminate Justin. I looked around the nearly all-white room and was confident about its sterility.

Justin spoke through his mask. "When can I go home?"

"As soon as you're feeling stronger and your blood count is higher," I explained.

Justin threw off his covers, sat up, and put one leg over the bed. "But I want to get out of this hospital. I've been sick too long."

"Justin, calm down. The staff here is trying to help you. They can't let you go home just yet. There is a risk of infection and bleeding. You—" I helped him lean back in bed.

Justin wiped his wet eyes. "Why is the leukemia still there?"

"I don't know, baby." I couldn't look into his eyes. "It's still there, but that's why we're here to get you a donor."

"I thought I'd be in remission after the chemo. You told me that I wouldn't have it after the chemo." Justin turned on his side.

"I'm sorry, baby. Mommy was wrong. The chemo didn't destroy everything, so now we need a donor." I rubbed Justin's hand, careful not to upset the IV.

Justin balanced himself on his elbow. "When are Grandma and Uncle Charlie coming?"

I answered through my tears. "I'm not sure yet. But don't worry, because Mom is here now. And your Aunt Ruby was just here yesterday, remember?"

"Yeah, but I don't know her," Justin whined.

"She knows you. She just hasn't been able to see you for a while." I fluffed Justin's pillow, then kissed his smooth, bald head. "But doesn't she seem nice?"

"Yes, ma'am," Justin agreed.

"Well, she is nice. She and I used to be really close and she'll be coming back to see you again today." I decided to explain my plan so Justin wouldn't be confused. "In fact, there'll be a lot of different family members you haven't seen since you were a baby coming by to see you really soon."

Justin looked into my eyes. "Why is that, Mom? Are they coming to see me 'cause they think I'm going to die?"

I thought my heart would break after hearing his words. "No, not at all. They're coming because we're in New Orleans now and you have some family here that I have to find. When I find them, everybody is going to be tested until we find you a match, okay?"

"Okay." Justin smiled, revealing his slightly crooked teeth.

Later in the day Aunt Ruby came by and sat with Justin, telling him funny old stories about the South while I listened and recalled her telling me the same ones when I was small.

Finally, we stepped out of the room into the waiting area.

Aunt Ruby sat down first. "Well, how did you make out earlier?"

"Well, first I started up by where we used to live and I walked the whole neighborhood. A lot has changed since Hurricane Katrina." I sat down next to her.

"Yes, so much was tore up by that storm. I've had to rebuild twice myself," Aunt Ruby said.

I nodded. "I didn't find Smooth, but I found Tyrone, one of his old buddies."

Aunt Ruby pushed the hair of her red wig out of her eyes. "That's good. I'm glad you made some progress today. "

"Yeah, I guess you could say that," I said, smirking because I had no idea how to find my roaming ex-husband.

Aunt Ruby smiled. "Believe me, if you've found one of his old friends, you'll soon find him."

"They're not really friends anymore, though." I fumbled around in my bag and pulled out the slip of paper with Tyrone's number on it.

"That doesn't matter. You're close on his trail, honey. Just keep sniffing him out. Men are like dogs that way." Aunt Ruby laughed.

"I'll agree with you on that." I eyed the paper, then giggled.

Aunt Ruby asked, "Have you talked to your mama yet?"

I sighed. "I called her, but she won't answer my call."

Aunt Ruby's eyes became serious. "Why not?"

"She's upset with me. She thinks I shouldn't be here in New Orleans. She's convinced there's something evil here that broke up her and my dad," I explained.

Aunt Ruby shook her head. "Now, that's a joke. The only thing evil here that broke up those two is *her*. Rosalee was always so unreasonable."

I stuffed the paper back into my bag. "Anyway, she's totally against my being here and especially against me teaming up with you."

"Of course not. I'm sure she's not happy about that at all." Aunt Ruby shook her head. "I don't know what's wrong with your mama. It was always hard to get along with that woman."

"No one knows, Aunt Ruby," I agreed.

"She'd turn even the most kind person into an enemy. Bitter, just plain bitter is what I call her. And I never understood why." Aunt Ruby waved her plump, diamond-ring-covered hands in the air. "If anyone should've been bitter, it should've been me."

I didn't expect Aunt Ruby to say that. "What do you mean?"

"I was the one with the short, kinky hair who got teased in school. Your mama had the long, soft, flowing hair. Yet despite my resemblance to him, my own daddy refused to claim me. He said over and over again that I wasn't his, even when everyone else said I was. Well, everyone except my rebellious mother. She should've never told him I belonged to someone else. That's not funny at all."

"No, it's not and I'm sorry 'bout that." At that moment I was ashamed of my grandfather.

"Sweetie, that's old news. Nothing for you to feel bad about. Your mama, Rosalee, and your Uncle Charlie had everything. Still, I ain't bitter, not much anyways." Aunt Ruby put her hand up in the air.

"I'm glad you're not bitter." I thought of Mama's hateful ways. "Mama lets hers eat her alive and it shows too."

"I'll bet it does," Aunt Ruby said.

I looked past Aunt Ruby. "She has a really bad attitude."

Aunt Ruby snapped her brightly manicured fingers. "I used my adversity to make me stronger, left Baton Rouge, and made myself a home down here in New Orleans. Worked three jobs and bought myself a piece of land with this old boarding house on it. That's how I got to where I am today, so I'm not bitter, honey."

I hopped out of my seat and spun around. "Oh, so that's what the Red House used to be, an old boarding house?"

Aunt Ruby turned sideways in her chair. "Yep, and I turned it into a classic bed-and-breakfast. Folks come from all over just to stay at the Red House and I make sure they're never disappointed."

"You're the friendliest lady I know. So I'm sure your customers are happy." I pushed back the curtains to look out of the huge bay windows.

"I looked at my sister and brother and I decided a long time ago that I could internalize that anger and let it ruin my life, or I could get rid of it and make my life turn out a different way." Aunt Ruby looked sad for a moment.

I smiled. "I'm glad you chose something different because those two—"

Aunt Ruby's cheerful countenance returned and she laughed. "Child, hush. Don't say another word about it." She put her thick finger against her ruby-red lips.

I sat back down and crossed my legs. "I'm just glad I got Mama and Uncle Charlie to test to be a donor before I left."

"Rosalee is so stubborn I'm surprised she did it without a fuss." Aunt Ruby threw her head back in laughter, then adjusted her wig around her ears.

I shook my head. "Oh , I didn't say there wasn't a fuss. I just said she did it."

"Well, thank goodness, my own results will be in tomorrow. So hopefully I'm all that sweet boy of yours needs." Aunt Ruby patted my hand with hers.

"Hopefully," I agreed.

"Now, you said you wanted to locate more family members." She sat down in an armchair. "Who else do you have in mind?"

I answered slowly. "Besides Smooth, I was hoping to find my father and my paternal grandmother, Nana."

Aunt Ruby's eyes grew large. "Do you at least know where to start?"

"Nope. Last time I saw Nana I was only ten years old. She did write me once, though, when I was in prison, but I never wrote back." I waited for Aunt Ruby's reaction. I'd felt guilty about it for so long.

Aunt Ruby leaned back in her chair. "Well, what did she say?"

"Not much, just that she'd missed me, that she was praying that God would make a way for me to be safe," I explained. "I never did finish reading the letter. It was too painful and I was too angry."

Aunt Ruby picked up a piece of caramel and ate it. "Hmph, and you're sitting here free today. I guess she sure was right about God making a way, huh?"

I nodded. "I guess so."

Aunt Ruby let the caramel roll around in her mouth before she spoke. "Why didn't you ever answer her?"

"She wanted to come and see me, but I was in a really bad place back then. I didn't want anyone to come see me. Especially not the ones like her and my dad, who abandoned me," I said.

"I wouldn't say they abandoned you, child." Aunt Ruby's eyebrows met in the middle.

I closed my eyes against the thought of abandonment. "Where were they all those years, huh?"

"I can't answer that, sweetie. You'll have to get your answers from them. All I can say is life isn't always black-and-white." Aunt Ruby patted my hand. "Sometimes there are shades of gray. Remember that."

I swallowed hard. "When I was locked up, I didn't want anyone to see me like a caged animal, like I was less than human, less than alive."

"I'm sorry." Aunt Ruby's eyes met mine.

"So am I," I agreed. "Anyway, if I could just find Nana and my dad, it would be great. My dad used to live down here so . . . Last time Nana wrote me from Maryland, though. I guess she moved up there, so I don't know if she's in Maryland or New Orleans or somewhere else."

Aunt Ruby didn't look at me. "Your dad is from Maryland."

"I know." I nodded.

Aunt Ruby snapped her fingers. "What about your sister?"

"She's coming down here tomorrow to be tested," I answered.

Aunt Ruby smiled. "That's good."

I raised my eyebrows. "I'm just glad she could fit me into her *bourgeois* little schedule."

"Oh, come on, don't be so hard on her. She can't help the way she is. She's accomplished a lot and coming out of your mama's house, she has a right to be proud." Aunt Ruby let out a giggle.

"I guess you're right. It's not that I'm jealous of her or anything, but I just wish she'd bring that big head of hers down to earth sometimes." I rolled my eyes, a habit I knew I needed to break.

"I know how you feel, sweetheart. People can be stuck on themselves," Aunt Ruby said.

"Maybe the two of you can put your heads together and come up with a plan to find your father. Haven't heard anything about him in years."

I stood up again and wrapped my arms around my waist. "Yeah, maybe. I don't think Alyssa cares like I do, though."

Aunt Ruby looked up at me. "What makes you think that?"

"It's what she says and the way she acts, like he doesn't even exist. She's angrier about it than I am, if that's even possible." I paced the floor as I talked.

"Oh, it's possible. I know. I used to be angry myself."
Aunt Ruby stood up and grabbed me by the arm. "She'll
come around."

"Maybe. I'm not even sure what I expect. Right now I
just want to find him, let him get tested for Justin, then
maybe I can . . . get to know him or something. I don't
know." I threw my hands into the air in mock surrender.

"Your father just might be a match himself." Aunt Ruby
patted me on the shoulder. "Who knows?"

"I sure hope so," I said. "If my father is a match, then
that would be great. Even if he isn't a match, I'd still like
to find him."

"Of course you would." Aunt Ruby fluttered her fake
eyelashes. "Or your nana or your sister. They might be the
match you're looking for. You never know."

"You're right. Either of them could be," I agreed. "We'll
see."

"By the way, here is that phone I promised ya." Aunt
Ruby reached into her purse and pulled out a cute little
silver phone. "Every girl needs one, honey."

"How can I ever thank you?"

Aunt Ruby looked down at the phone. "Don't worry
about it, darling. I just hope this helps with communica-
tion."

"It will." I took the phone out of its box, then twirled
it around in my hands, checking out its features. "This is
fantastic."

Aunt Ruby pulled herself from her seat. "I'm gonna go
now. I'll see you at home."

I hugged her again. "Thanks, Aunt Ruby."

"For what, child?"

"For being you," I said.

"Honey, that's easy." Aunt Ruby burst into laughter.
"It's all that other stuff that's hard."

I watched her walk away, laughing to herself.

Later on back at Aunt Ruby's place, I called Mama and Uncle Charlie answered the phone.

"Hold on, now. I'll get your mama." Uncle Charlie coughed uncontrollably into the phone.

I waited, held on, then heard the phone being hung up. At the sound of the dial tone, I was livid. How could Mama ignore me like this? I called back, but this time there was no answer.

I dialed over and over again, leaving numerous voice mails. As I called her for the last time, I looked up and said, "Lord, you know what I need." Could she possibly be so stubborn?

Finally, Mama answered. "What do you want?"

"Hello, Mama. I just wanted to see how you are and to tell you how I am." Sadly, I wasn't sure if she even cared.

"If you cared anything about me, you wouldn't be *there* in the first place," Mama whined.

"I didn't call to debate with you about why I'm here. But just to tell you that Justin is doing well and he's been asking for you. Also to tell you that Alyssa is coming down tomorrow to be tested also."

Mama sighed. "Well, I knows about that. She called me first."

"Okay." I held the phone close to my ear, planning each word before I said it.

Mama's voice was scratchy from years of smoking. "You staying with Ruby?"

"Yes, ma'am," I answered.

"Don't know how you're gonna stay there with no way to support yourself. When Ruby finds out you don't have no money she's gonna put you out on the streets."

"Aunt Ruby's not like that," I scoffed.

Mama taunted, "She is like that. How are you gonna tell me about my own flesh and blood? She's been mean like that ever since she was a little girl."

I folded my arms."Well, she's my flesh and blood too and she's not like that at all."

"You'll see." Mama cackled. "Still having them scary dreams?"

Why did Mama want to torture me with something so painful? "I don't want to talk about that."

"They're gonna get worse now that you're in that evil place and staying with that evil woman," Mama said.

"For the last time, Aunt Ruby is not like that and New Orleans is not evil, either. I'm here to get help for Justin and there's nothing that's going to drive me away until I find it."

"Well, I sure hope you know what you're doing," Mama spat out.

At that moment a vision flashed before my eyes. I was standing with Alyssa and my mother and we were holding each other, crying. Then it faded away. I didn't know what it meant, but it startled me. I hoped it had nothing to do with Justin.

"I'll talk to you later, Mama." I held the phone until Mama hung up. She never even said good-bye.

I took my shower, then slipped into my cotton pajamas. I curled up in the middle of the queen-size bed with my potential donor list. I crossed off myself, Uncle Charlie, Mama, put a question mark next to Aunt Ruby, then circled Alyssa's name. She was next in line to be tested.

It had been quite a few years since I'd seen my sister and despite my best effort, I had mixed feelings about it. After all, she and I were both products of Mama's pain-filled parenting.

I remembered the years after our father left, when Mama ran through a string of menfolk from all around town, using them to satisfy an itch she claimed to have. In reality, she used them for money, clothes, rides to and fro, or to take her out dancing from time to time. Each one, she claimed, brought something to her, but each one seemed to take something away even more. And as she was drained of hope or whatever was missing in her life, she proceeded to take that much more away from us, her helpless children. With all things considered, however, I thought that me and my sister turned out all right— if you subtract my prison record, that is, especially since I was falsely accused. I was still stunned at how one eyewitness testimony had nailed my coffin and left me buried for six whole years. Nevertheless, I was what I considered a pretty decent person and so was my sister, except that she thought she was better than everyone else. We each had our problems, but neither of us carried around the poison Mama tried to instill in us. Folks all around town used to say Mama was as mean as a rattlesnake and twice as deadly.

Maybe seeing my sister again wouldn't be as bad as I thought.

Chapter 9

True to her nature, Alyssa flew in bright and early. Aunt Ruby and I met her at the Louis Armstrong International Airport. She came walking down the crowded hallway wearing a gray plaid two-piece suit with a matching fedora hat. She looked like a chocolate Barbie with a fully made-up face, long, freshly permed hair, and long, shapely legs to match. She had dimples like mine, but she had Mama's gray eyes.

"Well, hey there, Ms. Business Lady." Aunt Ruby grabbed her.

"Well, hey, yourself." Alyssa hugged Aunt Ruby back.

"It's been a long time, sis." I opened my arms wide.

"Too long." Alyssa walked into my embrace.

I smelled Elizabeth Arden perfume on her neck. She'd been wearing it since college.

"Now that's about the nicest thing I've seen in a while." Aunt Ruby stood back and smiled.

Alyssa pulled away from me and snapped her fingers. "Let's go. Chop-chop."

Same old Alyssa. I shook my head and asked, "What about your luggage?"

Alyssa held up a laptop case and an overnight bag. "Nope. This is all I brought."

"Let's get to parking lot A then and we'll be on our way," Aunt Ruby instructed.

Alyssa walked ahead of us through the airport, to the parking lot where Aunt Ruby took the lead. I wondered how she could possibly walk so fast in what appeared to be four-inch platform shoes. After we found the car, Aunt Ruby unlocked the doors. I was already standing by the passenger door when Alyssa shoved me aside, then hopped into the front seat. It was just like when we were kids. It had started already.

First we went to the hospital so Alyssa could be tested. While we were there I received the results of Aunt Ruby's test. Unfortunately, Aunt Ruby was not a match and the strain of this search was already taking an emotional toll on me. Alyssa patted me on the back gently without saying a word. Out of pure necessity, I pulled myself together before I led Alyssa to Justin's room. Aunt Ruby stayed in the waiting area, so that the two of us could have more time with Justin.

Alyssa tiptoed into his room, grabbed a chair, flipped it backwards, and sat down beside his bed. She took off her hat and placed it in her lap.

Justin opened his eyes and sat up in bed. "Auntie, is that really you?"

"You betcha." Alyssa leaned over to hug Justin, careful not to disturb any of his tubes or equipment.

"Hi, Mom." Justin waved his little hand.

"Hey, baby." I sat in a chair behind Alyssa and touched his hand.

Justin turned his attention back to Alyssa. "What are you doing here, Auntie?"

"Well, I'm here for you, of course. I'm gonna spend some time with you first and then I guess I'll hang out with your old mom here."

I put my finger up. "Oh, I've got your old."

Justin laughed. "It's so cool that you're here."

"I think it's pretty cool that you're so big now." Alyssa paused. "What do you want to be when you grow up?"

Justin hunched his shoulders. "I'm not sure yet. Maybe a football player or a drummer."

Alyssa had a big smile on her face. "Well, whatever you do, make sure you do well in school. Then you can become anything you want."

"I don't like school so much." Justin forced his lips into a frown.

"I can understand that, but education is so important. You can become something really great one day. Then you can represent this family properly." Alyssa leaned in close to him and tapped him gently on the nose.

I wasn't sure whether or not to take offense to her comments or not. Sometimes you couldn't tell if my sister was being deliberately insulting or if her air of superiority was accidental.

In any case, we spent the rest of the visit talking to Justin about all of the things that he liked and all of the things that he wanted to do when he was able to leave the hospital. Then Alyssa hugged Justin and said, "I'm so proud of you for being so brave. This time next year, you'll be stronger and taller than me."

"Thanks, Aunt Alyssa." Justin's smile lit up the whole room.

That made me feel good about her visit.

We left the hospital and as we pulled up in front of the Red House, Alyssa's eyes grew wide. "Is this place really yours, Aunt Ruby?"

"Well, I certainly didn't name it Ruby's Red House for nothing." Aunt Ruby laughed.

"Pretty swanky, if I do say so myself," Alyssa said as she walked through the front door.

Magnolia met us at the door. "Pretty little Alyssa. Girl, it's been forever."

Alyssa stood back with her hands on her shapely hips. "How are you, ma'am?"

"Why, I'm just fine, but I'll bet you don't remember me any more than your sister did when she saw me." Magnolia laughed so hard that her cheeks jiggled.

Alyssa stared at Magnolia. "I'm sorry, but I probably don't."

Ruby interrupted, "Alyssa, this is my best friend Magnolia. We go way back. You were just a little girl the last time she saw you and Trinity."

"Ain't that the truth." Magnolia wiped tears of laughter from her eyes.

I could see Alyssa cringing inside her business suit. And why she wore a suit for an occasion such as this, I didn't know. But that was my sister: all business and no heart.

"Nice seeing you again, Ms. Magnolia," Alyssa said in her fake voice.

"You too, baby." Magnolia was still wiping her eyes with her apron as she walked away.

Aunt Ruby handed me a key. "Trinity, why don't you take Alyssa upstairs and help her get settled into suite twenty-five, which is right down the hall from you."

"No problem," I said. "We'll be back down in a little while."

Then we took the winding staircase to the second floor and found the empty suite.

"This is very nice." Alyssa took off her suit jacket and threw it on the bed, revealing a short-sleeved silk blouse. "Aunt Ruby has done well for herself."

"Yeah, she has, if you consider having money as doing well for yourself." I didn't know why I had to go there, but I did.

Alyssa smirked. "Well, I certainly don't consider being broke doing well."

I put both hands on my wide hips. "I just meant that there are other important things besides money."

"I know what you meant and I agree: there are some other things." Alyssa admired the expensive rings on her finger. "It's just that money is right up there on the top of my list."

"Really? Not mine."

"I can tell." Alyssa giggled. "Just kidding. I know you haven't been out long enough to really *do* anything yet. But I do know you've got a pretty large lawsuit coming to you. So tell me, what are your plans?"

I sat down on the edge of the bed. "I was thinking I'd wait tables for a little while just so I could go to cosmetology school and get my license. Then after a few years, maybe I could even have my own salon."

"Okay, that's not bad. You did always hook up my hair for me. That's not a bad plan."

Alyssa fluffed her curls with her hands. "This humidity is killing my curls."

"I can fix that right up for you." I pushed a strand of her hair out of her face. "Did you bring your curling iron?"

Alyssa shot me a look. "Do I look like a fool to you?"

We both burst out laughing as she took her curling iron out of her overnight bag. I began to work on her hair, running my fingers through it to massage the scalp, then adding the hair products she had brought with her.

"You were always good with a comb and a brush, Trinity." Alyssa took out her cell phone and started playing with it.

"Thanks." Memories of me doing my sister's hair made me feel warm on the inside.

"This is just like old times."

Alyssa shook her head. "Except that Mama is not in the background screaming."

"Girl, I know that's right." I waved the brush in the air like a flag.

Alyssa snapped, "Mama is really upset that you're here."

"I know. She told me." I kept parting her hair.

Alyssa continued tapping the screen on her phone. "I'm sure she did."

"I can't help that she's upset. Being here is something I have to do. I've got a list and I'm crossing off names as I go. New Orleans is just my starting point. I'm almost sure that Smooth is here and I believe our father may be here too." I reached over for Alyssa's hair oil and rubbed some onto her scalp.

Alyssa hunched her shoulders. "To be honest, I never cared where our father was."

I stopped rubbing to focus in on her answer. "Weren't you ever just curious?"

"When I was younger, yes. But after a while I gave up on dreaming about a father who was never around. It was obviously his choice," Alyssa spat out.

I stopped curling for a minute. "Still, I'd like to hear that from him. Mama's always talking about how bad he was and how ugly he was. I'd like to see and hear for myself. I want a chance to know him for myself."

Alyssa turned to face me. "Well, if you really want to find him so badly, why don't you just look him up on all of the social networks?"

I was confused. "What?"

"The social networks, like Facebook. I know you must've heard of that one at least, even in prison." Alyssa looked at me as if I was from another planet.

"Yeah, I've heard of social networks and Facebook, but I never knew how they worked."

I put my hand up to my face in embarrassment. "I've been gone so long that I'm out of touch with everything."

"No problem. I'll help you set up accounts with each of the most popular ones. Then I'll walk you through the steps." Alyssa unzipped her leather laptop case and took out a shiny black laptop. "I'm much too busy to fool with them personally, but I've heard a lot of people have been successful in finding their loved ones that way."

"Hmm. That's interesting," I let go of Alyssa's hair and began to put her items away.

Alyssa grabbed her hand mirror. "Ooh, girl, you've still got it. I look better than I did when I stepped out of the salon. One hundred-and-fifty-dollar hairdo, indeed."

"Thanks. I appreciate that." I fluffed and admired her hair.

Alyssa reached into her handbag and took out a tube of lip gloss. "Yes, being on Facebook is not the kind of image I want to portray, but it's fine for you." She applied some to her lips.

I squinted my eyes. "What's that supposed to mean?"

"Just that you've got nothing to lose and in terms of Justin, you have everything to gain."

Alyssa smiled as she put away the lip gloss.

"That's true," I agreed.

Alyssa laid down on the bed, turned on the computer, and began searching the Web. "If our father is out there, there's a good chance that these networks will help to locate him."

I laid down beside her on the bed. "Sounds like a great idea."

"First, we'll have to get you an e-mail account." Alyssa glared at me. "I don't suppose you already have one?"

I shot her a look. "Nope."

"Okay, let's just do this." Alyssa fiddled with the keyboard for a few minutes. "There, now you have an e-mail address at coolmail. We'll start with Facebook because it's probably the most popular."

I looked over her shoulder. "Facebook?"

Alyssa slid over so I could see clearly. "Yes. Now I need you to choose a password for Facebook."

I thought about it for a minute. "Oh, I don't know."

"What about Justin Mercy 2012?"

I nodded. "That's okay, I guess."

"Okay, cool. Now we're almost done." Alyssa tapped on the keyboard. "Then you can get on Facebook."

"I'm not sure I'll know what to do." I watched carefully to see what my sister was doing.

"It's easy and almost everyone is on it. I'll show you." Alyssa zipped through the Facebook search in seconds. "Now we put our father's name, Anthony Crawford, into the search box."

We waded through several profiles with the name Anthony Crawford, with Alyssa explaining everything as we went along, until we stumbled upon many people with that name.

"Hmmm. There are too many Anthony Crawfords." Alyssa shrugged.

"Wow." I pointed to the list of names on the screen. "All of those are Anthony Crawfords?"

"Yep. Who knew?" Alyssa started to click on each one, then she stopped. "This could take forever. Let's check the Anthonys in New Orleans, specifically."

"Sounds good," I said.

Most of them had profile pictures or descriptions that disqualified them from being our father. Except for one that had no profile picture. "Okay, what about this one? He's from New Orleans, but has no picture, no age. What do we do now?"

Alyssa's face brightened. "Now we need to communicate with this person. So we'll send him a friend request first."

I looked at Alyssa. "Then what?"

Alyssa pushed the laptop aside and stood up. "Now you'll have to wait until he accepts your friend request. Then we can check to see if it's really him."

"Wait?"

"Yes, wait." Alyssa continued to check Facebook profiles.

"That's all I've been doing lately, waiting and feeling helpless." I jumped up off of the bed. "I want to do something."

Alyssa continued to explain. "I hear you, but there's only so much we can do until we know for sure that it's him."

"In the meantime, can't I do the same thing with Smooth?" I sat back down on the bed, anxious. "I mean, can't I look him up too?"

"Sure, why not? "

I took control of the computer. "Should I look under Smooth McGee?"

"I don't know. Maybe." Alyssa guided me through the steps.

I checked. "Nothing."

Alyssa looked puzzled. "What's his real name?"

"It's Oliver Fitzgerald McGee." I ran through similar names.

"Whoa. No wonder he calls himself Smooth." Alyssa covered her mouth as she giggled.

"I would too if I had a name like that."

I hit her with my paper. "That's his grandfather's name."

Alyssa didn't smile. "You're still in love with him, aren't you?"

"I am not." I made my face look serious.

"I don't believe it. You're defending that hideous name. Don't make excuses for that name. It's horrendous, that's it and that's all." She chuckled.

I giggled as she made silly faces and tickled me. I'd never seen her act so silly. Not since we were kids. "What's gotten into you?"

"Nothing." Alyssa sat up and became serious. "I'm just glad to see you, that's all."

"You were never glad to see me before." I stared straight into her eyes, searching for an explanation.

Alyssa threw her arms around me and squeezed. "When you were gone for six years, I thought I'd lost you like we lost James."

I nodded, remembering our brother, James. He was two years younger than me and he was my best friend until the time he was killed. Light-skinned with light gray eyes, James looked very much like Mama, but acted very much like me. He dropped out of school after freshman year, hooked up with a gang, and left home before he was fifteen. By fifteen he was found dead in the streets.

The funny thing is that I'd dreamed about him dying about a month before he died. I wanted to warn him, to tell him to be careful, but I didn't know where he was. I didn't know how to get in contact with him. I couldn't tell Mama about it, because she wouldn't allow my brother's name to be spoken in the house anymore; besides, she cursed my visions. And I couldn't tell Alyssa, because we weren't friends at the time, just two enemies under one roof. So I kept my dream to myself and hoped that it meant nothing until the day Mama got the call.

Alyssa helped me to look up Smooth by his real name, and showed me how to register for a few other social-networking accounts. After searching for every variation of Smooth's first, last, and nickname, we realized we were having no luck, then shut down the computer.

After freshening up, we went downstairs to the dining hall for dinner. Magnolia waved to us from down the hallway. We waved back.

Aunt Ruby cornered us before we could turn the corner. "I'm so glad you ladies are here. I was just about to come drag you out."

"Oh, I'm sorry, we just got caught up on Facebook doing profile searches."

Aunt Ruby opened her mouth wide. "Facebook? Profile searches?"

"That's when you put in a person's name and hope their profile will show up," Alyssa explained.

"Oh, okay," Aunt Ruby laughed heartily.

"Trying to show her the ropes of social networking, you know." Alyssa threw up her hand for a high five.

"Now, I can't help you out there, darling, 'cause the only social networking I do is in person, mostly right here at the Red House." Aunt Ruby gave Alyssa the high five she was waiting for.

"Alyssa says lots of people have been found on Facebook," I explained.

"Come to think of it, I have heard that." Aunt Ruby put her hand over her mouth as if she was embarrassed. "But I don't know how to use those things. My secretary and accountant keep up with all of my computer business. I haven't got much use for it."

"I understand. Nevertheless, it might just be helpful in locating all the people she needs, for Justin's sake," Alyssa said. "It's a very efficient process."

"That's a good idea. I'm so glad you're here, Alyssa. So glad you're both here. Now it's time to eat. Come on, darlings." Aunt Ruby led the way to the dining hall.

It was semi-crowded, with guests cheerfully eating dinner.

As soon as Alyssa, Aunt Ruby, and I sat down at our table, someone came up behind me and tapped me on the shoulder.

Chapter 10

I turned around, wondering who it could be, then stared right into the face of Tyrone.

"Hey. What are you doing here?"

"I don't know. I was just about to ask you the same thing." Tyrone chuckled. "Good evening, ladies."

Aunt Ruby answered, "How are you, son?"

"Hello." Alyssa looked him up and down, suspiciously.

I pointed to both of them. "Oh, I'm sorry, Tyrone Freeman, this is my sister, Alyssa, who is visiting from Washington, D.C., and this is my Aunt Ruby."

Tyrone offered his hand to each of them. "I'm very pleased to meet you both. You're not Ruby, the owner of this place, are you?"

"The one and only." Aunt Ruby clapped her hands lightly.

Tyrone raised his eyebrows. "I'm impressed."

"So you see I have a legitimate reason to be here." I laughed. "Now, have you been stalking me?"

"Not hardly. I'm here with friends. He and his wife are in town for a church conference and it appears that they're staying here." Tyrone pointed to a table not that far away. "There they are."

I peered through the crowd. "That's nice. Where are they from?"

"They drove in from North Carolina, actually," Tyrone explained.

"Wow, all the way from North Carolina for a church conference," I said.

"It's kind of a big deal. People fly in from all over the country to attend this one," Tyrone explained. "It's called the Victory Conference."

"Well, I guess I'd fly in to get victory too." Aunt Ruby laughed so that her plump cheeks rose like half melons.

"I know that's right." I put up my fist in agreement.

Alyssa didn't comment.

"Well, I don't want to hold you up. It was nice meeting you, ladies—and Trinity, it was very good seeing you again." Tyrone began to reach into his pockets. "I remember giving you my number, but I forgot to take yours. Maybe I can give you a call sometime."

"Sure." I wrote my cell number on a napkin and handed it to him.

"Thanks." Tyrone smiled before walking away.

"He's not bad-looking at all," Aunt Ruby said. "You'd better watch him."

"Don't worry, Aunt Ruby, he's broke. I can tell." Alyssa twisted her lips and glanced sideways. "Then again, the view from over here isn't too bad."

"You're ridiculous." I shook my head.

Alyssa put on her *excuse me* face. "Oh, so like no one else noticed his biceps, triceps, and glutes except me?"

I continued to shake my head and sighed. "I didn't say that, but no one else is talking about him like you are."

"Oh, please. Get a life, girl. He's only good for eye candy anyway." Alyssa pounded her fist gently on the table. "There's absolutely no potential otherwise."

That was my sister, always skeptical about men. Sometimes I wondered if she liked men at all. She hardly dated, kept her emotions to a minimum, and very rarely complimented any man unless he was wealthy.

When we were done with dinner, we went back up to Alyssa's room and checked our social-networking progress. Our friend request had been accepted, but the man was clearly not our father. He was actually twenty-two years old and Caucasian. I fell back on the bed in frustration.

Alyssa hunched me in my side. "It's okay. There are still other ways. Let's look up our grandmother's name."

I hadn't thought of that. "Nana?"

Alyssa grabbed the laptop from me and began tapping on the keys. "Yes, Nana."

I reached into my purse and pulled out an old, tattered letter. "This is the letter she sent me. Her name is Pauline Crawford."

Alyssa snatched it from my hand. "Good, we'll start there. I'll look up all the Pauline Crawfords." She tapped a few keys. "Uh-oh, there are twenty-four of them. Most of them have pictures, though."

I leaned over her shoulder. "Any of them look like her?"

"Not in these pics. Again, about five people don't have profile pics, so I'll just do friend requests for them." Within seconds, Alyssa sent the friend requests. "Done."

"So we wait again?"

"Not necessarily. Now I can check other Crawfords in Louisiana to see if they're related." Alyssa searched vigorously.

I stared at the computer screen. "How are you going to know that?"

Alyssa curled her lips into a frown. "Well, we can see if anybody looks familiar or has some recognizable information. I don't know. I'm a corporate attorney, not a private detective."

"But you're doing a pretty good job, Inspector." I put my hand to my forehead to salute her.

"Cute." Alyssa looked up at me and smiled.

"Look, what about that person there, Anita Crawford?" I pointed at a particular person.

"Click on her profile."

"Okay, sure." Alyssa clicked, then was silent.

I leaned forward and squinted my eyes. "That's it?"

"Wait a minute." Alyssa scrolled down the profile page. I didn't know what she was doing. "What is it?"

"I think I saw something," she said.

I looked closer. "What did you see?"

I looked over her shoulder. "There's a house in one of these pictures that looks familiar. Do you remember this house?"

I looked closely. "You're right, it does look kind of familiar."

Alyssa nodded as she she tapped on the computer. "There's something about those white and blue shingles. Seems like I remember seeing that house before somehow."

I was so excited. "So what do we do?"

Alyssa responded, "I don't know. I mean, do we contact a stranger and say, Hey, one of your pictures has a house in it that I think I might remember? I mean, how crazy is that?"

Suddenly, it became clear to me. "No, we can send her a message, right?"

"Yeah, we can inbox her," Alyssa agreed.

"Right, we can inbox her a message and ask if she's related to Pauline Crawford."

Alyssa nodded. "You're catching on fast, sis. Not bad." Alyssa gave me a high five.

"Let's do it."

"Let's do it," I said, sending a message to Anita Crawford's inbox on Facebook.

Then we waited.

When we were children, the only time we agreed on anything was about how mean and unfair Mama was. Other than that, we were both opinionated and stubborn. Neither one of us would give in to the other. In fact, I was surprised we were now on the same team. Apparently, our mutual love of Justin had brought us together.

Before long, I left Alyssa's room for mine, showered quickly, then climbed into my own bed. Tomorrow we'd visit Justin early and receive my sister's test results. I fell asleep dreaming about Justin's recovery. I couldn't wait to see if Alyssa would be the answer to my prayers.

Early the next morning, Aunt Ruby banged on my door like the whole building was on fire or something.

"I'm coming. I'm coming," I said as I slipped out of bed and made my way to the front door.

"Good morning, child." Aunt Ruby held a tray of goodies out for me.

Alyssa trailed behind her, waving. "Morning."

"Oh. Thanks, but you didn't have to do that." I took the tray from her.

Aunt Ruby threw her hands in the air. "I know I didn't have to, but I wanted to serve the best nieces in the whole wide world."

"Aunt Ruby, you're just too much," Alyssa yawned.

"That's what most folk say, but as it turns out, I'm just enough." Aunt Ruby laughed before sitting down on the side of my bed. "Now, you two girls mean everything to me and it don't matter how your mama feels about me or how she's tried to keep us apart—the Crawford women are back together again."

"We love you too, Aunt Ruby," I said as I stuffed a warm buttered biscuit into my mouth.

"Absolutely. You're the best. They aren't cooking like this up in Washington, D.C. I'll tell you that." Alyssa waved a strip of bacon around in her hand.

Aunt Ruby nodded. "I'll bet they ain't. But you're in the Deep South now, gal, and Aunt Ruby's gonna take good care of you, both of you."

"Thanks for all of your help, including this phone." I took out the new cell phone she gave me. "I sure do appreciate it. When I first got here I didn't know what I was going to do. Then you gave me this room and even this cell phone is fabulous."

"That little thing—I'm glad you like it," Aunt Ruby said.

"Like it? They didn't make smart phones like this before I went away." I examined it like it was made of gold and diamonds. It was the nicest gift anyone had given me in a long time.

"Believe me, it can do a whole lot of cool stuff when you get used to it," Alyssa added.

"It's an Android."

"Well, all I know is that it's been so helpful to me so far." I smiled as I held it.

"Ms. Technology here will show you the way, I'm sure." Aunt Ruby turned to look at both of us. "And speaking of technology, any luck with your computer search?"

Alyssa and I looked at each other.

"No, not yet," Alyssa answered.

"Well, just keep trying. You never know what might turn up." Aunt Ruby picked up a muffin and stuffed it into her mouth.

We finished our breakfast, then the three of us piled into the car to go to visit Justin.

After each of us had a short visit with Justin, we found Dr. Stanford to ask about Alyssa's results.

"I'm sorry," he said. "Your sister is not a match."

"Oh no." I felt my heart fall into my stomach.

"Don't get discouraged. I'm sure you have many other family members who have not been tested yet." Aunt Ruby squeezed my hand.

"There are a few." At that moment, I couldn't think of any.

"See, I'm sure it will all work out," Dr. Stanford said. "Until then, I'm increasing Justin's dosage of chemo."

"Don't worry." Alyssa squeezed my hand.

"You still have Smooth," Aunt Ruby added.

"Yeah, Smooth, the slickster." Alyssa rolled her eyes.

Aunt Ruby shook her finger at her. "Alyssa, please."

I shot her a look. "Don't start, girl."

Alyssa grimaced. "What?"

"You're right. I do have Smooth." I smiled through the tears that were forming in my eyes.

As we were leaving the hospital, I stopped on the steps, looked up, and said, "Lord, where are you now?" We were only five weeks into the journey and I was already tired.

I took out the nearly crumpled piece of paper from my purse and crossed Alyssa's name off of the list.

Finally, I found the strength to walk down to the car. Alyssa sat in the front seat, fiddling with her phone. She was always obsessed with trendy, expensive clothes and gadgets.

Aunt Ruby sat in the driver's seat, speeding down the highway with the oldies station blaring. I sat back, with my hands behind my head and with my eyes closed, trying to relax.

Suddenly, Alyssa bounced around in her seat and tapped me on the knee.

When I opened my eyes, Alyssa was practically leaning over her seat into my lap. "What is it?"

She passed her phone to me. I looked at it and noticed that it was a Facebook entry. Anita Crawford had inboxed her back. She said she wasn't sure where Nana lived or what her number was, but that Nana was indeed her cousin and that she worked at Mercy Hospital right in New Orleans. She mentioned that a family member had run into her at the hospital not long ago and said that she wished us luck in finding her.

I looked into Alyssa's eyes.

"Yes." Alyssa high-fived me.

"What's going on back there, you two?" Aunt Ruby slowed down. "You girls leaving me out of something?"

"No, Aunt Ruby. I didn't want to mention anything until we were sure." I glanced at Alyssa.

Aunt Ruby asked, "Sure of what?"

"That we'd found Nana," I explained.

"We think we may have found our grandmother on our dad's side," Alyssa added.

"On Facebook," I continued.

"So she's on Facebook? Well, I'll be." Aunt Ruby's eyes grew large.

"We don't know if she is on Facebook, but a cousin of hers is. We put two and two together and contacted her. Now we have a good lead." Alyssa snapped her fingers in excitement.

"We think we know where she works," I explained.

Aunt Ruby peeped over her shoulder. "And where is that?"

"At the same hospital that Justin is in, Mercy Hospital." I was in awe.

Aunt Ruby briefly glanced over her shoulder at me. "You're kidding me?"

"No, I'm not. I can hardly believe it myself. According to this relative, Nana has been right under our noses all the time." I clapped my hands.

Aunt Ruby took one hand off the wheel and snapped her fingers. "That sure is something."

"Yes, it is something." Alyssa nodded.

"Maybe the good Lord is on your side, after all," Aunt Ruby said.

I closed my eyes and let hope run through my veins. "Let's hope this something leads me to my father and turns into a miracle for Justin."

Aunt Ruby asked, "What should we do? Should we turn around and go back to the hospital?"

"I don't know. Maybe we should." I looked at Alyssa.

"Why don't we come back when we're done with our errands. We'll go back and look her up," Alyssa suggested. "If she's really there, that shouldn't be too hard."

"No, it shouldn't. But convincing her to test—now, that may be a challenge." I hoped that Nana would be agreeable.

Alyssa shook her head. "Not necessarily. Maybe she's a nurse."

All of the pieces were coming together. "She could be. If she's a nurse, then she'll know the importance of a procedure like this.

"Either way, if she works at a hospital, surely, she must have compassion for the sick," Alyssa said.

"I sure hope so." I gave a quick nod of agreement.

Aunt Ruby nodded too.

I continued: "Well, I think we should go back now and at least ask the hospital about her. I won't be able to concentrate if we don't."

"Okay. No problem. We'll turn around." Aunt Ruby swerved, then did a broken U-turn in the middle of the intersection.

"We wanted you to go back, not kill us," I screamed.

"Aunt Ruby, we want to get there in one piece, please," Alyssa said. "Not be in a bed next to Justin, all busted up."

"Don't be making fun of my driving, girls," Aunt Ruby squealed. "I'm real sensitive about that."

"Sorry." Alyssa batted her eyelashes.

"Sorry, Aunt Ruby." I poked out my lips.

Aunt Ruby tossed the curls of her wig back. "It's all right. Been driving since I was fifteen years old."

"Yeah, but the laws have changed since then." Alyssa snickered.

Aunt Ruby raised her eyebrows. "You're still making fun of my driving?"

"No, now I'm making fun of your age." Alyssa chuckled. "I'm sorry, but I couldn't resist."

Aunt Ruby looked over at Alyssa with one eyebrow raised. "And if I put you out on the corner, could you resist then?"

"My lips are sealed." Alyssa put her nicely manicured finger up to her lips.

"You won't hear another peep out of me, really." I put my whole hand over my mouth.

Aunt Ruby fluttered her fake eyelashes. "Well, we'll just see about that."

When we arrived back at the hospital, we left Aunt Ruby in the car. We walked quickly through the double doors to the information desk.

The woman asked, "May I help you?"

"Yes, thank you, we're looking for a person," I explained. "She may be a nurse."

"You've come to the right place." She smiled. "We have plenty."

"No, I mean a particular nurse," I explained.

The woman leaned forward. "What's her name?"

Alyssa answered, "Her name is Pauline Crawford."

The woman pushed her glasses down on her nose and squinted. "What do you want with her?"

I looked into her eyes. "She's our grandmother and we've lost touch."

"Well, why didn't you say so from the beginning?" The lady paused. "My name is Maggie and Pauline is a friend of mine. A good woman, a very good woman, and yes—she's a nurse."

Alyssa and I looked at each other.

"Her shift doesn't start until six today, though. I know, because I invited her to my nephew's barbecue today and she said she had to work."

Alyssa took out a paper, a pen, and began to write. "So we should come back at six, then?"

"If you want to see the Pauline that I know, yes," the woman said.

"Great." I high-fived Alyssa.

"Cool." Alyssa grinned at me.

The woman added, "Oh, and ladies: one more thing."

I looked at the woman. "What is it?"

"You'll want to go to the pediatric center. That's where she'll be."

I was stunned. "So she works with sick kids, then?"

"Yes, she does." The woman smiled.

Alyssa and I looked at each other. "Thank you," Alyssa said, taking off running.

"Thanks so much." I followed her down the hall.

Alyssa ran to Aunt Ruby's car, but I stopped on the hospital steps to think for a minute.

I finally had a break in my quest to find my father and grandmother. It was odd how Nana was working in the same section Justin was in. What are you trying to tell me, Lord?

I looked up into the open sky and my prayer came pouring out.

Lord, I know you hear me. Something inside keeps telling me that you hear me. And no matter how desperate I get, I can't let go of that feeling. I can't shake it. A part of me cries out and remembers something sweet in my spirit from long ago. A part of me remembers a peace I knew when I was a little girl, one I rebelled against as I later grew up, one I rebelled against when the prison chaplain tried to pray with me. I want that touch again.

Chapter 11

Aunt Ruby put her foot on the gas pedal, pushing her Cadillac to its maximum capacity.

Alyssa and I just held on for the ride. With her nonchalance, I wondered if she ever feared being pulled over and given a speeding ticket.

When she finally reached her destination, she stopped the car by the river and told us all to get out. We weren't sure of what to think, but we reluctantly jumped out of the car. Following Aunt Ruby, we trudged along the dock until we came to a small car-repair shop.

Aunt Ruby got out and stretched. "I just wanted to have my say somewhere where it's peaceful and quiet."

"Well, I guess this is as good a place as any." I climbed out of the car, stretching also.

Alyssa folded her arms, looked down at her watch, and rolled her eyes.

"Alyssa, you'll be going back to your own home and success soon. I'm so proud of you for all you've accomplished. Now, I know you're self-sufficient, but if you ever run into any trouble or need me for any reason, I hope you won't hesitate to call me."

Alyssa nodded.

Aunt Ruby continued, "And please don't let it be so long before you come visit me again, you hear?"

"It won't be." Alyssa smiled. "I promise."

Aunt Ruby walked over to me and put her hands on my shoulders. "And Trinity, I know you don't really have anything to go home to right now. Life has been so hard on you. It gets like that sometimes."

"Hmph," I said, shaking my head.

"So I've been thinking about it and I've decided to offer you two things to help you along your way." Aunt Ruby shifted her weight from one leg to another. "First, I'd like to offer you a job as hostess at Ruby's Red House. I know it's probably not what you want to do with the rest of your life, but that'll take care of income as long as you need it."

I opened my mouth wide."Oh, Aunt Ruby—"

"Wait," Aunt Ruby led us into the shop.

An older, bowlegged man with a gray mustache and beard approached us. "Good ol' Ruby Jean." The man hugged Aunt Ruby tightly.

Aunt Ruby gave him a stern look. "Bruce, ain't nothing old 'cept that truck over there."

The man stepped back and looked her up and down. "I'm sorry, darling. I meant, *sweet* Ruby Jean."

"Now that's better." Aunt Ruby grabbed our hands like we were children. "I'd like you to meet my two nieces, closest thing I have to daughters, Alyssa and Trinity. Girls, this is my old friend, Bruce."

"Good to meet you, ladies." Bruce took off his mechanic's cap, revealing a mess of matted gray hair.

"Nice to meet you too," Alyssa and I said in unison.

"The next thing I wanted to tell you, Trinity, is that you can drive my old truck here until you can get your own. And I do mean *old*, 'cause it's a clunker, but it just needs a little tender, lovin' care. It's a 1975 Chevrolet pickup and as you can see, it's a classic." Aunt Ruby pointed at a truck in the corner of the shop. "It ain't pretty, but it runs."

I started, "I—"

Aunt Ruby handed me the keys to the truck. "Bruce here says we should be able to get it restored and on the road in a couple of weeks. Until then you can just drive the Caddy."

"I'm putting in new custom vinyl upholstery, a brand-new sparkling paint job, and a rebuilt motor and tranny. I'm also replacing all of the rusted parts with chrome ones. And of course, you'll have four brand-new tires." Bruce grinned with pride. "Now, you can't ask for better than that, can you?"

"No, I can't ask for more than that, Mr. Bruce. Thank you so much, Aunt Ruby. That's very generous. You've done so much for me already." I felt overwhelmed by her generosity.

Aunt Ruby pushed me over to the truck. "Nonsense. I've learned you take care of the ones you love. Now you just sit back and enjoy it."

"That's not as easy as it sounds for a person like me." I eyed the truck, trying to imagine what it would look like when it was fully restored. "I'm used to working for everything I've ever gotten."

"I know you're a hard worker, honey. You always have been. Just had some hard breaks in life, I think." Aunt Ruby walked over to the truck and tapped it on the hood. "This is a good, solid vehicle right here."

When she walked back to me, I reached forward to hug her. "You're very special to me and you've already done so much by helping with Justin's medical care and by letting me stay here. . . ."

Aunt Ruby didn't seem to be listening. "You'll have to get your license again before you can drive anything, though."

Alyssa finally broke her silence. "Well, it's no Porsche, but you'll be on the road in no time, I guess."

"I will and thanks again, Aunt Ruby." I felt safe in Aunt Ruby's arms.

Alyssa broke our embrace and joined in. "Can I get in on all this love?"

After the group hug, we had lunch in a little café by the river, then ran a few errands before going home. By five o' clock, Aunt Ruby handed over the keys to her Cadillac so Alyssa and I could go back to the hospital. This time we went to the pediatric wing to see Justin. He was groggy from the various medicines and wanted to sleep. *Please, Lord, keep my baby from slipping away.*

"Justin, Mommy and Aunt Alyssa are here," I said from across the room.

Justin's eyes lit up. "Hi, Mom."

"I can speak for myself, thank you." Alyssa moved closer to Justin. "Hey, buddy. Yes, Auntie is here."

"Hi, Auntie," Justin said before drifting back into a deep sleep.

After we left, it was time to go to the front desk. I asked for Pauline Crawford and we were told to wait, that she would be signing in shortly. So we found chairs and waited.

"Never thought I'd make it this far," I admitted.

"Neither did I. Other than finding our dad and grand-mother for Justin's sake, I had no interest, but I must admit that now I'm just a little excited." Alyssa fidgeted in her seat.

"So am I. Can't wait." I stretched my neck toward the corridor.

Alyssa sat still for a moment. "I just hope you're not disappointed."

I turned my attention to Alyssa. "What do you mean by that?"

"Well, people are people and in my experience, people let you down." Alyssa looked away from me and began digging in her designer purse.

"Alyssa, I've been let down my whole life. But something inside tells me that finding Nana will be a good thing." I turned away from her.

"Maybe." Alyssa curled her lips, without looking at me. Alyssa and I sat quietly as the tension mounted. She fumbled with her phone while I looked through a stray magazine.

It was nice to get a glance at the various hair styles, old and new. I couldn't wait to get my hands into someone's hair. Then the urge came to close my eyes and when I did, I saw a flash of bright turquoise almost blinding me. It was as if sunlight was illuminating the bold color. As suddenly as it came, the vision disappeared.

I opened my eyes, then blinked. I saw my sister still occupied with her phone. She'd put on her glasses and was carefully examining the screen. I wondered how a little thing like an Android phone could fascinate such an intelligent and professional woman like her. I shook my head and smiled. No matter how difficult she was, she was my sister. I was looking down at the magazine when I heard the voice and immediately, I knew it was her.

I tapped Alyssa and pointed discreetly. When I saw her, my eyes filled up with tears.

The woman had beautiful, shoulder-length kinky, curly, silver-streaked hair, smooth dark skin, and quite a nice figure for a woman her age. I knew it had to be her. I stood up quickly and walked over to her just as she was walking away. She turned around to face me and our eyes met.

As she approached me, I noticed that she had big, dark brown eyes like mine. "Trinity, is that you?"

"Yes, Nana. It's me." I moved closer to her.

She grabbed me and squeezed me tight. She finally let me go, only to see Alyssa standing behind her. Then she grabbed Alyssa and wouldn't let her go, either.

"These are my grandchildren." Nana looked at the lady behind the desk, then smiled.

"That's so nice." The lady smiled back.

Nana sat down in one of the chairs. "How did you two find me?"

Alyssa and I sat down also.

"We found a cousin of yours on Facebook and she told us you work here," Alyssa said.

"Oh my, Facebook. I don't do much social networking." Nana did not stop showing her sparkling teeth. "It's so good to see you two girls. I've missed you."

"I've missed you too." I looked over at Alyssa.

Alyssa hesitated before she spoke. "Can't believe you're real."

"I'm real, sweetheart." Nana looked solemn for a moment. "I tried to contact you both. I wrote to you while you were in prison. And Alyssa, you were a little harder to track down, but I wrote to you when you were at Smith and Sloan law firm. I imagine that you never received the letter."

Alyssa stuttered, "I haven't been with that company for a while—so—I—uh—"

"It's okay. By the grace of God, you're both here now." Nana took each of our hands.

"Yes, we're here now," I said. "We were actually trying to find our father too."

Nana's eyebrows came together. "Trying to find him?"

I nodded. "Yes. We'd like to connect with him also. Right, Alyssa?"

Alyssa shot me a look. "Sure, why not?"

Nana stood up quickly, rubbing her hands up and down her uniform pants. "I'll tell you what . . . I'm going to let my supervisor know that I've got to take care of a family emergency and take a couple of hours off. You can meet me in the cafeteria where we can get some coffee or something, if you'd like. That way we'll have time to talk. We need time to talk."

I noticed that she'd avoided eye contact in those last couple of minutes. "Sounds good." I tapped on Alyssa's hand.

"Okay, we'll meet you in the cafeteria, then," Alyssa said.

Nana nodded and looked away, then disappeared down the hall without another word.

I could sense that something was wrong, but was afraid to comment. We started walking to the elevator, wondering about what we would encounter next.

"I don't trust her," Alyssa snapped.

I was in no mood for one of Alyssa's tantrums. "Why would you say something like that?"

"Did you see the look on her face when you asked about our father? As if he was off limits or something, then she changes the subject and says, *meet me in the cafeteria.* I don't like it." Alyssa folded her arms against her chest.

"I don't see it that way at all. She's on her job, so she can't just have a private conversation right there on the floor she's supposed to be working. She just has to get permission to take some time off. I'm sure she'll answer all our questions about our father then." I pushed the down button.

When the elevator door opened, Alyssa and I stepped inside, and squeezed between four other people. Then she leaned over to me.

Her voice was a mere whisper. "I'm sure glad you're confident. I'm not even sure I want to know about either of them. I remember when that letter came to me at that law firm I was working at." Alyssa's lip quivered. "I was so angry I balled it up and threw it away."

I saw the raw emotion in my sister's eyes, but I waited until we were out of the elevator before I responded. "Why? At least Nana tried to reach out to you."

Alyssa stiffened her lips. "Too little. Too late. Why didn't you respond to her letter?"

I let out a long breath, then raised my voice in frustration. "I was on death row and very bitter about life."

Alyssa stopped in front of the cafeteria doors and began to pat her foot. "Oh, so you have a good excuse and I don't?"

"I didn't say that. Look, let's just let the past stay in the past. We have Nana here now." I extended my hand. "Let's just deal with now."

Alyssa shook my hand as if it had cow dung on it. "I'll try. But I'm telling you now, if something doesn't smell right, I'm out."

I shook her hand back. "That's fair enough."

The room was half empty, with a few nurses and doctors sitting in groups, eating. By the time Nana arrived at the cafeteria, we were already sitting at a table in the back. I stood up and waved to her as if she couldn't see us from where we were sitting. Then we watched Nana slowly slip through the maze of tables to get to us, with her head hanging low. Suddenly, she looked as if she had the weight of the world on her shoulders. What happened to her big smile?

Nana sat down and closed her eyes. "I kept praying the whole time I walked down here."

I leaned forward in my chair. "What's wrong?"

Nana took each of our hands in hers. "I almost choked up when you asked about connecting with your father."

Suddenly, I didn't feel hopeful anymore. "What is it?"

"I knew it. He doesn't want to be bothered with us, does he?" Alyssa pushed her chair back and stood up. "He probably has a whole other family by now. It's cool, though."

"Alyssa, please, calm down." I rolled my eyes at her in disgust. "Sit back down."

Alyssa folded her arms again and sat down.

"No, it's nothing like that." Nana put her hand up to her forehead.

I looked into Nana's eyes. "Then what is it?"

Alyssa glanced over at me.

Nana's voice was a whisper. "Your father passed away."

I closed my eyes, then opened them. "Passed away? What do you mean, *passed away*?"

"When did this happen?" Alyssa gritted her teeth. "Why weren't we told?"

"I'm sorry, but he's gone." Nana's hand moved from her forehead to her eyes.

"Apparently your mother never told you."

I swallowed hard. "Mama knew?"

"I don't believe this." Alyssa slammed her hand down on the table.

I jumped, but Nana didn't budge.

I fought to hold back the tears. "What happened to him?"

"It was a very bad accident." Nana looked into my eyes, then to Alyssa's. "Your father used to drive trucks for a while, you know?"

"No, we didn't know. We really don't know anything about him." I slumped down in my chair, not knowing what to do or how to feel.

Alyssa sighed, then crossed her legs. "That's an understatement."

Tears welled up in Nana's eyes. "Well, one day he was riding with someone else in an eighteen-wheeler and there was a terrible accident, through no fault of his own. It all happened so fast. Anyway, you girls must've been about fourteen and fifteen years old."

Tears began to run down my face too. "Fourteen and fifteen?"

"Yes, about that, I'm sure. I remember thinking that the both of you should've been in high school during that time. I tried to call your mama, but she'd changed her number. I sent two letters and I sent messages by other family members." Nana reached into her purse and pulled out a package of tissues. She dried her face with one, then passed the package along to me.

"I don't understand." I took a tissue, then handed it to Alyssa. "Why couldn't you just come by?"

Alyssa pushed the tissues away from her.

"Are you kidding me? The last time I saw your mother, she fought me, threatened me, then when I tried to protect myself, she set the police on me. She told me she hated me, that she always would, that I would never be allowed to see either of you again—and she did a great job with that, I must say." Nana wiped a lone tear from her eye. "In fact, the first thing she did after filing a false police report was to take out an order of protection against me. Besides the fact that I was living in Maryland at the time."

Suddenly, it all made sense to me. "So that's how she kept you away?"

"No, honey, that's how she kept us both away. Your father wasn't a perfect man, but he did love you girls. He wanted to see you, but Rosalee wouldn't let him come by." Nana was visibly shaken. "He tried to fight it for a while, but soon he just got frustrated and gave up."

Alyssa tapped her feet frantically. "So you're saying he just gave up on his kids? He gave up on us?"

"He wasn't a strong man. He had many personal problems, including gambling, but despite them all, he loved you two." Nana bit her lip. "Just a shame your mother never told you."

"*Shame* is not the word." I shook my head as I tried to process what was happening.

"After he died, I promised not to give up. I knew I had to find you and somehow try to get back the time that was stolen," Nana explained.

Alyssa stood up and shoved her chair in. "And just how do you plan to do that?" Then she yelled, "Our father is dead, for goodness sake. How in the world can you get that back?"

"Alyssa—" I signaled her by putting my finger over my lips.

People stopped eating to look over at us.

"Don't *Alyssa* me. I don't care who hears us. She's just as guilty as Mama, because she should've found us, made a way. I don't care—something. She let us stay and rot in that house with that demon of a mother of ours." Alyssa turned to Nana. "As far as I'm concerned, you're just what I expected—a hypocrite." Alyssa waved her hands as she sped through the cafeteria and out of the double doors.

I looked at Nana. "I'm sorry."

"No, don't apologize. You two have every right to be angry. I just hope you can forgive me," Nana said with sadness in her eyes.

"I already have." I blinked away the tears that were forming.

Nana reached for my hand across the table. "You were always special."

Through the ache that was in my heart, I managed a little smile. "I'd better catch up with my sister before she drives away without me." I stood up shakily. "But I will stay in touch."

Nana slipped me a piece of paper. "This is my address and my telephone number. Call me any time."

I nodded. "Okay, thanks."

I stood stiff as Nana hugged me, refusing to lift my limp arms to hug her back. In my heart, I was numb. When she let me go, she walked out of the cafeteria without looking back. I stood there frozen, feeling the sting of deceit and betrayal. Once again, my world had come crashing down.

Chapter 12

It was the quietest drive back to Aunt Ruby's place. I didn't dare start a conversation, because Alyssa was livid. I knew that the least little thing would cause her to explode, so I kept my thoughts, good and bad, to myself. When we finally arrived, Alyssa went straight to her room and I went straight to mine. I knew that we each needed to be alone for a while.

Being alone with my thoughts didn't help much, though. I was so angry and so confused.

How could Mama do something like that? The truth of my father's death made me sick to my stomach, because I'd had so much hope for our future relationship. Now my hopes were all buried six feet under in a cemetery I'd never even seen. I laid on my bed, staring up at the ceiling, determined not to cry.

At dinnertime, Aunt Ruby knocked on my room door. "Aren't you coming down for supper, sweetie?"

I got up and opened the door just a crack. "No, thanks. I'm okay."

"Are you feeling all right?"

"I don't really want to talk about it right now, Auntie. It's been a rough day, though."

Aunt Ruby didn't give up. "Your sister didn't answer her door at all. Do you know anything about that?"

"Yeah. She's not doing too well either, " I explained.

Aunt Ruby raised her painted eyebrows.

I looked Aunt Ruby straight in the eye and said, "We'll talk to you about everything tomorrow. I promise."

"I understand. Get your rest then." Aunt Ruby closed the door.

I could tell that she lingered by the door for a while before moving. I didn't mean to seem mysterious, but I certainly wasn't about to go through the range of emotions as I poured out my heart to her, either. Not tonight.

The next morning, I scrambled out of bed, jumped into the shower, then threw on a pair of jeans and a T-shirt before I headed down to my sister's room. As soon as she opened the door for me I noticed that she was throwing clothes into her overnight bag.

I walked over to the bed. "What are you doing?"

"Packing." Alyssa continued to fling her clothes. "What does it look like I'm doing?"

"But I didn't know you were leaving so soon," I whined.

Alyssa huffed, "I've been here long enough now. Too long."

I started, "But—"

"Look, I'm sorry I was no match for Justin and maybe Nana may be better for that than me, but I've had enough of all of this. I'm ready to go back to Washington and live my life and forget that any of this ever happened." Alyssa zipped her bag and picked it up. "I'm done."

I took the bag from her hand and set it down. "But how can you do that?"

Alyssa grabbed her bag back from the floor. "I don't know. The same way I was doing it before, I guess. The same way I—"

"But he was our father," I said. "That must mean something to you."

Alyssa shouted, "Of course it means something to me, but I can't let it stop me."

Tears welled up in my eyes. "But he was our father and he's dead."

"So what? He's dead, but we never knew him, anyway. We never even knew him." Then Alyssa broke down as the truth overwhelmed us both.

We sat on the bed holding each other like we did when we were little girls.

"How could Mama not tell us our father was dead? Why? And why didn't she let us have a relationship with him when he was alive?" Alyssa dried her face with her a tissue. "I just don't get it."

"Neither do I." I closed my eyes to help alleviate the pain.

Alyssa pounded her fist into her hand. "What I really want to do is confront Mama about it. I want to know what she was thinking all this time."

I nodded my head as I slowly parted my eyelids. "So do I."

Suddenly Alyssa's face filled with excitement. "Maybe we can drive back to Baton Rouge to see Mama before I go on my way, because, given everything that has happened, I don't know when I'll be back in Louisiana again."

I squinted my eyes. "You mean go now?"

"Yeah, why not? She owes us at least an explanation," Alyssa said.

I was hesitant at first, but I knew that I would have no peace until I heard Mama admit to what she'd done. "What about Justin?"

"I'm sure he'll be fine until we get back. I promise we won't be gone that long." Alyssa snapped her fingers.

"Okay. I'll go," I agreed. "His condition is stable and we'll come right back, right?"

"Right." Alyssa nodded.

Before I knew it, we had borrowed Aunt Ruby's car and were on the road to Baton Rouge, with the wind in our faces and an ache in our hearts. It took us a little over an hour since we stopped for gas, which gave us time to cool down.

Tyrone called while we were on our way to Mama's house.

I answered the phone hesitantly. "Hey."

Tyrone's voice was vibrant and full of life. "Hello. How are you?"

"I'm okay, I guess," I answered.

"You don't sound okay. Are you with Justin?"

"No, I'm with my sister, actually." I looked toward Alyssa in the driver's seat. "We're on our way to take care of some family business."

"Oh, I'm sorry," he said.

I paused before answering. "No problem."

"Well, I'm gonna let you go and handle your business. If you need me, you know where I am." Tyrone sounded awkward.

"I'll keep that in mind." I sighed. "Thanks."

"Cheer up, Trinity." Tyrone's voice was strangely encouraging. "I don't know exactly what's bothering you the most today, but just remember that joy always comes in the morning."

"So they say." I sighed.

"So I know." Tyrone paused. "I'll call you later, okay?"

"Sure." I hit the end button.

Alyssa glanced over at me. "Who was that?"

I looked at my phone. "Oh, that was just Tyrone."

Alyssa grinned. "Oh, the hottie who showed up at Aunt Ruby's yesterday?"

"Hottie? No. And I thought you didn't like him." I twisted my lips to the side.

"I never said that. I just said he probably doesn't have any money, that's all. I never said he wasn't cute."

"Cute?" I shook my head. "I don't see him like that."

Alyssa pointed to me. "Well, I'm sure he sees you like that."

"Nah, we're just friends," I protested.

Alyssa looked at me and put on a fake grin. "You used to be friends, but I saw more than that in his eyes."

I squinted my eyes. "Now you're imagining things."

Alyssa twisted her lips. "Okay then, explain it to me."

"He's just really friendly and we talk a lot. I mean, he's a really nice guy. I'm just not in the mood for his cheery attitude right now." I couldn't remember Tyrone being this positive back in the day.

"Cheery sounds good to me." Alyssa bounced up and down in the driver's seat.

"He always makes me feel better and right now I want to stay mad for a little while longer." I turned toward Alyssa. "I think I've earned that."

Alyssa took one hand off the steering wheel and snapped her fingers in a circular motion. "Hmph. You're right about that."

By the time I put my phone away, we were approaching Mama's house. I swallowed hard. "Well, here we go."

"Yeah, into the battle zone," Alyssa responded.

Alyssa parked the car, then we jumped out and walked toward the front door.

The screen door looked as if it was falling off the hinges. I swatted a mosquito before knocking.

As usual, Uncle Charlie came to answer the door. "Hey there, girls."

"Hey, Uncle Charlie." I threw myself onto the couch.

"Hi." Alyssa hugged Uncle Charlie. "It's good to see you."

"Good to see you too, sweetheart. It's been a while since you've been home." Uncle Charlie looked at me. "Trinity, did you find what you were looking for in New Orleans?"

I shook my head. "Not yet. Alyssa tested, but she's not a match."

Uncle Charlie shook his head. "Sorry to hear that."

"It's okay. I've still got others on my list." I looked around the room for signs of Mama.

"But we're here to see Mama. Is she here?"

Alyssa added, "We need to see her."

Uncle Charlie spat out a wad of chewing tobacco into a tin can. "She was still asleep a little while ago. Not sure if she's up yet."

Before I could turn around, Alyssa was banging on Mama's bedroom door like the police. "Mama, come on out here."

Suddenly the door opened and Mama poked her head out. "What's all of that noise about? And what are you two doing here?"

"Now that's a very good question. I've been asking myself that the whole ride down here. However, it seems that I'm here for answers," Alyssa yelled.

Mama stepped out of her bedroom, wearing her raggedy robe. "What do you mean, answers?"

I interrupted, "We found Nana."

Mama squinted her eyes. "Who?"

"Our paternal grandmother, that's who." Alyssa rolled her eyes.

Mama sucked on her gums as she often did when she didn't have her teeth in. "So you found that witch, huh? What has she done now?"

I stood boldly in front of Mama. "She's done nothing. But you have. Why didn't you tell us that our father was dead?"

Alyssa continued, "How could you keep something like that from us?"

Mama squinted her eyes at us. "What are you two talking about?"

"You know what we're talking about. You knew I wanted to find him. Ever since I was a teenager I wanted to find him. You said you had no idea where he was." I put my hands on my hips. "That was a lie."

"Watch your mouth, you hear?" Mama raised her hand as if she was going to swing at me. "It wasn't a lie, cause I never knew where that man was. Never wanted to know. No good, cheating, troublemaking . . . And even to this day, I still don't know where his body is buried."

Alyssa circled Mama. "What a piece of work."

I ignored Alyssa's comment. "Really, Mama? Is that all you have to say?"

Alyssa stopped in front of Mama's face. "How could you withhold that kind of information from us?"

"We're your daughters, for goodness sake." I couldn't stop staring at her.

"You don't have to remind me." Mama frowned up her already lined face. "I just knew I was glad to be rid of him when he was finally gone, that's all."

Alyssa circled Mama like she was on the witness stand. "Was it that bad, Mama? Really?"

I jumped in. "Did you hate him that much that you couldn't even tell us that he died?"

"Yes, I did. I hated him worse. And you're just like him. Even now you look just like him, standing there, fresh out of prison with your high talk and your high-mindedness." Then she tightened her jaws and went in for the kill. "You even smell like him. You smell like that city. How dare you question me about him."

I swallowed, then stepped back.

Alyssa stepped in front of me. "And all of those years you kept him away from us, what were you thinking?"

"It was for your own good." Mama shook her finger in my face. "I was protecting you."

Alyssa rolled her eyes. "Our own good?"

I went out on a limb. "Protecting us from what, exactly?"

"From the truth, the truth of what a horrible man he really was." Mama sat down in the corduroy armchair.

Alyssa placed one hand on her hip and the other in the air. "You've got to be kidding me. We must look like fools to you."

"I'm not sure what you look like right now." Mama squinted her eyes and and poked out her lips.

"I am nobody's fool, believe that." Alyssa's eyes were red with anger.

"And you kept us away from our grandmother," I added. "She loved us and you sent her away."

"She's a wicked woman," Mama sneered. "She never cared about you."

"I used to think that, but now I know the truth." I paced around the room. "She's not the wicked one."

"Hmph," Alyssa huffed. "Got that right."

"She has brainwashed you two," Mama shouted at a volume that probably alarmed the neighbors.

I didn't like to hear her talk badly about Nana. "Oh, Mama, please. You've been the ultimate brainwasher since the day our dad left."

"That's the key word, *left*." Mama's voice was calmer now. "He's the one who left and I'm the one who stayed."

"And you've been making me pay for that my whole life." I shook my head in disbelief.

Mama squealed, "Making you pay? What about me? I've been paying since the days y'all was born."

"I guess you have been, *paying* since I was born," Alyssa spat out. "Well, I don't have to bother you anymore and we can just call it even."

I bit my lip to hold back the anger that was about to erupt in me, then walked out because I couldn't stand to look at her anymore. I got into the passenger's seat of Aunt Ruby's Cadillac and buckled myself in. Alyssa followed close behind me, hopped in, and sped away without a word.

Alyssa drove nonstop back to Aunt Ruby's.

I finally broke the silence. "Can you believe her?"

"It is what it is." Alyssa quickly ran inside, then straight up to her room to get her bag.

Aunt Ruby and I followed her upstairs. I filled in Aunt Ruby on the details as Alyssa got ready.

"I still can't believe Rosalee would do something like keep your father's death from you." Aunt Ruby sat down on Alyssa's bed and kicked off her shoes.

"Yeah, well she did it, and now it's over." Alyssa straightened her hat in the mirror. "He's dead."

Aunt Ruby stood up in front of Alyssa. "Things will get better, Alyssa. Your mama—"

Alyssa closed her eyes in frustration. "Please. Spare me the lectures, Aunt Ruby."

"What I mean is, I'm sorry about what happened to you girls. I don't know what your mama was thinking." Aunt Ruby fell backwards on the bed.

"Neither do we." It was clear that Mama had reached a new low.

"Hmph. I've already called a cab to drive me to the airport." Alyssa continued to gather the last of her things.

Aunt Ruby leaned over on one elbow and shook her car keys. "Are you sure? I can drive you; it's no trouble."

"I know and thanks." Alyssa shook her head and smiled. "But I want to be alone right now. I want to clear my head on my way to the airport so I can be ready to work on the plane. I've got to get my head back in the game before I land."

Once again, Aunt Ruby stood up and nearly smothered Alyssa in her thick arms. "I understand, sweetie. And don't forget what I told you about calling me."

Alyssa nodded. "I remember." Then Alyssa reached out and then pulled me to her. "Take care of yourself now."

"I will." I nodded. "I'm gonna miss ya."

"I'm gonna miss you too. I'll call you," Alyssa whispered.

"Okay," I whispered back.

Within minutes we had walked Alyssa downstairs and she was gone. Only the Elizabeth Arden scent remained.

"Come on, darling. Let's get some food in ya." Aunt Ruby put her heavy arms around me.

"I'm really not hungry yet." I stiffened underneath her embrace.

Aunt Ruby insisted, "You've got to eat something to keep up your strength."

"If you don't mind, I'd just like to go to my room." Then I began to squirm in Aunt Ruby's grasp. "I want to freshen up before I go to see Justin."

"Okay, baby. I'll save you a plate." Aunt Ruby loosened her grip on me.

I went upstairs to my room and fell onto my bed. It was still early and yet it had already been such a long day. I yawned as exhaustion threatened to overtake me. As I was stretching, trying to snap out of my fatigue, my cell phone rang. I rolled over and answered it.

"Hello," I said.

"Hi, this is Tyrone." He paused. "I hope I didn't catch you at a bad time."

I sat up in bed. "Hi. No, I was just resting."

Tyrone chuckled. "Then why do you sound so sad?"

I rolled over onto my back. "To tell you the truth, I just had an unpleasant confrontation with my mother."

"That's too bad," Tyrone answered.

I spoke quickly. "As it turns out, she kept a big secret from my sister, brother, and me."

"I never knew you had a brother."

"Well, I don't anymore, but I used to. His name was James and he died in a gang fight, a stabbing when he was just fifteen." My mind brought back the gruesome imagery.

Tyrone groaned. "Aw, man. That's messed up."

"Yeah, it is. But anyway, Mama never told any of us that our father died quite a few years ago," I explained. "I mean, we were in high school and we couldn't even attend his funeral or keep his obituary."

"Oh, that's terrible. I'm sorry to hear about your loss," Tyrone said. "Maybe your nana kept a copy of the obituary so you can look at it."

"Maybe and thanks. I just regret that I never got to know him and now he's gone." I felt like bringing Tyrone into my pity party now. "Gone just like my brother."

"I'm really sorry." Tyrone's voice was warm and sincere.

"I know you are. My brother and I were very close. Now I'll never have a chance to be close to my father." I turned around on the bed.

"Well, everything happens for a reason," Tyrone responded.

I paused before answering, "And the reason is that my mother is miserable and selfish—"

Tyrone interrupted, "No, that's not exactly what I mean."

Suddenly, I focused in on what he was saying. "What do you mean?"

Tyrone spoke softly. "I mean that God has a way that we may not understand, but it's for the best."

I wasn't sure what he meant. "How do you know that?"

"I know because the Word of God tells me." Tyrone paused for a moment. "Hey, why don't you join me this evening?"

I sat up on the side of the bed. "This evening?"

"We're having a gospel concert down at my church," Tyrone explained. "It's very informal."

"I don't know." I held the phone in silence for a few seconds. "Will you be playing?"

"I'll be there with my bass guitar." Tyrone chuckled.

"Really? As tempting as that sounds, I don't know if I can . . ." I started.

Tyrone coaxed, "Oh, come on. You can't just stay in and sulk."

"Yes, I can." I held the phone closer to my ear. "That's all I feel like doing—sulking. And why can't I?"

"I wouldn't be a gentleman if I let you go through this alone." Tyrone cleared his throat.

"Come on. You can even bring your sister and aunt also if you'd like. I'm sure they could use some entertainment too."

"My sister left town a little while ago and I doubt if my aunt will be interested." I looked around my room. "But what time is the concert?"

"It starts at six o' clock," he said.

I looked up at the wall clock. "I want to see Justin. We drove to Baton Rouge earlier so I haven't seen him since last night."

Tyrone snapped his fingers. "Of course. I can meet you at the hospital."

"I don't know." I stood up and began walking around the room.

"I'd like to meet your son," Tyrone continued. "After all, I was almost his godfather."

"Yes, almost." I threw my head back and laughed. "If your boy, Smooth, hadn't gotten all crazy acting and stuff and broke up the whole friendship."

Tyrone chuckled. "Come on, give the guy a break."

I rolled my eyes as I walked. "Does he deserve one?"

"You can't blame him for trying to protect his family." Suddenly, Tyrone's voice sounded very serious.

I stopped walking. "Is that what he was doing?"

"No, but that was probably his intention," Tyrone answered.

"Hmph," I snapped. "And all this time I just thought he was being jealous, paranoid, and controlling."

Tyrone almost choked with laughter. "Well, maybe when I see you we can come up with some clues on how to find Mr. Smooth."

"Now that would really be helpful." I switched my phone to the other ear, because I had begun to perspire. "I've got to find him and soon."

Tyrone didn't waste any time. "So we'll meet at the hospital, then?"

I decided to give in. "Okay, meet me at the front entrance of the pediatrics ward at five."

"Fine. Five it is, then," Tyrone confirmed.

I hung up the phone, then flung my head down on my pillow. Why was I wasting time going to a concert with Tyrone when there was so much else to do? I did need something to take my mind off of my problems for a little while. Church was as good a place as any to start. I climbed off the bed and looked through my closet at my pitiful wardrobe. I took a dress off of a hanger and held it in front of me, looking into the full-length mirror. It would be too short for church, so I shook my head. How could I show up at a concert looking like this? Then I found the one decent black skirt and white blouse that I had hanging in my closet, and slipped into them. It was the outfit I wore when going on interviews, although it now fit a little snug. Taking out my black pumps to go along with the ensemble, I tried them on, looked at myself from both side angles, then twirled in front of my reflection. Finally, I smiled with satisfaction.

Then I stared at my cell phone for a few minutes before I picked it up and called Nana.

Since I was heading out to the hospital, I decided that I needed to see her again. I hoped that she would be available, so I asked. Thankfully, she was as anxious to see me as I was to see her.

Nana and I met in the cafeteria at 3:30. She was sitting at a table for two, sipping on a cold drink when I arrived. I walked up behind her, tapped her on the shoulder, then placed my face against hers. It felt strange being so close to her after all these years, but for some reason I felt that I needed to do that. Her skin was unreasonably soft and so was her long, curly hair. I took in her same vanilla scent.

Nana reached around and patted me on the shoulder. "Thanks for meeting with me again."

"I'm sorry about what happened the last time." I took a seat across from her.

"No need to apologize. None of this is your fault. It's not your sister's fault, either. You're just victims of the devil's devices." Nana smiled before her look turned desperate. "And Alyssa always was the more headstrong of the two of you."

"Alyssa should've stayed to listen." I had trouble hiding my embarrassment.

Nana shook her head. "She's just upset and rightfully so. You girls never should've been left that way."

I leaned closer to her. "Why did he leave us, Nana?"

"Well, your father never wanted to leave you girls, but when things didn't work out between him and your mother, your mother became very bitter. She didn't want him to see you. Now, my son never was perfect—as none of us are—but he did try to see you for a while."

"What happened?" I looked into Nana's eyes and saw compassion. "Why did he stop trying?"

Nana look me straight in the eyes. "Well, there were child-support issues, court orders, false allegations, and restraining orders. Eventually, being the weak man that he was, he got frustrated and he gave up. I'm not proud of that and I'm not making any excuses for it. But that's the truth about who he was."

"Sounds kind of sad." I looked down at my hands as I clasped them together.

"He had his own demons, for sure. I tried to get him to surrender his life and his problems to the Lord, but he said he couldn't see himself being saved from something he could handle on his own. So you see, that's what he tried to do and it destroyed him." Nana grabbed my hands with hers. They were unusually soft. Almost like cotton.

I braced myself. "Tell me about the accident."

Nana squeezed my hands, then let go. "Your father was riding in the truck with two of his buddies, unsavory characters, to say the least. I knew both of them from the old neighborhood. They were always troublemakers and I always warned your father about keeping company with such hooligans, but you know birds of a feather do flock together. And they were his type of folk." She took a deep breath, then let it out. "He wasn't the driver, but the driver was under the influence. So was your father."

"So they were drinking?"

Nana continued, "Among other things, yes. But the driver lost control of the truck and went skidding all over the highway, causing multiple collisions and ending up crashing into a utility pole. Your father was thrown ten feet from the car. All of them were flown out to the county hospital by helicopter. The driver died in surgery the same day."

I searched Nana's face for the truth. I needed closure. "What about my father?"

"Your father remained in a coma for several weeks until the decision was made to remove him from life support. He always told me if anything happened to him, he wanted to go and not be kept alive artificially. So after three weeks of no brain activity, we let him go," Nana explained.

I was confused. "We?"

"My husband and I." Nana spoke softly.

"I don't remember having a grandfather," I said.

"Well, I remarried two years after I last saw you. I was living in Maryland when I met him. We've been married seventeen years now. John is a good man."

I nodded. "Oh, I see."

"I'd like you to meet him when you're ready," Nana offered. "Anyway, the third man lost both his legs, but he survived. Lives out in Alabama with his family." Nana shook her head. "It was a horrible accident . . . just horrible."

"I'm just sad that we didn't know."

Nana bowed her head. "So am I."

I put my hand over my eyes. "We would've been there for the funeral and everything."

"I know you would've if you could've." Nana let out a deep breath. "I figured she wouldn't let you come, but I thought she would've at least let you know that he was gone."

"Nope. Not a word." I hit the table with my hand.

Nana took my hand. "I'm so sorry about that."

"I guess the day she found out my father died was just another day for her." I stared at the wall ahead of me.

"Your mother is a very troubled woman." Nana took a sip of her coffee.

"That's not even the half of it," I agreed.

Nana smiled despite her tear-filled eyes. "I'm still praying for her, though."

"Don't bother. " I shook my head violently. "She doesn't deserve it."

"The truth is that none of us do." Nana loosened her face. "No, don't be angry with your mother."

I raised my eyebrows. "Are you kidding me?"

"Forgive her and move on." Nana had a slight smile.

I pounded my fist on the table. "She doesn't even care that she did us wrong."

Nana patted my fist. "Put it all in God's hands."

I twisted my fist away from her touch. "But how can I do that?"

Nana paused, then pushed her glasses up on her nose. "It's definitely easier said than done, but first you've got to put your whole life in His hands. Then little by little He'll give you the answers you need."

I nodded. Then I remembered Justin. "Nana, maybe you could pray for my son."

"Of course I can, sweetheart. I didn't even know you had a son." Nana smiled again.

"What's his name?"

"His name is Justin. He's nine years old and he's very sick," I said. "In fact, he's a patient at this hospital."

"Really?" Nana looked around her. "At Mercy?"

"Yes," I answered.

Nana's eyes became wide. "Oh, my. What's wrong with him?"

I didn't blink. "He has a very serious form of cancer."

"All cancer is serious." Nana nodded.

"He's dying fast," I added.

Nana put her finger to her lips. "Don't claim that, honey. My God is a healer."

"He has acute myeloid leukemia and he needs a bone-marrow transplant from a matching donor, which is why I'm here in New Orleans."

"My goodness." Nana put her hand on her heart.

"Every family member that I have contact with has already been tested. Still, there's no match." I closed my eyes and saw a vision of the turquoise wall again.

Nana pushed her chair away from the table. "Say no more. Just tell me where and when I can be tested."

"Thanks, Nana." I stood up and hugged her.

"No, sweetie. You don't have to thank me. It's the very least I can do. The most I can do is pray. Now, that'll bring down power from heaven." Nana grabbed my hand. "We'll get through this."

I liked the way she said *we'll get through this*. There was something sweet about her. It was different than Aunt Ruby's warmth, so I couldn't pinpoint what it was. But it was nice to feel.

"So are you here in town to stay?"

"Well, at least until Justin gets well." I paused, then explained, "My Aunt Ruby had him transferred down here so it would be easier for me."

Nana took off her glasses. "Is that right?"

"It'll be easier for me to locate as much family as possible here in New Orleans," I explained.

Nana's eyes met mine. "So that's why you came looking for your father?"

"Only partly." I looked down at the table, then lifted my eyes. "I really hoped I could get to know him too."

Nana smiled slightly. "I know you did, sweetie."

"My Aunt Ruby has been very kind. I'm staying at her bed-and-breakfast off of Route Nine, Ruby's Red house." I pushed my chair away from the table.

"I know that place. Never knew it belonged to your aunt, though." Nana chuckled.

"Yep, it's a nice place." I pulled out my cell phone. "She's given me use of her car, a job, and a cell phone."

Nana smiled. "Well, it sounds like you're well on your way to restoration."

I folded a napkin in my hands. "It's Justin's restoration I'm concerned about."

Nana nodded.

"I'm trying to find my ex-husband, Smooth, Justin's father." I looked directly into Nana's soft eyes.

"Yes, I see." Nana's eyes lit up. "He may be the perfect match."

I nodded. "There's as good a chance as any and I won't be satisfied until he's tested."

Nana finished her drink and wiped her mouth daintily. "Of course. I'll do whatever I can to help."

"Thank you. I have an old friend of Smooth's who I'm meeting with later this evening. His name is Tyrone. I am hoping we might be able to come up with something in regard to Smooth's whereabouts."

"I'm sure you will." Nana stood up. "When can I meet my grandson?"

I forced a smile as tears rose up in my eyes. "Right now is a great time."

I didn't have to tell her about the protective gear she needed to wear, because being a registered nurse, she already knew what to do. I led her to Justin's room and made an awkward introduction. I explained that his great-grandmother, who he never knew about, was a nurse at Mercy Hospital.

Justin seemed excited. "Really?"

"Really," Nana confirmed.

"I think that's kind of cool," Justin said. "I never knew I had a great-grandmother."

"And I never knew I had a great-grandson." Nana giggled. "Well, now we know."

Justin shot me a look as if he was having a hard time believing it. "And you're a nurse here on this floor?"

"Yeah." I smiled at him, proud of Nana's profession.

Justin chuckled. "Looks like somebody is looking out for me after all."

"Not just somebody, son, God is working in mysterious ways." Nana grabbed Justin's frail hand. "He knew before you were admitted here that I'd be working here with you."

Justin looked to his left, then his right. "Are you saying He planned it this way?"

"Yes, that's exactly what I'm saying." Nana patted him on the hand.

I didn't know what to say and I wasn't really sure whether I believed it or not. But I knew I was glad Justin had a great-grandmother who was warm and caring and able to check in on him when I wasn't there. Even if it wasn't a miracle, it was pretty big in my eyes.

Chapter 13

After Nana left, I waited with Justin until I heard a text coming through. When I saw that it was from Tyrone, I ran through the corridor, then took the elevator downstairs to meet him at the front entrance. It was exactly five o'clock.

"Hey there, lady." Tyrone was wearing a contemporary-looking suit without a tie. He opened his arms for a hug. "You look very nice."

Apprehensively, I hugged him back. "So do you. But you could've let me edge up that hairline a little."

Tyrone reached for his hair. "Oh, I—"

I couldn't hold it in any longer so I burst out laughing. "I'm just kidding. That's a joke. Don't you remember I used to always get you like that back in the day?"

"Yeah, that's right. I remember now. Then you'd offer to *really* cut everyone's hair for free." Tyrone followed me to the elevator.

I pressed the up button, still smiling from my little joke. "At which time Smooth would catch an attitude. All I wanted to do was cut some hair. Not run away with one of the band members."

Tyrone chuckled. "But he wasn't having it."

"No, he wasn't." My smile disappeared. "I'm glad those days are over."

The elevator door opened and we walked inside. "Do you still think about cutting hair?"

"Almost every day," I answered.

Tyrone leaned in close. "Really?"

I whispered so the other two passengers on the elevator wouldn't hear me. "Yes, really. I'm hoping to go to beauty school at some point."

"Cool." Tyrone nodded as we left the elevator. "Never give up on your dream."

I paused, because no one had ever told me that before. *Lord, please help me not to give up.*

Finally, we reached Justin's room.

Tyrone put his hand on the doorknob. "I hope I'm not bothering him by coming."

"Don't be silly." I pushed past him and opened the door myself. "My son is very friendly. He likes meeting new people." I walked over to Justin's bed, then pulled up a chair and sat down.

"Justin, remember when I told you I had one more person for you to meet—well, this is an old friend of mine. He and your father used to play in a band together. His name is Mr. Tyrone Freeman." I leaned out of the way.

"Hello, Justin." Tyrone extended his hand.

"Hi, Mr. Freeman," Justin said, shaking his hand.

Tyrone pulled up another chair and sat down. "Why don't you call me Mr. Tyrone instead? It makes me feel a little younger."

"Okay," Justin answered.

Tyrone continued, "How are you feeling today?"

Justin spoke slowly. "A little weak."

"That's okay, buddy." Tyrone grinned as if he had a big secret. "Do you know what Jesus says about the weak?"

Justin shook his head slightly. "No. What does he say?"

"He says, *Let the weak say I'm strong.*"

Justin stared at Tyrone. "And why is that?"

"Because He is stronger than we are and if we cast all our cares on Him, He can handle it. He can make us strong as long as we stick with Him," Tyrone said.

Justin squinted his eyes. "Oh, okay. Are you a preacher or something?"

Tyrone bowed his head. "Not at all. Just a man who loves the Lord."

Justin's face lit up. "You sound a lot like my *new* grandma."

Tyrone glanced up at me. "Oh really? You have a new grandma?"

"Yes, she's my great-grandma and I just met her today, but she seems pretty nice." Justin smiled. "And guess what?"

Tyrone widened his eyes in anticipation. "What?"

"She works here at this hospital, so she's kind of like my guardian angel or something."

Justin looked in the direction of the door as if his great-grandmother would be coming back soon.

Tyrone looked over at me. "Is that so?"

Justin continued: "She kept talking about how good God is and stuff."

"That's because He is," Tyrone said.

"I hope He'll be good to me, then." Justin put his head back on his pillow.

Tyrone chuckled. "Whether you know it or not, He already is."

At that moment I wondered if what Tyrone said was really true. Had God already been good to him, to me? Maybe He had been. Today, I was alive and so was Justin. And today I was not in a jail cell. I was a free woman. No matter what I was going through, I decided that Tyrone was right.

Justin showed his dimples, something he'd inherited from me. "What instrument did you play in the band?"

"I played the bass guitar. Still do." Tyrone pretended to play an imaginary guitar. "I love music."

"Wow." Justin propped himself up against his pillow. "Me too."

Then Tyrone pretended to play an imaginary saxophone. "Your dad always played the saxophone. I'm sure your mom has told you that already."

Justin nodded.

Tyrone grinned. "Your dad is one of the best musicians around these parts."

"Oh yeah?" Justin looked into Tyrone's eyes. "Why don't you play in the same band anymore?"

Tyrone shot me a look. "Well, sometimes people have different things they have to do and because of that they have to go their separate ways."

Justin scratched his head. "What things did you have to do?"

"I was called to play for the church and other gospel events, so that's what I do now."

Tyrone held up his hand for a high five. "I even teach music to kids at a rec center."

"Oh." Justin bit his bottom lip. "I get it."

Tyrone playfully punched the air. "Of course you do. You seem like a very bright boy and you're going to be getting well and leaving this hospital very soon."

Justin smiled. "I hope so."

Tyrone smiled back. "I know so."

I was glad to hear such empowering words spoken over Justin's life.

Tyrone slid the chair back a little, then stood up. "I'm not going to stay long enough to wear you out or take up all of your time you want to spend with your mother, but I just wanted to meet you. I knew you had to be special if you were Trinity's son and just like I thought, you are."

"Thanks." Justin propped himself up on his pillow. "Are you coming back again?"

"Sure, if you want me to," Tyrone answered.

Justin nodded. "Cool."

"Cool," Tyrone said.

Then Tyrone quietly left the room and let me say good night to my son. I met him in the waiting area.

Tyrone cornered me as soon as I came out of Justin's room. "That's a great kid you've got there."

I smiled with all of the maternal pride I had inside of me. "I know. Thank you."

Tyrone shook his head. "Smooth doesn't know what he's missing."

I put on a fake smile. "Smooth never does, does he?"

Tyrone didn't respond.

We walked outside to the parking lot and got inside of Tyrone's black Chevy Silverado pickup truck. It was kind of plain, but strong, just like Tyrone. We drove away from the hospital, uptown past the Audubon Park and the campuses of Tulane and Loyola Universities. I saw the St. Charles streetcar roll through the streets. Finally we arrived at Mt. Sinai Deliverance Church.

Then he hopped out of the truck, went around to the passenger side, and helped me to get out. It was a medium-sized church made of light-colored stones, with beautiful stained-glass windows.

A crowd had already began to gather in front of the church. Tyrone took my arm as he led me inside. Before long, I was being introduced to friendly church members.

"Sister Jefferson, this is Trinity Crawford, an old friend of mine. Trinity, this is Sister Jefferson, the sweetest woman who ever walked the earth."

She hunched him in the ribs. "Oh, now go on and hush, boy. It's so nice to meet you, Ms. Trinity. And what a lovely name, I must say. You do know what that means, don't you?"

"Yes, my grandmother named me and explained the meaning to me at least a gazillion times before I was five years old." I showed her my biggest smile.

Sister Jefferson chuckled. "Your grandmother is a wise woman."

I nodded politely.

"It's good to see you two getting along so well." He kissed Sister Jefferson on the cheek.

"I'm going up to play now. Would you please take care of her for me?"

"Now, you know me." Sister Jefferson squeezed his arm. "That's no problem at all."

"Hey, wait a minute here," I said, smirking. "You two are talking about me like I'm either an invalid or a child."

"No, that's just how we take care of each other here at Mt. Sinai Deliverance Church."

"I see." I eyed both of them playfully.

"I'll be back in a little while." Tyrone tapped my hand. "Enjoy the program."

"I will." I backed into a seat.

Sister Jefferson leaned over to me. "If you need anything, dear, anything at all, I'll be right over there with the ushers."

"Thank you, but I'm sure I'll be just fine." I gave her a reassuring smile.

Tyrone positioned himself in the band section. Shortly thereafter the music began and the choir marched in through the aisles.

A mixture of strong perfumes and colognes assaulted my nostrils as they went by. They wore black-and-white robes with silver trimming.

I watched Tyrone play song after song and it was nothing like the old days. It was nothing like listening to Smooth crank out loud tunes in smoke-filled clubs for a half-drunk audience. A sweet feeling came over me during the service as I remembered going to church with my siblings and grandmother. For a moment, I wondered what kind of woman I would have become if my father and grandmother had not been chased away.

In any case, the music—although different from what I was used to—excited me. It wasn't just the rhythm, but it was also the words that moved me: *unconditional love, healing, and forgiveness.* I kept listening to them over and over again, until I stood on my feet and started clapping along. Then they sang a song about breaking chains and something stirred on the inside of me as I thought about my years of imprisonment. Now I knew God was good because, although my heart was breaking at the condition of my son, He had given me this song to know that the chains over my life were broken. And it touched me in a way I hadn't been touched before. I knew it was more than a great performance. It was more than the prowess of an experienced music ministry. Underneath it all, I knew it was a God thing and throughout the concert, I remained eager to enjoy this feeling. *Lord, what are you telling me?*

When the concert was over, Sister Jefferson came over and hugged me. "Thank you for coming out."

"It was my pleasure." I hugged her back, hoping she could feel my gratitude.

A few minutes later, I saw Tyrone pushing himself through the crowd. "Well, what did you think?"

I laughed at the sight of him, with his jacket half on and half off. "I think it was very nice. I had a lot of fun."

Tyrone wiped the sweat from his face with a napkin. "You did?"

I gave him a playful punch in the arm. "Don't act so surprised. My grandmother used to bring me to church all the time when I was young."

Tyrone pretended to fall backwards. "Really?"

"Yes, really." I put up one finger to confirm it.

Tyrone chuckled, then led me out of the sanctuary. "I guess you could say that I brought you back to your roots, then?"

I followed him happily. "Yeah, I guess you could say that."

Tyrone looked back once we were outside. "Well, all of that playing sure did make me hungry. How about you?"

I looked down at my stomach and gave it a little pat. "Me too."

Tyrone smiled. "Good, then let's go grab something to eat."

"Sure. Why not?" As usual, Tyrone was so nice it was hard to turn him down.

I looked into his brown eyes and saw a gentleness I'd never noticed before . . . or maybe I had seen it before when I was married to Smooth. In any case, I certainly wasn't allowed to acknowledge it or admire it in any way. Smooth was never the kind of man who would share his glory. Instead, he was jealous and controlling. Sad part is, I didn't even realize it at the time.

He held the door open for me as I hopped into the truck. "Where do you want to go?"

Again, I patted my stomach. "Wherever you want. Doesn't matter to me as long as they have food."

"Let's go to Bayou St. John and Mid-City. They've got a lot of inexpensive restaurants out there," Tyrone suggested.

"Yeah, you're right. I do kind of remember something like that. Isn't that out by that park . . . uh . . . ?"

"Yep. Rambling City Park," Tyrone answered.

I nodded. "Yeah, that's it."

Tyrone continued to look straight ahead. "You remember when me and Smooth had that gig over there?"

"How could I forget?" I threw my hands in the air in mock surrender. "We were so young."

Tyrone shook his head. "And so dumb."

"I know that's right." I snapped my fingers.

Tyrone stopped by a strip of small restaurants and parked on the street.

Before I could hop out of the truck, he had run around to my side and was shaking his head. "You should've waited for me."

"Oh, I can handle it." I held onto his strong shoulders as he helped me to step down from the truck.

Tyrone shook his head. "That's not the point."

I unsuccessfully tried to stop myself from blushing. "I guess I'm not used to being with such a gentleman."

Tyrone shut the door behind me. "I wasn't always a gentleman myself, but thanks to Christ, it's a new day."

I straightened out my dress. "Yeah, I guess it is, huh?"

Then I allowed myself to smile as he took my arm and led me into the restaurant. We sat at a table in the middle. There was a stage at the back and we didn't want the music to drown out our conversation.

Tyrone jumped right in. "So how have you been, really? I mean, you must be going through a lot with your son and all?"

"I'm making it." I drummed my fingers on the table.

Tyrone stared into my eyes and it seemed as if he was staring into the depths of my soul. "Are you?"

I gave a tight-lipped smile, without revealing any teeth. "I am."

"Good." Tyrone looked a little sad. "I'm glad you're getting back on your feet after . . ."

I stared back and didn't blink. "After six years in prison?"

Tyrone paused. "I'm sorry . . ."

"No, it's okay. Most people want to know too. They just don't know how to bring it up. It's rough sometimes, you know. Dealing with the outside world, things I haven't had to deal with in a long time. Like having freedom and making decisions. Like the fact that I now have to reapply

for my driver's license, wait in lines and fill out forms."
I looked at the menu in front of me. "Like this menu, for
example. Tonight I get to decide what I want to eat. But
when I was on death row, everything was decided for me."

"I can't imagine." Tyrone shook his head. "If you don't
mind, what was it like in there?"

I swallowed before answering. "My cell was like a
concrete-and-steel cage about four feet by nine feet tall.
I was locked in for nineteen hours a day. Two hours a
day I was let out into a larger cage of about seven feet by
eleven for recreation."

Tyrone never took his eyes off of me. "Wow, I don't
know how you dealt with it."

"It wasn't easy." I began to shift positions in my seat.
"I spent some nights pacing the floor or staring out into
the darkness, listening to the vibrations of other inmates'
cages or the constant cursing of inmates on other tiers. I
was treated like I was less than human. There were times
I really wanted to die."

Tyrone was relentless. "What kept you going?"

I bit my bottom lip. "I held onto the fact that my son
needed a mother. I felt like if I kept appealing, maybe
someday some judge would realize I was innocent. No
matter how far-fetched it was, I had to hold onto that."

"So you held on in faith?" Tyrone smiled as if he was
coming back to life.

I shook my head. "I don't know if I'd call it faith."

"But it was. You had faith that you would be vindicated
and you were," Tyrone said. "I'm glad that's over for you."

"So am I." My heart beat faster as I remembered my
past. "You don't know what it's like to be one of the
walking dead."

Tyrone stopped smiling. "Actually, I'm afraid I do.
You see, I was never on death row, but I was once dead
spiritually."

I nodded, hoping he wouldn't start a full-fledged conversion attempt.

"Now, I'm alive." Tyrone looked absentmindedly at the menu.

I didn't know how to respond to that, so I didn't say anything.

A young waitress with pale peach skin, freckles, and light brown hair came to take our orders. She spoke with a Creole accent. "What can I get for y'all today?"

"I think I'm gonna have the catfish." Tyrone handed the menu to the waitress.

I stared at the menu. "Sounds good. Maybe I'll have the catfish and the Cajun fries platter."

Tyrone laughed. "You always did have a healthy appetite."

I balled up my fist and put it in his face. "Watch it, now."

Tyrone chuckled. "No, I mean that in a good way."

"You'd better." I pushed away from the table. "I'm going to take a little trip to the ladies' room. I'll be right back."

Tyrone pointed straight ahead. "The restrooms are at the back near that stage area."

"Okay. I'll find it." I left the table.

I pushed my way through the crowded eating area and saw the restroom signs ahead.

Looking down, I nearly toppled over in the black pumps I hadn't worn in six years. Ironically, Aunt Ruby had offered to let me borrow a pair of her shoes, as if our feet could ever actually be the same size. Smiling at that thought, I let my eyes wander across to the stage area. There was one man standing, already assembling his drum set, while another was bent down on the floor of the stage. My eyes involuntarily traveled upwards. The back of his head and broad back looked familiar. My eyes moved down to the spider tattoo on his neck. I knew then that it was him and I took a deep breath before making my decision.

Chapter 14

Unpacking his saxophone, Smooth McGee was bent over and never even looked up.

When I saw him, I didn't feel quite the way I thought I'd feel. I didn't stare at his fine lips or obsess over the way they used to feel on mine. I didn't care that he had two scantily-clad women on stage with him or that they were staring at him like he was tonight's dinner.

The last time I'd seen him I was so tormented from sitting on death row, I practically ignored him. Mama would have actually been proud of me for once. She never did like to see me make a fool out of myself over a man, especially not one who was so dark in complexion. Either way, our visit was short and ended with a whisper of *I love you* under his whiskey-soaked breath. I knew he didn't mean them, yet I took his words back with me, trying not to let them settle into my heart.

My thoughts brought me back to the present. And there he was on the stage, holding his saxophone with his strong hands. And I observed his dark chocolate, brown skin, shaggy dark hair he wore in a fade, and those red alligator shoes. Nothing had changed.

So I slipped past him as I walked to the restroom. There I relieved myself and lingered in the stall for an extra two minutes, trying to decide what to do. Finally, I decided that I would do nothing until after dinner. So I exited the restroom and covered my face with my hands, so I wouldn't be spotted. I carefully squeezed through the crowd, taking the long way back to my table.

Finally, I sat down, leaned over to Tyrone, and whispered in his ear. "I just saw Smooth."

Tyrone sat up straight. "He's here?"

"He's at the back and he's about to play." Sweat formed around my eyebrows.

"I'm sorry, but I didn't know." Tyrone shook his head like a child who was in trouble.

"This place definitely didn't seem like his style."

I tried to be calm yet I kept looking straight ahead. "I know. I was surprised too at first, but I'm okay now."

Tyrone didn't look convinced. "Are you sure?"

"Yes, I'm sure. I wanted to find him." I nodded. "Now I've found him. "

Tyrone took a sip of water. "Well, I guess the mission is accomplished."

"Thanks to you." I smiled and tapped his hand.

Tyrone held up his hands. "This was not my doing, but I'm glad you've found him for your son's sake."

"Yeah, so am I."

Suddenly, our waitress appeared with our plates, so we stopped talking and thanked her.

"How do you want to handle this?" Tyrone wiped his mouth with his napkin. "Do you want me to leave?"

I looked into his eyes. "No, why would you do that?"

"Well, you know how Smooth is. I don't want to start any confusion." Tyrone backed his chair away from the table and stood up.

I signaled him to sit back down. "There's no confusion here. I'm going to eat my dinner, then talk to him." Despite my brave words, I couldn't stop shaking.

Tyrone sat down, but still looked unconvinced. "You know what I mean—how paranoid he always was. I don't want him to get the wrong idea about us, you know?"

"Oh, right." I squeezed my eyes shut as I remembered Smooth's jealous tantrums and the fights we had because of them. Then I reached out to take Tyrone's hand. "But we're old friends and Smooth is my ex-husband. I refuse to spend the rest of my life hiding from his suspicious eyes or worrying about what he might think about me or my life. It's just that: my life." I pulled my hand away from his, curled my fingers into a fist, and slammed it down on the table.

"Okay, if you say so. I'll just get myself prayed up." Tyrone raised his eyebrows.

"Now, that's not a bad idea." I stretched my arms wide, maintained eye contact with Tyrone, and took a deep breath, but I couldn't stop thinking of *him*.

For years he had been the biggest thing in my life, the only man I'd ever truly loved.

There was a time, after our divorce, that I wondered if I could even make it without him or if I could ever hear music again without crying. I'd been stuck on Smooth McGee since I stole him away from Madison Douglass during the senior prom. And he'd been everything I thought I needed: strong, charming, and dark like chocolate, with a smile so bright he could make any woman's day.

Finally, the band began to play and I turned my body to face the stage. I didn't understand why my heart was beating so fast, but I prayed that it would slow down before I passed out. Then I crossed my legs and for the first time in my life, I let Smooth's music soothe me, but not seduce me. I drummed my fingers on the table to the rhythm and imagined myself getting through this evening successfully. *No drama*, I decided. I remembered Mama's last words: "Gal, don't you go down there and get caught up with that ol' Smooth McGee." And for once, Mama was right. I had come too far to turn back now. I had to stay focused for Justin's sake and not get caught up in his games.

Our waitress circled us again. "Ma'am, can I get you something else?"

"No, I'm okay. Thanks, honey." I took a sip of my lemonade.

The waitress smacked her gum. "Sir, what about you?"

"I'm good, thanks." Tyrone grinned at the waitress.

The lights were dim but I could still see his silhouette through the darkness. I leaned forward as I listened to Smooth's band. There was a drummer, a keyboard player, a trombone player, a lead singer, and two background singers. The tunes were mellow and the lyrics were about love. What did Smooth ever know about love? Had he ever loved me? No. I was convinced that he only loved himself.

I could hear Tyrone talking in the background, but I was so preoccupied that I couldn't make out what he was saying. I kept taking shallow breaths, trying to relax as Smooth caressed his saxophone. The three young ladies positioned themselves in front of the stage. They wore hip-length weaves, red-leather miniskirts, and red halter tops with white polka dots. The lead singer, who stood in the middle, wore a red-and-white bow in her hair. They sang, but I didn't focus on their voices. Instead, I watched Smooth as *he* watched them. His dark eyes seemed to dance with excitement.

When the show was over, the band received a standing ovation. I made my way through the crowd, back to the stage.

Nervously, I walked past the other band members and went right up to him. "So it's been a while, huh?"

Finally, Smooth looked up at me. Sweat glistened off of his thick eyebrows. "Puddin'?"

"Yeah, it's me." I swallowed hard.

Smooth jumped down off the stage and took me in his arms. "It's so good to see you."

I let myself be hugged, but did not hug back. I had been down that road before.

He loosened his embrace and stared into my eyes, grinning. "What are you doing here?"

"Actually, I've been trying to find you for the past couple of weeks, but tonight I just happened to stumble upon this place."

Smooth looked me up and down as if I was a piece of meat. "Oh yeah?" He put his hand on my shoulder and squeezed.

I removed his hand and shot him a look. I knew what he was thinking and I was determined to make my position clear. "Yeah, I was having dinner with an old friend."

Smooth's grin disappeared. "An old friend?"

"Yes, our old friend, Tyrone," I explained.

"Tyrone?" Smooth squinted his eyes at me. "You mean Bingo, that Tyrone?"

I looked behind me. "Yep. And here he comes."

Smooth's eyes narrowed in on me as Tyrone approached.

Tyrone went right up to him and opened his arms for a hug. "What's up, man?"

Smooth didn't smile or blink. "You tell me, brother."

Tyrone put his arms down. "What?"

"I mean, you're here with my wife, trying to disrespect me." Smooth took a couple of steps back as if he was bracing himself. "You tell me what's up."

"Aw, Smooth, you've got it all wrong, man." Tyrone waved his hands. "It's nothing like that."

"There you go, acting the fool again." I shook my head. "Jumping to conclusions. And besides, I'm not your wife anymore."

Smooth kept his eyes on Tyrone. "Yeah, you're a free woman now, huh? Free to be with this clown?"

I jumped in front of Tyrone. "Smooth, it's sad to see you're still the same after all these years. But I guess I had to see it with my own eyes."

Smooth turned his attention to me. "What do you mean by that?"

"I mean, you didn't have good sense when we were married and you still don't."

"And he does? I suppose Tyrone has got plenty of sense. He sure knows how to be a backstabber and steal a man's woman." Smooth started to crack his knuckles as if he was about to throw a punch.

"I am not your woman." I stood between them and put my hands on my hips. "No one has stolen me because I am not a piece of property."

Tyrone tried to get around me. "Smooth, I—"

"Stay out of this." Smooth tried to walk around me, but I kept shifting positions.

I turned to Tyrone. "I'll take care of this. Why don't you just meet me in the car?"

Tyrone started to object, but I put my finger to my lips and signaled him with my eyes.

"Okay, but I sure hate it turned out like this, though." Tyrone turned to walk away.

Smooth shot him an angry look. "I'll bet you do. Just keep on walking, bruh."

I rolled my eyes in disgust. "You ought to be ashamed of yourself. Tyrone is our friend."

"Was. He's no longer a friend of mine." Smooth paced the stage area.

"Well, that's too bad, because he was always a good friend to you. And he has been nothing but respectful, even now." I looked around to make sure I wasn't talking too loud.

"Whatever." Smooth took me by the arm. "What are you doing with him, anyway?"

I twisted myself out of his grasp. "I told you I ran into him when I was looking for you."

Smooth stared at me. "And why were you looking for me?"

"Because you're my son's father." I let out a deep breath.

As if he had forgotten all about him, he asked, "How is my boy?"

I looked him in the eye. "Justin isn't doing well at all. That's why I'm here."

I had to hold it together.

Smooth's face hardened. "What do you mean, he's not doing well? What's wrong with him?"

"He has cancer," I blurted out.

He led me over to a quiet corner. "Cancer? You've got to be kidding me."

"I wish I was, but I'm not. He has an aggressive form of leukemia called acute myelogenous leukemia." I leaned against the brick wall.

Smooth put his hand on the wall, leaning over me. "When did you find out?"

"Just going on two months now. That's why I came to New Orleans, to find you and other family members," I explained.

Smooth's expression changed from rage to confusion. "Other family members?"

"Anyone who could be tested. Justin needs a bone-marrow donor and it has to be someone close to him. Obviously, you would be a good candidate. But I've found my paternal grandmother and she's been tested also. I was hoping to have my father tested, but in talking to my grandmother, I found out that he passed away some years ago."

"Hmph. That's too bad." Smooth took a lighter out of his pocket and lit a cigarette.

Looking at the rings of smoke he blew into the air, I secretly wondered when New Orleans would enact their own ban on smoking in public places.

"My mother never even told me about my father's death, but never mind about her for now." I waved my hands as if to clear the slate and start over. "Anyway, Justin is in a race against time and we need you."

Smooth grabbed my hand. "What do you need me to do?"

I pulled my hand away. "I need you to go down to the hospital where he is and be tested."

"I don't know about all of that. You know how I feel about hospitals. The last time I was in one I almost—"

I rolled my eyes once more. "I know. I know. You almost died."

"Then why are you asking me to do this?"

I pulled the cigarette out of his mouth and held it between my fingers. "Because I'm desperate. Because you may just be Justin's last hope. If you're not a match, Justin may die."

Smooth took the cigarette from me and placed it back into his mouth. Then he turned his back to me and began to walk away. "This is all too much to handle right now."

I followed him. "Where are you going?"

Smooth kept walking. "I'm going home to get a drink."

"And where is home, Smooth? Where can I find you when I need you?"

Finally he stopped and handed me a card. "I'm staying in a boarding house on Canal Street. What about you?"

I looked at the card to make sure that what he was saying was legitimate. "I'm staying at Ruby's Red House. It's my aunt's place."

Smooth took the cigarette out of his mouth and blew out another ring of smoke. I fanned it out of my face. I much preferred the buzz of actual nicotine to the smut of mere secondhand smoke. Thankfully, I'd never become addicted; besides, I was determined to be a better example for my son.

I stayed right on his heels. "Will I hear from you soon?"

Smooth murmured something under his breath and kept walking. I waited until he left the building before I eased out and walked down the street to where Tyrone's truck was parked.

As soon as Tyrone saw me, he jumped out, ran over to the passenger's side, and opened my door wide. It was nice to know that chivalry was alive and well.

"I saw Smooth when he left and he looked like he was still fired up." Tyrone put his hands on my shoulders and looked into my eyes. "Are you okay?"

"Yeah, I'm fine." I broke the awkward moment by smiling. "You know Smooth is all talk. He wouldn't really hurt a fly."

Tyrone helped me into the car, shut the door, and went around to the driver's side. "Well, I don't know about that, 'cause the Smooth I remember would hurt someone *if* he had to—that is, to protect who or what he loves."

I looked over at him. "So you really think he still loves me?"

Tyrone hunched his shoulders.

"Let me answer that for you. He doesn't love me. He just loves to have control over me." I folded my arms. "He'll never have that again."

It was silent in the truck for a while until Tyrone turned on the radio. Surprisingly, it was gospel music blaring from the station.

I was curious. "Is that the kind of music you listen to?"

"Not all of the time, but mostly gospel, yes. I can turn it off if it bothers you." Tyrone reached for the radio dial.

I grabbed his hand and guided it away from the radio. "No, it's kind of nice. Different than what I'm used to, but nice."

"Cool." Tyrone smiled and put his hand back on the steering wheel. "Were you able to tell Smooth about your son?"

"Yes, I did and I know where he is staying now too." I smoothed out the wrinkles in my dress.

"Great." Tyrone quickly glanced over at me.

I smiled. "Yes, I'm pretty hopeful."

Tyrone's eyes seemed to be full of concern. "I know that coming to New Orleans hasn't been easy. I'm just glad it's all working out for you."

"I just hope that Smooth is a match and that we can get everything done in time." I fumbled with my purse in my lap. It was a worn black leather purse with a long strap. I'd purchased it at a discount outlet in Miami on my honeymoon and it had been one of my favorites ever since.

"Remember that God created time, but He's not defined by it." Tyrone glanced over at me and grinned with the pearliest white teeth I'd seen in a while. "He's got this."

He didn't cease to impress me. "How did you get so smart, Bingo?"

"Same way you did, I guess, Puddin' . . . by the grace of God." Tyrone laughed.

"Yeah, I guess you're right. By the grace of God." I made a mental note to look up the word *grace* when I got home.

Tyrone pulled up right in front of Aunt Ruby's, got out, opened my door for me, then hugged me good night. "Thanks for coming out to support me."

His hands were firm, but gentle. When he let me go, I gave him a light punch in his shoulder. "Anytime. After all, what are old friends for?"

I watched him hop back into the truck and drive away as I stood in the doorway, waving.

"Trinity Anne Crawford," the voice screeched.

I squeezed my eyes shut and cringed, because I'd recognize that voice anywhere.

Chapter 15

Had she really driven all the way from the middle of Baton Rouge in Uncle Charlie's old station wagon? Sure enough, I went inside only to find Mama standing in Aunt Ruby's lobby.

She was dressed in an oversized muumuu, a pair of worn-out sneakers, and a purple head scarf.

"Mama, what are you doing here?"

Mama walked right up to me. "What am I doing here? The real question is how could you and your sister roll up on me the other day like that, trying to trick me and scandalize my good name?"

"No one was trying to trick or scandalize you and you know it," I said, calmly.

"Maybe we should take this somewhere a little more private," Aunt Ruby said, leading us into her own private suite.

"Well, why are you still here?" Mama rolled her light eyes at Aunt Ruby. "This is all your fault, anyway."

Aunt Ruby rolled her neck. "How in the world is this my fault?"

"If you hadn't encouraged Trinity to come back to New Orleans, none of this would've happened," Mama yelled.

"None of *what* would've happened?" Aunt Ruby maintained her cool. "Do you mean she wouldn't have found out about her own father's passing? Because if that's what you're talking about, that's ridiculous. You must be out of your mind to hide something like that from your daughters."

Mama moved closer to Aunt Ruby and put her finger in her face. "And you must be out of your mind talking to me like that."

Aunt Ruby moved Mama's finger and got even closer to her. "I'll talk to you anyway I want. I'm not scared of you, Rosalee. Never was."

Mama fanned Aunt Ruby away and started in the other direction, toward me. "This ain't even about you."

"I know that, but why don't you just give the girl a break? Trinity is dealing with so much right now," Aunt Ruby pleaded.

Mama pointed her finger at her sagging chest. "And I'm not? I had Trinity and Alyssa come in yelling and screaming at me like I did something wrong, when it was their no-good fa—"

Something ugly was about to rise up in me. "Look, I have nothing to say to you. I don't know why you even came down here."

"I came to get you out of this place, to bring you back. I told you there was something evil down here and now it has already turned you against me," Mama said.

I squinted at her. "Are you serious right now?"

Mama pushed her long, straight hair from her face. It was becoming more gray as each day went by. "Yep. Same wicked place that destroyed my marriage to your good-for-nothing father."

I came close to Mama, but not close enough that she could swing at me. "First of all, none of this has anything to do with New Orleans. This has to do with you lying to Alyssa and me for years; lying to us about our own father. You could've at least told us he was dead."

Mama's eyes looked like those of a cat. "He'd been dead to me long before that accident."

Despite my best attempt, tears began to run down my face. "I know that, but he was still our father." I didn't want her to see my reaction because I knew she'd feed on it.

Aunt Ruby shook her head. "I'm going to go back to work. Trinity, you know where to find me if you need me."

"Bye." Mama waved her hand. "She won't need you. You're trying to turn her against me too."

Aunt Ruby threw up her hands as she exited the room. "I give up."

"Why are you here? Nothing is going to be solved now." I paced back and forth in front of her. "You kept my father away from me and now he's gone. He's been dead and buried and there is nothing you can do to change that for me now."

"That ain't even true." Mama smirked.

"It is true and I have nothing else to say to you about it right now. Nothing, except that I'm angry and that's between me and God. Not me and you." I opened the door for her. "Good-bye, Mama. Go back to Baton Rouge."

"I want you to come back with me." Mama had a sadness in her eyes.

"Why? So you can dog me even more? No, I've got people who are helping me. I'm staying here until I have a blood donor for Justin," I said.

Mama closed one eye and lifted her chin. "I hope you're not talking about that witchcraft-working grandmother of yours."

"She's a good woman, Mama. Good-bye," I pointed to the hallway.

When she'd left, I quickly closed the door behind her and locked it. Where was big-mouthed Alyssa when I needed her? She'd missed everything. Now I would have to explain all of this to her over the phone. I stayed in Aunt Ruby's room, trying to recuperate from the attack.

I looked out of the window and saw Mama leaving the Red House with Ms. Magnolia close on her tail. I knew then that they must've put Mama out. She left people no choice. I watched her walk far down the street, with her head scarf falling off of her silky gray hair. When Mama finally disappeared from my view, Ms. Magnolia turned around and headed back to the building.

It was now safe for me to go upstairs to my own room.

The first thing I did was jump into the shower and let the warm water take away the stress of the day: no donor match with Alyssa, a confrontation with Smooth, then one with Mama.

What a day. As I caressed my tired body, the apricot-scented soap soothed my tight muscles. Under the shower's spray, I saw a vision. It was Tyrone's face, but I couldn't see anything else. Then it faded as quickly as it came.

I stepped out of the bathroom and picked up my phone to call Alyssa. I wanted to tell her about Mama's surprise visit. Her phone rang three times, then went to voice mail. By the time I ended the call, a text had come through from Tyrone: THANKS AGAIN FOR COMING OUT. KEEP YOUR HEAD UP. That was enough to make me smile.

But keeping my head up was easier said than done. I curled up in bed and dreamed about my son, that he was well again and running through a grassy field.

The next day I left Aunt Ruby's early, heading out to see Justin. I took the streetcar down to the hospital, then slowly walked the long hallway to his room. I swallowed hard before entering, then found Dr. Stanford and a team of doctors examining Justin.

"Ms. Crawford, we're going to have to ask that you not wear him out. He needs time to rest. His blood count is very low," Dr. Stanford said.

I wiped Justin's forehead with a napkin. "I won't. I promise."

Justin's voice was just a whisper. "It hurts, Mom."

I was leaned over him gently, afraid to hug him for fear that I would break him. He was so fragile. "But what about pain medication? He's been complaining."

Dr. Stanford looked over his glasses. "I'll increase the dosage in his IV. But I'm afraid that I have a bit of bad news. "

I let out a big sigh. How much disappointment could I possibly take? "What is it?"

"The results are in for Mrs. Pauline Crawford and she's not a match," Dr. Stanford said.

I gasped as I searched his face for answers. Then reality set in: Nana wasn't a match for Justin.

"I'm sorry. We'll have to talk about the possibilities," he said.

I wasn't ready to accept anything other than a cure. "I'll talk to you later, Doctor."

He nodded before he and the other doctors exited the room.

I spent my last few minutes with Justin, careful not to excite him.

"You know, I've loved you since the day you were born. When I was away, you were the only thing that kept me alive." I stroked his hand.

"Okay, Mommy," he said before he dozed off to sleep.

"I love you, Justin." I kissed him on his forehead before leaving the room.

By the time I reached home, I was drained. I curled up on my bed and buried my face in my pillow. After a few minutes, I sat up and reached across the bed to retrieve my backpack.

From it I pulled out my list. I stared at it for a moment as if it was a foreign object, then let my eyes glide over the inevitable. Mama, Uncle Charlie, Aunt Ruby, Alyssa, and Nana had all been tested. Everyone else's name had already been crossed off. Now I hesitantly crossed Nana's name off of the list too. The walls seemed to be closing in on me. I was running out of potential donors. I was running out of family members. As I closed my eyes, an image of Justin crying in the hospital flashed before my eyes.

I tried to shake away the image, but it wouldn't move. I left my bed completely, but it followed me around the room. I put my fingers against my temples and rubbed, but it wouldn't go away. I blinked my eyes for clarity, but I couldn't get rid of the vision. I couldn't let my son die. I had no choice. I had to go to visit Smooth and force him to be tested.

Nana called and left a message on my voice mail, but I didn't have time to talk to her yet.

I didn't want to talk to anybody. I looked at my phone and ignored the call, deciding I'd call her later.

My impending issue was getting ready to see Mr. Smooth McGee again. I went to my closet and looked at the few old and outdated outfits I'd brought with me. I finally settled on a sleek black cocktail dress, which always accentuated my curves while making me appear slimmer. Wearing it also made me feel somewhat sophisticated.

All the years I was growing up, while Mama was telling me I was too wide, I learned to adore the color black. For me, as for a lot of women, it was my secret weapon. I could hide my imperfections under it and come out shining and elegant, at least in my mind. So I wore black everything as if I was going to a funeral all of the time. And the way I felt dead on the inside most days, wearing black was like me mourning the loss of me. Mama hated it, though. She said I'd lost what little mind I did have and that I had picked up witchcraft. Sometimes I almost wanted to be what she said I was, just so she'd be quiet for a change.

But now I realize why I never could be what Mama said I was. I was what I was by the grace of God, at least according to Tyrone. I looked up the word *grace* using my phone and thought about it for a few minutes. Then I popped open my Bible and found all the references to grace that I could find.

Maybe reuniting with Tyrone, finding Aunt Ruby, Nana, and even finding Smooth was a part of this *grace*. And maybe this grace had a purpose. I was determined to find out.

Chapter 16

It was almost noon the next day when I found myself in front of Smooth's building. It was an older French-style building and I could see that it was badly in need of repair. I figured Katrina had contributed to its decay. I went through the front door, which, for some strange reason, was open, then I followed the numbers on the doors: A-1, 2, 3, 4, 5, 6, 7, and finally A-8. It was located at the end of the hall, by a window. I knocked on Smooth's door and hoped that he was home. I hadn't wanted to warn him.

Smooth yelled out, "Who is it?"

I leaned against a wall and waited. "Why don't you open the door and find out?"

Smooth came to the door bare-chested and glistening with water. "Puddin'?"

"I don't go by that nickname anymore. It's Trinity," I said.

"Oh, right. Come in." Smooth grabbed a T-shirt and pulled it over his head.

I stepped into the room to find clothes thrown everywhere and an untidy bed, among other unorganized items.

"You look really nice." Smooth eyed me like I was candy.

"Thanks." I smiled as if I was a teenager.

Please, have a seat." Smooth picked up a can of beer off of the side table.

I looked around the room and frowned. "Where?"

"Oh, I'm sorry. Right here." He picked up a pile of clean laundry from a wooden chair.

I sat down on the edge of the chair and crossed my legs sideways, afraid to lean back for fear that bugs would crawl over me.

Smooth kneeled down in front of me, biting his bottom lip. "To what do I owe this pleasure?"

I uncrossed my legs and looked him directly in the eyes. "Hey, save your little sweet talk for the other women you have coming up here."

Smooth shook his index finger from side to side. "Now there you go, bad-mouthing me again."

I fluttered my eyelashes."You're right. I'm sorry."

"No problem." Smooth grinned.

It was time to get down to business. "I'm here about Justin, of course. I would think you'd know that, since I told you he was very sick."

Smooth stood on his feet. "Where is he?"

"He's at Mercy Hospital." I rolled my eyes. "I would've told you that yesterday, but you walked out on me, remember?"

"Sorry about that." Smooth took out a cigarette and lit it. "It's just that you were just shooting out a whole lot of bad news at once."

"I understand. It's been a lot for me to handle too." I leaned forward and patted his hand slightly. "Since when did you start smoking so much?"

Smooth took the cigarette out of his mouth and blew out a puff of smoke. "Since you left me all alone."

I rolled my eyes again."Yeah, right."

"No, really, baby. All those years of you being in jail, I—"

I held my hand up in front of his face. "Stop. I'm not one of your little groupies, remember? I used to be, but I'm not anymore."

Smooth curled his lips into a frown. "What are you talking about?"

"I'm a big girl now." I gave him a fake smile. "I can take care of myself."

"I can see that." Smooth rubbed his hands together. "Hey, now that you're out and it was all a big mistake, you must be about to get paid?"

"I have an attorney handling things for me, but my concern right now is Justin." I blew out a breath of frustration. "That's all."

Smooth grinned at me. "Still, that money must be sounding pretty good, huh?"

I backed him into a corner and put my finger in his chest. "Have you heard anything I've been saying? I don't care about any lawsuit money. I care about my son."

"I know that. It's just that when I heard about all of this on the news, I was curious, that's all." Smooth raised both hands in mock surrender.

"Curious about what?" I put my hands on my hips. "How much money I'd be getting in the end?"

"Nah, it's nothing like that. How did Justin get to New Orleans anyway if he's so sick?"

Smooth put the cigarette back into his mouth and inhaled. "Or did he get sick here?"

I sighed. "No, he became sick in Baton Rouge, but my Aunt Ruby had him transferred here. Anyway, that's not the point. Have you decided to be tested yet? It's been long enough. Justin doesn't have time to waste."

Smooth exhaled. "What do you mean, doesn't have time?"

"Fool, are you ignorant or something?" I was losing patience. "I told you he needs a donor or he'll die."

Smooth swallowed hard. "Oh, I didn't realize it was that serious."

"That's probably because you were drunk when I explained it to you," I snapped.

"I wasn't drunk." Smooth banged his fist against the wall.

"Look. Whatever. What you do with your life is none of my business. Just like what I do with mine is no longer yours." I leaned closer to him. "But Justin is our son and I'll do anything to keep him alive."

Smooth sat down in another wooden chair. "You sure are fine." He reached for my knee.

I moved it just in time. "Look, don't get it twisted. That's not why I'm here. I'm here because Justin needs you. I was tested. So was Mama, Aunt Ruby, Alyssa, and even Nana. My father is dead and there's no one else to test but you."

Smooth leaned back. "All right, what must I do?"

"Well, first they're going to have you fill out a form. Then they're just going to take your blood, that's all," I explained.

Smooth opened his mouth wide. "Take my blood? With a needle?"

"Yes, just a little blood, you big baby." I swatted my hand at him.

"Then what?"

"Then they'll be able to tell us if your blood is a good match for Justin's," I explained.

Smooth put his hand against his broad chest. "It should be. I'm his father."

I took a deep breath before explaining. "It doesn't exactly work that way. Siblings usually have a better shot at matching, but since we didn't have any more children, you're all we've got." Tears welled up behind my eyelids.

Smooth put his hand on mine and squeezed. "And how much time does he have?"

"None," I answered. "He's so weak and . . . you've got to go down there today."

Smooth nodded. "Okay, I'll go."

"Good." I put my other hand on top of his.

When we got to the hospital I stopped at the nurses' station to call for Nana. I wasn't sure if she would be on duty, but she was.

Within minutes, she turned the corner. "What's going on? Is Justin all right?"

"Yes, he was fine when I left him this morning. But I wanted you to meet Justin's father, Mr. Smooth McGee."

"Well, it's so nice to meet you, son." Nana leaned in for a hug.

"Good to meet you, ma'am." Smooth hugged her back.

It made me feel strange that two of the most important people in my life were meeting for the first time.

"I'm going to go by Justin's room when I'm on my rounds." Nana tapped me on the hand.

"Thanks, Nana." I didn't know what I would do without her.

Then Nana patted Smooth on the back. "Don't worry, son, Justin is in God's hands. Everything will be just fine." Nana waved and sped off down the corridor.

Smooth nodded but didn't say anything.

"Well," I said. "Are you ready to see your son?"

"I am." He nodded.

"We've got to put on these so we don't spread germs to him." I handed him a gown, cap, gloves, and a mask.

Smooth held up the protective gear as if it was an alien suit. "Is all of this necessary?"

"Unfortunately, it is." I showed him how to put it on.

Smooth watched me and followed in silence.

Finally, I pushed the door open and we went inside. Justin was awake and immediately turned toward the door. "Mom?"

"I'm back." I spoke softly. "And I brought someone."

Smooth walked straight over to him. "How are you doing, son?"

Justin sat up in bed and looked at me. "Is that . . . ?"

"Yes." A sadness grew inside me. "It's your father."

Justin's eyes filled with tears. "Dad?"

"I've missed you, son." Smooth hugged Justin gently.

Justin tried to sit up. "I haven't seen you in two years."

"Yeah, I know and I'm sorry about that, son. It's just that your grandma, Rosalee, and I never did get along very well." Smooth fiddled with his fingers. "And while your mother was away, she made it real hard for me whenever I came to town."

Justin smiled a weak smile. "I know how Grandma is."

"Still, that's no excuse, though, for me not keeping in touch. I always promised myself I wouldn't be a deadbeat dad and—"

Justin put his finger up to his father's mouth. "I'm real glad to see you."

Smooth grabbed hold of Justin's finger and kissed it. "I'm glad to see you too."

It was a touching reunion and it did my heart good. For the first time in years things were really looking up. We were all together again as a family and surprisingly, something in my heart began to flutter. I just wasn't sure exactly what it was.

Finally, Smooth and I left Justin's room and I introduced him to Dr. Stanford. Then he went to be tested while I waited. Aunt Ruby called to ask how everything was going. So did Tyrone. There was no word from Alyssa yet, though, other than a text saying she'd made it home safely.

By the time Smooth emerged from the examination room, he looked a little frazzled. I wasn't sure if it was because of the procedure or because of the stress of Justin's condition. It was probably a combination of both, I decided.

Smooth strutted out as if he had already saved Justin's life. "I'm all done."

"Good." I stood up and began adjusting my clothing. "Now what happens?"

"Now we wait," I answered.

"So do you want to go get something to eat?"

I took two steps back. "We wait—separately."

"Now that's cold." Smooth put two hands over his heart. "Don't you even trust me anymore?"

I didn't smile. "Is that a trick question?"

"Very funny." Smooth smiled that same smile that used to get to me.

"I'm not trying to be." I held out my arm in front of me so he couldn't come any closer.

"I have to protect myself for the sake of my son."

"He's my son too." Smooth moved closer to me.

I took two steps back. "You're right. So you, of all people, should understand."

"Understand what?"

I gave a fake smile. "Understand why I don't have time to play games."

"Games?" Smooth grabbed his heart and pretended to be wounded. "What's wrong with the two of us comforting each other during this difficult time?"

I shook my head and crossed my arms. "Oh, please. Now you sound like a greeting card. I'm not falling for any of your lines, sorry. Been down that road before and I'm not going back."

Smooth snapped his fingers. "So it's just like that?"

"Look, let's get something straight." I put one hand on my hip and the other a few inches away from his face. "I'm only here for my son. Nothing more. Don't waste your time."

Smooth gently pushed my finger down. "So you can't hang out with me for old times' sake, but you can hang out with Tyrone?"

I rolled my eyes toward the ceiling. "For the last time, whatever I do with Tyrone is none of your business, but for the record we are just friends. Just like we *all* used to be."

Smooth raised his eyebrows. "Hmm. Just friends, huh?"

"Yes, friends," I said. "He's been very helpful since I've been here and you need to think about getting together with him yourself."

Smooth took a step forward. "Why in the world would I want to do that?"

"Because you and Tyrone used to be buddies and he's a really cool guy." I could still feel his breath on my skin.

"I'll bet."

"Oh, you're hopeless. Just go home or something." I fanned him away with my hands. "My Aunt Ruby is expecting me."

Smooth started walking toward the elevator, then turned. "All right, I'll go, but are you sure it isn't Tyrone you're rushing off to?"

I rolled my eyes. "Ugh, you're impossible."

"Wait." Smooth chuckled. "Let me take you home."

"No, thanks. I'll take the streetcar." I waved my hand without looking back.

"The streetcar can't treat you like I'll treat you, baby," Smooth called out.

Chapter 17

I returned to Aunt Ruby's only to find her in her office, fussing with Mama on the phone.

I could tell by the way she kept saying, "Now Rosalee, be reasonable. Rosalee, come on now."

I kept on walking by. There was no way I wanted to be a part of that mess.

Ms. Magnolia met me in the dining room. "Hello, sweetheart. May I get you something to eat?"

I pushed my chair back and started to stand. "That would be nice, but let me help you."

Ms. Magnolia put her big hands on my shoulders and guided me back into my seat. "Oh, no. That's my job. That's why I'm the cook around here."

"You sure make the best food I've ever tasted."

"Thank you, dear. Now you'll be helping out around here soon enough, 'cause your aunt's gonna have you start your job as hostess."

I smiled. "Yes, ma'am. She's been more than generous."

"No worries, darling. Your aunt told me you'll start working tonight with the dinner crowd." Ms. Magnolia opened her arms wide. "Big convention coming in town this evening."

My mouth dropped open. "Oh, I didn't know."

"Ruby must've forgot to tell you. So much on her mind you know, chile. But she did tell me. She tells me everything, ya know?" Ms. Magnolia clapped her hands. "Yep, tonight's the night. I just saw your name and today's date circled on her calendar."

"Wow, I didn't know."

Ms. Magnolia handed me a sheet with a list of respon-sibilities on it. "I know you didn't, baby, but we really need the help so you just eat up and get ready for tonight, you hear?"

"Yes, ma'am." I quickly looked over the list.

"Now what can I get for ya, baby?"

Knowing she wouldn't take no for an answer, I decided to choose something simple. "Maybe some popcorn shrimp and fries."

"Don't you want no biscuits with that?"

I smiled. "No ma'am."

Ms. Magnolia formed her dumpling-shaped cheeks into a smile. "That's fine, then. I'll be right back in a hurry."

"Take your time, Ms. Magnolia," I said, but she had already walked away.

Just as I had begun to relax, my cell phone rang. I con-templated not answering it, but decided against it. I looked into my bag and saw that it was Tyrone calling. As busy as I was, I wondered what he wanted.

"Hey," I started.

He laughed, then answered, "Hey, yourself."

"You sound mighty happy." I eyed the phone curiously, surprised at his enthusiasm.

"Well, this is the day that the Lord has made. I will rejoice and be glad in it."

I wondered what he was up to. "Huh? Really?"

"Sorry to hit you with something like that, but that scripture has been bursting through my spirit since I got up this morning," Tyrone explained.

I slowly blinked. "Okay."

"Sorry, but I get like this sometimes." Tyrone chuckled. "It's been a good day for me so far. I've finished all of my workload and I'm just about ready to leave for the day."

His peculiar behavior made me more curious about him. "I never asked you what you do for a living besides music."

"Actually, music is all I do." Tyrone paused. "I've got a job down here at the rec center where I teach music to kids, remember?"

"You're kidding? When you mentioned it to Justin I assumed you were only a volunteer."

Tyrone explained, "Nope. A friend of mine hooked me up with the position a couple of years back and I've been there ever since."

"Oh, that sounds really interesting." I wanted to hear more.

"Yeah, I enjoy it. I like working with the kids. They keep me laughing, so my work isn't like work at all," Tyrone answered.

"Wow, I don't know if I'd have the patience for that, but I definitely applaud you for doing it." I giggled at the thought of me working with a bunch of kids.

"Well, my love of music helps." Tyrone asked, "What about you? How has your day been so far?"

"Productive. I went to see Smooth and got him to agree to take the donor's test." *Jesus, help me.*

"So he took it?"

I closed my eyes and thought of Justin. "Yes, and now we wait."

"That's great. I'm sure this will all work out."

"I hope you're right," I responded.

"You guys have got a great kid." Tyrone said.

I snickered. "Yeah, I'm just glad I finally convinced him to go. Smooth never did like hospitals or needles."

Tyrone paused before speaking. "But for his son, surely he'd do anything. I know I would if I had a family as beautiful as you two."

"Well, I'm no longer his family, but I guess I know what you mean and thanks," I explained. "But I need him just to focus on his son."

"I understand. What are your plans for the rest of the day?"

"Well, I just found out that I'll be working tonight."

"Congrats on the job," Tyrone said.

I leaned back in my chair. "Yeah, my Aunt Ruby is the best, except I hear we'll be packed out with a big convention."

"Aw, man, that's too bad on your first day."

"I'll get through it, I guess. I'm no stranger to hard work." I paused. "Why? What did you have in mind?"

"Oh, nothing too important. I thought that maybe I could swing by and we could maybe roll through the French Quarter, but that was before I knew you had to work."

I held the phone away from me and thought about it for a moment. It certainly did sound like fun. "I've got a few hours before it's time for the dinner crowd to come, so I can probably get out for a little while. I need to get my mind out of the hospital right now."

"Okay, cool. I'll be there in about fifteen minutes," Tyrone suggested.

"Cool." I ended the call and ran upstairs to change clothes. I threw off the black dress and changed into an old pair of jeans and a checkered blouse. Then I pinned my hair up in a high ponytail. I spun around in front of the mirror and gave myself the final approval. Yes, I certainly looked plain enough. I didn't want anyone, including Smooth, to get the wrong idea about Tyrone's and my relationship. When I was satisfied, I went back downstairs to the dining area to wait for Tyrone.

Before long, Tyrone and Aunt Ruby entered the dining room simultaneously.

"Child, I want to talk to you about your crazy mama." Aunt Ruby threw her hands in the air as if she was giving up.

Tyrone extended his hand. "Hello, Ms. Ruby."

"Oh, I'm sorry." Aunt Ruby pushed his hand away and grabbed him into a tight bear hug. "Hello, darling. And call me Ruby. I'm not that old." Tyrone chuckled, but didn't answer.

"Aunt Ruby I'm going out for just a little bit, but I'll be sure to be back long before it's time for my shift," I said.

"Oh my goodness. That's right. You'll be working tonight and I haven't even explained anything to ya." Aunt Ruby hit herself in the forehead.

"It's okay. Ms. Magnolia told me." I showed her the list Ms. Magnolia gave me. "And like I said, I won't be long."

Aunt Ruby leaned forward. "Okay, baby. Mr. Tyrone, you take good care of my niece, ya hear?"

"Will do, ma'am. Will do." Tyrone smiled before opening the front door for me.

I followed Tyrone outside and looked for his truck. "Where did you park the truck?"

"Oh, I didn't bring it. I figured it would be more fun going by streetcar or cab. Is that a problem?"

I never did mind walking. "No. Not at all. I could use the exercise."

Tyrone moved back and forth, shifting his weight from one foot to another. "Where do you want to go?"

"It doesn't matter to me."

Tyrone put up his finger. "Okay, I have an idea. What about taking a ride on the Algiers Ferry?"

"I've never been there, but it sounds like fun," I said.

Tyrone shook his head. "Never been? Wow, I can't believe you used to live in New Orleans and never experienced the Algiers Ferry."

I smiled. "Nope. Never got a chance to."

Tyrone continued to shake his head. "Well, we've definitely got to change that."

First, we took the streetcar and paid the $1.25 fare to ride uptown to the riverfront. I noticed that some of the streets were still raggedy and some traffic lights malfunctioned as a result of Hurricane Katrina. We passed by swamps and bridges before we reached Canal Street.

The pedestrian entrance was on the plaza at the foot of Canal Street. It was right across from Harrah's Casino.

"Come on. Since we're not driving, there's no charge."

"Oh, cool." I shook my purse.

"I know you remember this place." Tyrone pointed to the casino.

"Yeah, how could I forget." Memories came rushing back as we walked. "This was Smooth's favorite place to gamble. And according to my mother, it was my father's favorite, also."

"Really?"

I tried not to let my emotions overcome me. "Yep. Sad thing is, that's all she ever told me about him, that he was a gambling fool who ruined her life."

"I'm sorry to hear that." Tyrone looked down at the ground.

"I'm sorry too. I'm just feeling a certain type of way about everything that's going on right now."

Tyrone finally lifted his head up. "I understand. I never knew my dad, either."

I stopped and looked at him. "Doesn't it still hurt?"

"Sometimes, but not so much since I've found my heavenly Father. I know it probably sounds corny to you, but it's the truth. Things are different now." Tyrone stretched out his hands, with his palms facing upwards, as if he was about to pray. "I still miss him, but I'm not angry about it anymore."

I kept my eyes on him as we started to walk again. "That's good. I guess I just wished I could've gotten to know him before he died. Mama always talks about him in the negative."

Tyrone closed his fingers into a fist. "Hold onto the good things you know about him."

"I don't know any good things about him." I don't know why I was relieved that he didn't pray.

"Then find someone who does and ask," Tyrone responded, matter-of-factly.

"Thanks." I felt my smile coming back. "That sounds like good advice, actually."

Tyrone stepped backwards. "You sound surprised."

"Well, you're not like the old Bingo." My smile grew wider.

"The old Bingo is gone. But I'll have you know I graduated at the top of my high school class."

"Really? I'm impressed." I never pictured him as the scholastic type.

"No need to be." Tyrone gave me a quick wink. "Now I'm taking a few college music courses over at the community college."

"You're really doing your thing." I elbowed him in the ribs. "Good for you."

"I can't take any credit for any of it." Tyrone quickly glanced upwards. "God is my source."

I didn't know how to answer him when he started talking about *his God*.

From the ferry we could see the magnitude of the river. I closed my eyes and saw Justin's face again. He was floating and his eyes were closed. And then I saw a flash of turquoise before the vision dissipated. I shook my head and opened my eyes wide. When I looked at Tyrone, he was staring out at the river. He had his hands in his pockets as if he didn't have a care in the world. I wondered how I could get that kind of peace.

Now it was my turn to get into his head. "Tyrone, I hope this isn't too personal, but why don't you have a family of your own yet?"

Tyrone hunched his shoulders and made a funny face. "To tell you the truth, I haven't really been looking. I've been so consumed with music and ministry that I haven't had much time to get out and have fun."

"But a nice guy like you should have a nice wife. I know a lot of single women back in Baton Rouge looking for a single guy like yourself." I elbowed him again.

"Ow." Tyrone grabbed his side with his hands and chuckled. "No, thanks. I don't like matchmaking. I feel when the time is right, God will send me whoever I'm supposed to have," Tyrone said.

I patted him on the arm and noticed how rock-hard it was. "Fair enough. I'll still be keeping my eye out for you, though."

Tyrone smiled. "Okay, you do that, my sister."

Finally, the ferry docked on the west bank at Algiers Point and we took the streetcar back to Aunt Ruby's place. Tyrone walked me to the door and gave me a quick hug. His arms were gentle and his cologne was intoxicating. Then he jumped into a yellow cab, which quickly disappeared down the street.

As soon as I went inside, Aunt Ruby met me at the door. "Your husband was here."

"I beg your pardon." I put up my hand. "You must mean *ex-husband*."

Aunt Ruby seemed annoyed. "Whatever."

I quickly grasped the seriousness of the situation. "Smooth came here?"

"Yes, he did and when I told him you'd stepped out with his old friend, Tyrone, he went ballistic, started talking loud and . . . bad mouthing Tyrone and—Why didn't you tell me Smooth had a problem with Tyrone?"

"Because it's no big deal." I rummaged through my purse for my phone, then let my purse drop to the floor. "Why didn't you call me? Why didn't he call me?"

"He said he wanted to surprise you and left those roses over there." Aunt Ruby pointed to her desk. "I tried to call, but it kept going to voice mail."

Feeling ashamed, I immediately checked my phone and sure enough, there were two voice mails from Aunt Ruby. There was one from Smooth. I let out a big sigh as I checked my settings and realized what went wrong.

"Oh, I'm sorry, I must've had it on silent by accident."

"It happens sometime, sweetie. I just don't know what you're going to do about that man of yours." Aunt Ruby shook her head until her wig became twisted.

"Auntie, he is not my man anymore. Trust me," I insisted.

Aunt Ruby put her jewel-covered hand on my shoulder. "Still, I don't think he knows that."

I curled my lips into a frown. "Well, he should by now. We've been divorced for years. Besides, I just told him the same thing this morning; that I'm only here for my son and that's all."

Aunt Ruby had a devilish grin on her face. "His ears heard you, but maybe not his heart, baby."

"I don't believe Smooth still loves me. I think he just wants what he wants because he can't have it." I picked up my purse and threw it across my shoulder.

Aunt Ruby chuckled. "Either way, you've got yourself a little problem."

I nodded. "I've got myself a bunch of problems."

Aunt Ruby hugged me before leaving the room.

I went upstairs to shower, then came downstairs, ready to work.

Aunt Ruby had a black-and-red uniform ready for me. Surprisingly, it was a perfect fit.

"The last girl who had this position was about your size. I had just ordered these for her days before she quit."

I held the uniform up in front of me and smiled with confidence. "Well, I won't let you down, Aunt Ruby."

Aunt Ruby stood back, smiling. "I know you won't, dear."

Aunt Ruby demonstrated several of my basic duties, then left me on my own. "Anything more complicated than that, I'll handle until you get the hang of it," were her parting words.

And I transitioned into my new job as hostess as easily as I had left the St. Gabriel's penitentiary. Living life as a free woman was easy in comparison to the life I used to live behind bars. The only thing that caused me pain and discomfort now was the pain and discomfort of my son.

At the end of the evening, I was so exhausted that I took a quick shower, then crawled straight into bed. I didn't go to sleep before calling the hospital to check on Justin once more.

"His condition is stable," a nurse reported.

"Thank you, ma'am," I turned over onto my side.

I breathed a sigh of relief and closed my weary eyes. If my tired soul could make it through the night, I'd be at his side first thing in the morning. *Good night, my angel.*

I woke up to the sound of my cell phone. With one eye open, I glanced at the wall clock.

It was 1:30 a.m. Still groggy with sleep, I reached for the ringing phone and attempted to make out the caller ID: Mercy Hospital. I answered it quickly, desperately waiting to hear what the voice on the other end of the line had to say.

"Ms. Crawford?"

"Yes, what is it? Is my son okay?" I held my breath.

"I'm afraid that Justin has begun hemorrhaging internally and he's fallen into a coma.

We've moved him into the ICU," the nurse said.

I shot up out of the bed and grabbed my backpack. "I'm on my way."

Chapter 18

I grabbed my bag and nearly knocked over Aunt Ruby as I was going downstairs.

Aunt Ruby held the sides of her nightcap. "Chile, where are you going in such a hurry and in the middle of the night?"

I must've been staring because I hadn't seen her without her wig before. "The hospital just called. Justin has taken a turn for the worse." I continued down the stairs.

"Then I'll go with you." Aunt Ruby let go of her cap and started back up the stairs. "Just let me get my shoes and I'll meet you in the car."

Within minutes, Aunt Ruby was in her Cadillac and driving faster than I'd ever seen her drive before. I just knew we'd get pulled over for a speeding ticket, but much to my surprise, we didn't. I'd called Smooth on the way, but he didn't answer, so I left him a voice mail.

By the time I arrived at the ICU, Nana was already sitting with Justin.

I squeezed her hand. "Nana, I'm so glad you're here."

Nana's eyes looked pink and puffy. "And where else would I be but with my great-grandson?"

Nana and Aunt Ruby spoke to each other briefly.

"I can't believe he's in a coma just a few hours after I left him. Maybe I shouldn't have left him." I wanted to punch something. "I should've stayed right here by his side."

"Oh, don't be ridiculous, dear." Nana patted my hand. "You couldn't have known this was coming. He was stable when you left him, right?"

Aunt Ruby pursed her lips. "She's right about that."

"Yes." I nodded.

Nana's voice was stern. "Then there'll be no more foolish talk about how you shouldn't have left him."

"Yes, ma'am," I answered.

Nana stood up and hugged me. "I'll be doing rounds if you need me."

I nodded.

Then Nana looked at Aunt Ruby. "You take care now, Ruby."

"You too, Ms. Crawford." Aunt Ruby nodded also.

I watched Nana walk toward the door. As soon as the door closed behind her, I turned my attention back to Justin.

"Justin, baby, wake up, it's Mommy," I pleaded. "Please wake up. You're all I've got."

Justin didn't move. His eyes remained shut and his body remained still.

After an hour of sitting, I stepped out of the room to make a few phone calls. Aunt Ruby stayed with Justin. First I called Mama.

"Justin has been put in the ICU," I said.

Mama sucked her teeth. "So you finally messed that boy up with your black magic, huh?"

I cringed at her voice. "What in the world are you talking about?"

Mama cackled. "You know what I'm talking about and I warned you, didn't I? I warned you about going back to that wretched place."

I closed my eyes. "Mama, please. Not now."

"I'll bet you're back with that wretched man too. That *smooth* black man." Mama wouldn't stop her taunting.

I spoke in a very quiet voice. "Mama, I called to tell you that Justin is very ill. He's in a coma and he might die."

"Well, if he does, you've caused it on yourself." Mama paused. "You and those demonic powers you have."

"I don't have demonic powers," I whispered into the phone. "Good-bye, Mama."

I wiped away the tear that ran down my face, but kept it moving. There was no sign of Smooth yet, so I called him a second time and left another message. I paced the waiting area as I called my sister to let her know what was going on. There was no answer there, either. Then I thought about calling Tyrone, but I decided against it. Calling him at this hour would be totally inappropriate. So I went back into Justin's room, relieved Aunt Ruby of her watch, and made her promise me that she'd go home to get some rest. She finally gave up arguing with me.

Somewhere between three and four o'clock in the morning I fell asleep in my chair and awoke with a cramp in my neck. When I opened my eyes, Smooth was standing beside me.

I wiped my sleep-blurred eyes. "How long have you been here?"

"Just a few hours." He squeezed my shoulder.

I sat up straight in the chair, trying to get comfortable. "Aunt Ruby was here with me for a long time, but I made her go home."

Smooth yawned. "Good, because I think the two of us should be here now for our son."

I nodded, then placed my face in my hands. So much had happened in such a short time. My head was spinning like a Ferris wheel.

I stretched my arms over my head. "Why didn't you answer your phone when I called?"

Smooth yawned. "You know why."

"No, I don't." I stood up and put both hands on my hips.

"Because I was still upset with you. I came by to see you, to bring you some flowers."

Smooth was chewing gum, something he liked to do whenever he wasn't smoking.

"Oh, thanks for the roses." I didn't look at him when I said it. "Aunt Ruby put them in a vase for me."

Smooth hardened his face. "I wanted to see you, but what I heard instead was that you were gone with that Bingo again."

I rolled my eyes. "He doesn't go by Bingo anymore. It's Tyrone. And do your remember that I told you we're just friends? Not that it's your business, anyway."

Then Smooth took a deep breath and the frown disappeared from his face. "I'm sorry for acting so stupid. Can you ever forgive me? I had no idea that you were calling about Justin. I swear. When I calmed down enough to listen to your messages, I came right over."

"I'm sure you did." I shifted my eyes to avoid eye contact.

Smooth moved his face closer to mine. "Doesn't that mean anything to you?"

I moved away from him. "Yeah, it means that you love your son."

"It means more than that." Smooth stopped chewing and stared at me.

"I don't think it does," I snapped.

Smooth grabbed my arm. "Don't you feel anything for me?"

I could feel the heat of his breath on my neck, stirring a million different emotions. I closed my eyes and counted to five in my head, then I resisted his grasp. "I don't know what I feel anymore, except that I want my son to live. That's it and that's all I want to focus on right now."

"Fair enough." Smooth backed away.

"I'm going to find someone to tell me if your test results are in." I fled from Justin's room. I went by Dr. Stanford's office, but he wasn't in yet. Then I went to see the head nurse.

The head nurse put on her reading glasses as she looked through a stack of papers. "You're here for Justin's lab results, aren't you?"

"Yes." I was almost out of breath. "Have you seen them?"

"I'm so sorry, but Mr. McGee is not a match, either," the head nurse said, shaking her head.

I almost lost my balance at hearing these words. "No, there has to be some mistake. His father has to be a match." I snatched the paper from her hands.

She retrieved it back from me and pointed out the line with the lab results.

"Sorry." I leaned away from the counter in silence.

"It's okay, I understand." The head nurse continued to organize a handful of papers.

I stopped listening to her words and stumbled across the room to a seat. There, I took out my list and scratched out Smooth's name. He was the last name on the paper and he was my last hope. Nothing short of a miracle could save Justin now. I began to cry in that moment harder than I had ever cried since Justin had been diagnosed. The cancer was eating away at Justin's body and now it was eating away at my soul.

When I was satisfied with my tears, I went back to Justin's room and told Smooth the news.

"That's all right." Smooth swallowed hard. "We'll figure something out."

"Don't you understand?" I was determined to make him feel as badly as I did. "There's nothing else to figure out. There's nothing else to do now except search the stupid national registry."

Smooth grabbed hold of both of my arms in order to calm me down. "Well, at least we have that."

"*We* have nothing. *I* have that. You're not a match and as far as I'm concerned, you can just go." I couldn't stop myself from saying it, even though I knew it was wrong.

"Wait a minute, now. He's my son too," Smooth protested.

I snatched my arms away from him. "Oh, you don't care about Justin. You only care about yourself."

Smooth's face hardened again. "You can't talk to me like this."

"I can talk to you anyway I want." I paused. "Just go home. You're not needed here anymore."

Smooth opened his mouth to respond, but didn't. Then he walked out, gently closing the door behind him.

I put my head onto Justin's bed and closed my eyes. Time was running out.

A few hours later, Nana showed up again. "Trinity, it's time for you to go get something to eat."

I shook my head."No, I can't. I'm not leaving him anymore."

"You can't stay here forever. You'll wither away to nothing. Then you won't be able to help Justin at all. Now, your Aunt Ruby is here now, so she can take over for a while." Nana pointed to the door. "You, come with me."

I got up and followed Nana, speaking briefly to Aunt Ruby as she entered Justin's room. Before I knew it, Nana had taken me through the parking garage and to her car. I didn't even object. After about ten minutes driving, we pulled up in front of a lovely little house. It had peach-colored vinyl siding with brown shutters around the windows and a pretty garden in the front yard. The front door was brown too with a decorative oval glass window.

"This is my home." Nana circled the room with her arms stretched out wide. "Now, make yourself comfortable here. I'm going to warm up something for you to eat."

"Thanks." I was so hurt I couldn't manage to say much else.

Nana returned with two bowls of shrimp gumbo. "You've got to stop looking sad and pray."

I took one of the bowls. "I've prayed, Nana."

"Not your little wimpy prayers, but prayers of real faith. You're going to have to come back to your faith, baby." Nana sat down with the other bowl. "You had it when you were a little girl and all you've got to do is turn and come back to it."

"I probably don't have time for that, Nana." I barely blinked.

"You don't have a choice. You'd better make time." Nana balled up her fists and threw them both onto the air. "Your son is dying in there and without real power, you're going to lose him. I didn't just bring you here to eat. I brought you here to change your life. Now, you can sit around here feeling sorry for yourself if you want, or you can take authority over this sickness and help me kick the devil's butt."

Nana lifted her hands to the ceiling. "Dear Awesome God, I come on behalf of my granddaughter, Trinity. She once knew you and she's forever yours. You've always had your hand on her life, even when she was in dire straits. I pray that you would reveal your power to her today. Shower her with your unconditional love and let it fill her heart like it once did. And Father, look down on that wonderful boy, heal him, and make him strong. Only you know the answers and we trust you and your will, in Jesus' holy name. Amen and amen."

I began to tremble. "Thank you, Nana. And thank you, Lord." Despite my resolve, tears burst through. I was all choked up, not knowing what to say or what to feel, but knowing that above all, I needed God.

Nana took my hand and led me to another room. The walls were bright turquoise, which immediately startled me. It was the exact color from my visions. There were several built-in bookcases with stacks of Bibles and religious textbooks.

Suddenly, I was filled with excitement. "Nana, have I ever been in this room before?"

Nana giggled. "Nope. I bought this house about six months ago when I moved back here from Maryland. Why do you ask?"

I walked around the room, touching the walls. "I've seen this room before. I don't know how or why, but I have."

Nana didn't seem at all surprised by what I said. "You've had the gift of prophesy since you were a little girl. God is going to use you greatly if you let Him."

Once again, I didn't know exactly what she meant by that, but it sounded like something good. I stared at the turquoise walls, then I asked her why she chose that color in the first place.

Nana smiled peacefully. "Oh, I didn't choose it. It chose me. It was already painted like that when I first saw it. I thought it was such a vibrant color. And from that first day, I fell in love with this room. It's the brightest room in the house and it's where I do most of my prayer and meditation."

"I see." I sat down on the ivory-colored love seat.

Nana walked over to one of her shelves. "I have something to show you."

My eyes followed her. "What is it?"

"You'll see." She reached up and pulled out a picture album.

There was a picture of my brother on the cover. "First of all, I'd like to say I was heartbroken when I heard about what happened to your brother."

"You knew?"

Nana's eyes filled up with tears, but not one fell. "Word got back to me, but your mother had already buried him."

"I'm sorry." I fell into her arms.

"Baby, none of this is your fault." Nana propped me up on a throw pillow, then opened the album.

We spent the next fifteen minutes looking at pictures of Alyssa, my brother, my father, and me, riding tricycles, having barbecues, and just playing outside. We were so young. It seemed like it all happened a million years ago. "Mama was right. I sure do look like my dad."

"Undoubtedly. You're smart like him too."

I looked at her. "Was he smart?"

Nana had a faraway look in her eye. "Very smart. He was class president two years in a row in high school. And he loved to cook all of the time. He'd follow me around in the kitchen and get such a kick out of helping me. When you all were little, he'd bake pies and cakes for you. Too much sugar, you know." Nana appeared to get misty-eyed again. "He always said he wanted to go to culinary-arts school and open up his own restaurant. Maybe even a bakery. Such a shame he wasted his life away with gambling the way he did, but he had his own choices to make." Silence filled the room as Nana put the photo albums away.

As she was leaning over, I noticed how unkempt her hair was, with several strands of silver-streaked hair falling all over the place. "Nana, why don't you let me do your hair really fast, before I go back to the hospital?"

Nana immediately put her hand up to her head. "Oh, does it look that bad?"

I shook my head. "No, I'd just like to get my fingers into your hair. It's so thick and beautiful."

Nana smiled her biggest smile. "So you still like to do hair, then?"

"Yes, ma'am. I plan to go to beauty school as soon as I can afford to."

"That's a good thing. " Nana took off the ponytail holder that was holding her hair and let all of her kinky curliness fall around her shoulders. "Do what you do, dear."

In less than ten minutes, I brushed, combed, and moisturized Nana's hair. Then I put in some of her hair gel and styled it in an updo. I handed her the mirror.

Nana looked at herself in the mirror she'd brought into the living room. "Why, my hair is so soft and so elegant."

"I'm glad you like it. Now I can go back to the hospital happy."

"Are you kidding me?" Nana stood up and looked at her hair from all angles. "It's much more elegant than what I'm accustomed to."

"Thanks, Nana." I squeezed her hand.

Nana stepped back. "For what, dear?"

I closed my eyes for a moment and imagined what he was like. "For telling me something good about my father."

"You're quite welcome." Nana hugged me and her vanilla scent reminded me of when I was a little girl.

Nana walked over to her shelves and began searching for something. "I'll have to find a copy of his obituary for you." She looked frazzled. "It's in one of those boxes in the attic."

I was ready to get back to Justin, but when my phone rang I was afraid to look at it.

Chapter 19

Thankfully, it was Aunt Ruby on the line. "You'll never guess what happened."

I was shaking. "No, I won't. What is it?"

"Justin came out of his coma." Aunt Ruby was breathing hard. "He just opened his eyes and looked right at me."

"Oh, my goodness. I'm so grateful. I'm on my way." I hung up on Aunt Ruby and started jumping up and down. "Justin is awake."

Nana held up her hand for a high five. "Of course he is. God is faithful and prayer changes things."

I gave Nana a high five before turning to leave.

On the way back to the hospital, I called Smooth to tell him the good news and he met me there.

Dr. Stanford was in the middle of examining Justin when we arrived. He stepped out into the hall to speak to us. "Thankfully, Justin is no longer comatose. He's awake and alert. The internal bleeding had been caused by low platelets in the blood. So although he's conscious, we're not out of the woods just yet. Unfortunately, there's still the threat of infection while we're searching for anonymous donors."

"I understand." I glanced at Smooth.

Smooth didn't answer. He looked defeated.

Dr. Stanford looked over his glasses. "In any case, it is imperative that we find a donor. And in the meantime, I'll be increasing his chemo dosage."

"But he's so weak already," I pleaded.

"I'm afraid it's the only way." Dr. Stanford stuck his pen behind his ear.

Smooth and I answered in unison. "Thank you, Doctor."

I ran back into Justin's room and watched him sleep until noon. When I wasn't staring, I was reading scriptures from the Bible to him, hoping that the words would seep into his subconscious spirit.

Smooth left at about three o'clock for a gig he'd booked weeks before. I thought of him playing his saxophone at this local event, wowing the crowds, and I felt warm inside. I wasn't sure why. Was I just genuinely happy for my son's father? Or did I really have feelings that ran deeper than I was willing to admit?

Aunt Ruby came to pick me up late in the evening and by this time I was ready to go home. I needed a break and most of all, I needed to do something to help my son. I wasn't sure what that was, though, other than praying. Back at Aunt Ruby's I locked myself in my room and cried out to God like a newborn baby cries for his mother. I called out for strength, for wisdom, for peace. I stayed on my knees until I felt satisfied.

At that moment I remembered that Tyrone didn't even know what had happened and he had been so nice to Justin. I dialed him quickly and waited as the phone rang. Once, then twice.

He answered by the third ring. "Hello."

It was good to hear his voice. "Hi."

"How are you?" Tyrone sounded cheerful enough.

I thought of all of the day's events. "Not so good."

"What's wrong?"

"I've been up since last night. Justin started bleeding uncontrollably and went into a coma," I explained.

"Wow, why didn't you call me?" He sounded genuinely concerned. "I would've come."

"It was so late that I didn't want to bother you. And then everything happened so fast." I bit my lip.

"I understand. How is he now?"

"He's out of the coma, thank God, but he's still in very serious condition." I held the phone as the words made their way to my mouth. "He still needs a donor."

"So I guess his father was no match?"

I tapped my fingers on the side table. "No, he wasn't."

Tyrone's voice was calm. "Of course, you must be very disappointed."

"You can only imagine." I looked at my list with all of the names scratched out in black ink, then crumpled it up and threw it in the trash. I had run out of resources. I was still running out of time.

"How can I help?"

"You can pray," I whispered.

"No problem." Tyrone paused, as if he was thinking. "Do you need anything else? I'll be passing through the area on my way home from work."

"I guess you could stop by for a few minutes. I'll probably need another shoulder to cry on."

"One shoulder coming right up." Tyrone chuckled.

I couldn't even manage a smile. "I'll see you when you get here then."

I went downstairs to the dining room.

Aunt Ruby stood behind the podium. "Listen, I just wanted you to know that you don't have to worry about going back to work until you're ready, at least until Justin is out of the ICU."

"Thanks, but this is a business you're running here and I intend to pull my own weight. I'll do the dinner shift tonight if you'll give me another chance." I leaned against the podium.

Aunt Ruby's eyes said it all. "But what about Justin?"

"Smooth is with him now. Then Nana promised to do the second shift. And I'll be back first thing in the morning." I held up three fingers to indicate the three shifts.

"We'll see." Aunt Ruby fanned me away. "I still don't think you should be working right now."

"Why are you so stubborn? Let me help you. Let me work." I grabbed a bunch of menus off of the podium and straightened them. "I need to keep my mind busy."

Aunt Ruby waved her big hand. "You'll have plenty of time for that, believe me."

"But I need to keep my mind busy." I rubbed my hands and moved from side to side.

"Stay still, child." Aunt Ruby reached out to stop me. "Everything will be all right."

I formed a weak smile.

At that moment Tyrone walked into the room, followed by Ms. Magnolia. "Look what a gem I found wandering around the streets."

"Good evening, ladies." Tyrone looked embarrassed.

Aunt Ruby squeezed him. "How are you, son?"

Tyrone grinned. "I'm good, thanks, ma'am. What about y'all?"

"I'm about as good as I'm gonna be today." Aunt Ruby threw her head back and laughed.

Magnolia laughed so hard both of her chins folded. "I'm even better now that you're here, darling."

I was shocked to see that Ms. Magnolia was being flirtatious and at her age. I never would've figured her for a cougar.

"Well, you certainly know how I am." I left the two women laughing and slowly led him over to a quiet table toward the back. "I think this is private enough."

"Thanks for rescuing me from Ms. Magnolia." He pulled out my chair for me.

"Oh, no problem." I smiled as I sat down.

Then Tyrone went to sit in his own chair. "So tell me everything about Justin's condition so I'll know how to pray specifically."

I folded my hands on the table. "Well, it's like I've already explained. He needs a blood match so he can have a bone-marrow transplant. "

Tyrone's eyes were glued to mine. "And you've tested everyone in the family?"

"Of course." I shook my head slowly. "Smooth was the last one."

Tyrone looked sad for a moment. "Man, that's rough."

I let out a big sigh. "If only Justin had a sibling."

Tyrone's eyes seem to grow larger. "What did you say?"

"I said it's too bad Justin doesn't have a sister or brother, because siblings are usually the best matches," I repeated.

"Really? I didn't know that." Tyrone seemed to be thinking. "So a sibling would be more likely a match?"

"Yep, but it's too late for that now." I put both elbows on the table and placed my face into my hands. "Maybe Smooth and I should've had another child. Then I could take him to court to sue for twice the child support." I laughed at my own joke, but noticed that Tyrone had become uncomfortably serious.

Suddenly Tyrone began to squirm in his seat, rub his hands together, and shake his leg under the table.

"What?" I searched his face, but he wouldn't look into my eyes. "What's wrong?"

Tyrone put his hands up to his face, then peeked out from behind them. "What if I told you something you probably didn't want to hear, but needed to know?"

I sighed again. "I'm in no mood for riddles. Please just say whatever it is you're trying to say."

"I don't know. You might hate me afterward." Tyrone drummed his fingers on the table.

I managed a half smile. "A nice guy like you, that's impossible."

Tyrone scratched his head. "I don't think so."

"Spit it out," I snapped.

Tyrone finally stopped moving and shaking. "Well, it happened about eight-and-a-half years ago."

Now I was getting annoyed. "What happened eight-and-a half-years ago? What in the world are you babbling about?"

Tyrone continued to shake his leg underneath the table."Smooth and I were on the road a lot, you see, and—"

"Okay, spill it." I didn't take my eyes off of him.

Tyrone swallowed hard one last time before speaking. "I know where you can get another potential donor for Justin."

I sat up straight in my chair and directed all of my attention toward him. In fact, if I could've glued my ear to his mouth I would've. "Just tell me, who?"

Tyrone shook his head. "Maybe I shouldn't be telling you this."

I leaned over and grabbed him by the collar. "Why not?"

"Because it's not really my place." Tyrone loosened my grip with his hands. He held them for a minute before letting them go.

"Say it," I insisted.

Tyrone's eyes saddened as they focused in on mine. "Here goes . . ." He paused. "Smooth has another son; therefore, Justin *does* have a brother."

Chapter 20

The air seemed thicker than it ever was. Everything around me seemed to stop, including time. All of my greatest fears swirled around me. I was suspended in Tyrone's words and they were suffocating me. I couldn't breathe. I began coughing uncontrollably, then took a sip of water, only to choke on that.

"What do you mean, Smooth has another son? Justin is his only son." Suddenly, the smell of Tyrone's cologne seemed to nauseate me.

Tyrone pushed back his chair. "I'm already sorry I said anything."

"No. Tell me what you're talking about." I looked him in the eyes. "Another son?"

"Forget that I said anything." Tyrone started folding a napkin nervously.

I leaned over and put my finger in his chest. "Uh-uh. What other son?"

Tyrone didn't answer. Instead, he gently removed my finger from his chest.

I poked out my lips. "I'm waiting. What son?"

"I'm talking about the one he had with another woman when he was still married to you," Tyrone finally spat out.

I shook my hands in his face. "No. You're lying. You're just like all the rest. Jealous of Smooth's music. Trying to hurt me."

Tyrone looked around at the other customers. "Whoa." He put his hand up as if he was trying to halt me. "Listen to yourself. That doesn't even make any sense. Why would I want to deliberately hurt you?"

I balled up a paper napkin and threw it at him. "That's what I'd like to know."

Tyrone sighed deeply. "Why would I want to hurt a friend?"

I rolled my eyes. "Good question. I guess we're not friends, then. My mistake."

Tyrone started, "Trinity . . ."

"Don't even call my name. Just get out. " I looked in the direction of the door.

"Please, I—"

I stood up and pointed toward the door. "Out. Get out, now."

Aunt Ruby came over. "Is there a problem, dear?"

Tyrone stood up and pushed his chair under the table. "I'm sorry, Ms. Ruby, but it's my fault."

"Yes, it is," I agreed.

Aunt Ruby stood in front of Tyrone. "Well, what happened?"

"I'd better go." Tyrone gently guided Aunt Ruby out of his way.

"Yes, let him go," I said, pouting.

Aunt Ruby continued, "But what happened?"

"I said something to upset her and I should've minded my own business. I'm sorry."

Tyrone left without looking back.

"You're not sorry. You're a liar," I mumbled.

Aunt Ruby's mouth was wide open. "What in heaven's name is going on?"

I was so angry. "Oh, this ain't got nothing to do with heaven, Aunt Ruby."

"Gal, come with me." Aunt Ruby pulled me back to her office. "Now, what is it?"

"Tyrone just told me that Smooth has another child," I explained.

"Is that all?" Aunt Ruby shook her head. "That's not the end of the world. Y'all have been divorced for a long time now."

I was still shaking. "This is a child he supposedly had while we were still married."

"Oh, I see." Aunt Ruby didn't blink.

"I know we're not together anymore, but it still hurts. He kept this from me all these years. How dare he do this to me? And then Tyrone is no better, because he covered for him back then when he knew what he was doing. Now he has the nerve to try to play hero by telling me Justin has a sibling to be tested," I whined.

"A sibling, that's right. Trinity, that's wonderful news. Take what you can from it. Take what will help Justin. Chew the fat and spit out the bones," Aunt Ruby hollered.

I paced back and forth. "But I feel so betrayed by everyone."

Aunt Ruby shrugged her plump shoulders. "It happens, dear."

I shook my head at Aunt Ruby. "Not you too?"

Aunt Ruby's eyes followed me around the room. "I ain't saying that it's right, just that it happens. Smooth ain't never been no saint."

"I can't believe this. And all this time Tyrone was sitting in my face, talking and laughing, when all along he knew. He knew. And New Orleans is a small, gossiping town. Everybody probably knows *except* me."

Aunt Ruby pleaded, "So what if people know? What did you expect Tyrone to do? How could he tell you something that wasn't his secret to tell? But at the same time, how could he continue to keep it hidden when he knows the information might save your son's life?"

"Whose side are you on, anyway?"

Aunt Ruby smacked her gum furiously. "I'm on the right side, honey."

"Everyone is against me. I might as well just give up. " I walked out of Aunt Ruby's office and through the front door, headed over to Smooth's place.

This time I took a yellow cab and I had time to think on the way over. Was it really true?

Had Smooth really fathered a child during our marriage? And was that child truly out there somewhere, possibly to save my son's life? There was so much to consider, so much to doubt. I didn't know where to begin. *Lord, help me.*

When I arrived at Smooth's building, I walked quickly to his door and banged on it like I was the police. He didn't answer at first, so I began to wonder if he was even home. I'd seen his Mustang parked outside, though, and for a few minutes, I'd contemplated busting out his windows. I knocked again. Then I wondered if he had female company over, which made me even more furious. Finally, Smooth cracked the door open, and stuck his head out, looking disheveled.

"Puddin', I—"

I pushed my way past him and looked around, fully expecting to see a woman. "Let's get one thing straight, I'm not your Puddin'. It's not like that between us anymore. My name is Trinity. Not Puddin'."

Smooth straightened himself up fast. "All right, I'm sorry. What's the emergency? You could've called."

"Yeah, I could've, but I chose not to." I circled him, looking him up and down.

"Okay, why did you come here, then? I thought that after I didn't match up as a donor, you were done with me."

"I was." I stopped and stared at him.

Smooth squinted his eyes. "So what changed your mind?"

"I'm desperate to save my son." I was breathing hard.

Smooth had a smug look on his face. "I know, but that doesn't have anything to do with me anymore, does it?"

The way he stood there, so anxious to be detached to his child made me feel sick in the stomach. "Just because you don't match up doesn't mean you're free and clear of being his father."

Smooth stood in front of me and looked into my eyes. "I didn't mean that, but you told me you never wanted to see me again."

"I'm sorry. I was angry," I explained. "Don't you care about your own son?"

"Of course I do," Smooth answered. "I just left the hospital. You know that."

I came up close to him. "Then why won't you help me?"

"What else can I do?" Smooth threw his hands up in the air. "I was tested and I'm not a good match, remember?"

"I know that. And I've come to terms with that." I composed myself. "But since I've been down here I've been told some very important information."

Smooth looked confused. "What information?"

Tears began to fall despite my inner protests. I spoke calmly. "Information about you and our sham of a marriage."

Smooth lifted his hand to wipe my eyes. "Is that why you've been crying?"

I pushed his hand out of my face. "Don't worry about my tears."

Smooth stepped away from me. "Okay, what important information?"

I swallowed hard, but couldn't answer. The words would not come up.

Becoming impatient, Smooth walked away from me. "What is it?"

I closed my eyes and let the stabbing words roll off of my tongue. "I've been told that even though you're not a match, someone else may be."

Smooth shook his head in confusion. "You told me everyone else has already been tested?"

I folded my arms. "Everyone on my side of the family, but not on your side."

"My side? I don't have any siblings." Smooth turned up his lips.

I paused to catch my breath. "No, but Justin does."

Smooth came a little closer, leaning his neck forward as if he couldn't hear me clearly. "What did you say?"

I managed to fake a smile even through my tears. "You have another son, remember?"

"Now, wait a minute, " Smooth started. "Not those silly rumors again."

"Silly rumors? I don't think you having a son is silly." I tapped my foot, waiting.

"What I mean is, uh—"

I closed my eyes to gather strength. "Don't bother to deny it or anything. It has already been confirmed. I probably couldn't have handled it when we were together, but you certainly owe me the truth now."

Smooth darted his eyes to every corner in the room. "All right, where are you going with this?"

I dropped my arms to my side and moved closer to him. "I need you to be honest with me for once and I need you to think of Justin above your foolish pride."

Smooth chuckled. "Believe me, I got over pride a long time ago."

"Good, then you won't mind admitting that you have a child, a son," I continued. "A son who shouldn't be much younger than ours. Don't worry; I can handle it. Believe it or not, I've spent the last hour coming to terms with what you did."

"Okay, I do have a child. His name is Desmond and he lives here in New Orleans."

Smooth took a cigarette out of his pocket and shoved it into his mouth. "Are you satisfied now?"

I was a little shaky after that statement, but I refused to show it. "Not quite. Now, I just need you to get the baby's mama to let her son be tested."

Smooth shook his head. "No."

I walked over to him and grabbed his arms. "No? Why not?"

"That's impossible," Smooth answered, flinging my hands off of him.

I blinked before I spoke. "What do you mean, impossible?"

Smooth shook his head adamantly as he turned and walked away. "I can't do that."

I followed him across the room."Can't or won't?"

"Both," Smooth said.

I stood in front of him. "Both? Are you kidding me?"

"Nope."

I exploded. "What in the world are you afraid of?"

"Neither Desmond nor his mother knows that Justin exists," Smooth explained.

"He doesn't even know he has a brother?" I nodded. "Hmph. That sounds about right."

Smooth continued, "Look, I didn't mean for things to turn out like, this but there's nothing I can do to change it now."

"What do you mean, there's nothing you can do? You can go to the child's mother, tell her you have a son, tell her your son is sick, then ask her to have her son tested as a donor. It's that simple."

"It's not simple." Smooth let out a long sigh. "I can't."

I couldn't believe what I was hearing. "So you'd let your son die to spare the feelings of the other?"

"It's not about the child's feelings. It's about the mother. She'll never listen to me. She won't allow it." Smooth turned his back on me.

I walked around to face him, backing him into a corner. "Won't allow it? How do you know that?"

"Because I know." Smooth took one last look at me, then turned away again. "She doesn't like me anymore."

"No kidding? I don't like you anymore, either. I see that we have a lot in common." I rolled my eyes at what I was hearing.

Smooth hung his head down low, shaking it back and forth. "She won't help me."

I walked right up to him and got in his face. "Then you'll just have to make her help, won't you?"

Chapter 21

Rosalee had been walking the worn linoleum floors all night, hoping with everything she had in her that the boy would live, despite his hardheaded parents. She'd practically raised Justin since his mother had been away so long. Of course, she had deep feelings for him, but that didn't change the way she felt about certain things, about certain people.

Sometimes people would really let her down. They'd have her believing they were in her corner and as it turned out, they weren't really with her at all. Folks had all kinds of ulterior motives, things she could never even imagine. She'd think they were genuinely interested in her well-being, but the next thing she knew she'd find out they were just trying to protect themselves. The same thing went for children. Sometimes she believed her own flesh and blood were against her. Why else would they torture her with such defiant actions? How else could she explain it?

Rosalee shook her brother, awakening him out of his sleep. "Charlie, are you all right?"

"I was until you woke me out of my dreams." He opened his eyes, then looked up at his younger sister. "Goodness, Rosalee, what is it now?"

Rosalee folded her arms. "I was just wondering if you've heard from those girls."

"No, I haven't and I don't blame them no way." Charlie sat up straight on the couch.

Rosalee peered at him from the corner of her eye. "What do you mean by that?"

Charlie twisted his pale lips. "You've been so spiteful to them, so selfish. I suspect neither one of them want anything to do with ya and I can't blame them."

Rosalee frowned up her already lined face. "Don't you talk to me like that, Charlie."

"What are you gonna do to me that hasn't already been done? Ain't nothing you can do to me, Rosalee." Charlie displayed his toothless grin. "Threaten me all you want, but I'm an old man and none of it matters to me no more."

"You're an old fool." Rosalee walked away from him.

"That may be, but I know enough to know you've done them girls wrong. Ain't nothing you can say that's gonna change that."

Rosalee's eyebrows met in the middle. "You're talking crazy, Charlie."

"Am I really talking crazy or is you just too stubborn to see the truth?" Charlie reached into his pocket and pulled out his pipe. "Now you've abandoned them when they need you the most." Charlie shook his gray head. "Just a shame, that's all."

"Hmph," Rosalee mumbled as she went into the kitchen.

For years the kitchen had been her sanctuary, not because she particularly liked to cook, but because she found refuge there. When it was time to prepare the family meals, she moved with accuracy and precision. It was here that she knew how to make everyone happy, even if she wasn't happy herself. She didn't obsess over food one way or the other, but she did enjoy the comfort it brought other people. As a result, it brought her comfort also.

Rosalee began by chopping the celery, the green and yellow peppers, one whole red onion, then a clove of garlic. She mixed them all together in her bowl, added a pinch of salt and black pepper, parsley, and oregano before she threw in her eggs. Before she added the ground beef, she paused for a moment. Rosalee sat on her stool and wiped her hands on her apron. Was Charlie right about her doing her daughters' wrong? Had she really gone too far this time?

When the phone finally rang the next morning, she shuffled over to the side table and answered it. Her heart beat fast. Then she heard her Ruby Jean's voice and instantly caught an attitude.

Rosalee spat out, "What do you want, Ruby Jean?"

Ruby asked, "Why do you have to always answer me like that? Why must you be so rude?"

"Ms. Ruby Jean, don't worry about how I answer my phone. How I talk to you or anybody else is my business."

Ruby raised her voice a notch. "You should be ashamed of yourself still acting the fool at your age."

Rosalee gasped. "Now, you listen here, just because you're a couple of years younger than me—"

Ruby burst into laughter. "A couple?"

"You take that back," Rosalee snapped.

"I will not." Ruby laughed even harder.

Rosalee huffed, "You will take it back, or so help me I'll—I'll—"

"You'll do what?" Ruby raised her ring filled hand up to her face. "I'm not afraid of your threats, Rosalee. Give it up."

Rosalee put her hands on her hips and spun around on the linoleum floor. "You think you're pretty smart don't ya?"

"Actually, I do think I'm smart. Smart enough to leave your miserable self by yourself."

"See, that's what I'm talking about." Rosalee tapped her foot on the kitchen floor. "What did you call me fer anyway?"

"Oh, I almost forgot, thanks to your mouth. I called to

let you and Charlie know that Justin is out of his coma. He's stable and he's resting."

"Hmmm," Rosalee murmured.

"Trinity is resting also."

"Well, good for her," Rosalee said, slamming the phone onto its hook. On the outside she protected herself with harshness, but on the inside, she was glad.

Chapter 22

By the time I made my way home, it was time for the dinner rush. Although Aunt Ruby offered to relieve me, I insisted that she let me do my job. She tried to talk to me, but I managed to slip away. If she was walking down one hall, I'd walk down another. It had been like that ever since I found out about Smooth's son. I was in no mood for a lecture.

Ms. Magnolia walked around wearing a pink, spandex dress she obviously had to squeeze into. As usual, she flirted with all of the male customers. Six of Aunt Ruby's guests came down to eat dinner and two of them came down for a little snack. The entire dining room smelled like cinnamon since Ms. Magnolia had baked her infamous cinnamon buns.

When my shift was over, I took the elevator upstairs and flung myself onto my bed headfirst. I couldn't help but remember my conversation with Smooth and the way he brushed me off. Maybe he'd change his mind once the shock of me knowing about his love child wore off.

There were so many things I wanted to say to him; yet I hadn't been able to fully express myself. It was like there was something stuck in my throat, holding me back. Something wouldn't let me say what I wanted to say. But I was hurt in a thousand different ways. I squeezed my pillow and put my face into it. There was Justin and there was Smooth, each one causing a different kind of pain, but pain nonetheless.

I found myself standing under the water in the shower, crying until I couldn't cry anymore. I had lost everything: six years of my life in prison, my opportunity to know my father, Justin's health and safety, my only friend, Tyrone, and now the sanctity of my past marriage.

Maybe Smooth's infidelity shouldn't have mattered anymore, but it did. Was it because I still had feelings for him? Or was it just the embarrassment? I was a proud woman. Always had been. I guess I got that from Mama.

My phone rang and when I looked at it I saw that it was Tyrone. I refused to answer it.

The next thing I knew a text came through: PLEASE FORGIVE ME, TYRONE, with a sad face. I pressed the power off button and shut the whole phone down. There was no way I wanted to talk to a traitor, someone who knew for years that my husband was cheating on me, someone who stood in my face but never said a word. It was unforgivable.

I folded my arms and said, "Hmph." Then I decided to get down on my knees and pray.

Nothing was going to be made whole without prayer. Not Justin's situation, not Smooth's situation, not Mama's situation. As I thought about thing after thing, issue after issue, I realized that I still needed God.

"Lord, I don't know what to do or even how to pray at this point. So much has gone wrong. I've messed up so many relationships. Mama and I are mad at each other. I'm not speaking to Tyrone anymore. I want to kill Smooth for what he's done to me. And Justin's condition is deteriorating. Help me, Lord, please. Help me to be better than what I am. Help me to be better than who I am. Change me into what I should be. In your name, Jesus. Amen."

The next morning I awoke to the sun streaming through my window. I threw on my clothes, grabbed my phone, and went downstairs. Magnolia was coming out of the kitchen.

"Morning, darling." She whizzed by with a pan of pancakes in her hand.

"Morning." I kept on walking.

Then Aunt Ruby caught me as I was passing by her office. "Slow down, girl. I've been looking for ya."

"Morning, Aunt Ruby."

"Sweetheart, are you all right? You've been avoiding me for a while."

"I haven't been avoiding you." I looked away. "I just have a lot of things on my mind.

"Sometimes it helps to talk about them." Aunt Ruby closed the door to her office.

"Not this time. I'm done talking." I dared to put on a fake smile.

Aunt Ruby placed her thick hands on her wide hips. "Is that so?"

"Yep," I snapped.

Aunt Ruby gestured for me to sit. "Do you think you're the only one who has ever had problems, or more specifically, marital problems?"

I let out a long breath. "Aunt Ruby, you wouldn't understand."

Aunt Ruby shook her finger at me. "Oh, I wouldn't understand, huh? Well, I'll have you know I used to be married too."

This shocked me. "You were?" I sat down in one of her Queen Anne guest chairs and crossed my legs.

"Yes, when I was very young. I was young and in love. His name was John. John Wilkins." Aunt Ruby's mood seemed to change to sadness.

I leaned forward. "Well, what happened to him?"

Aunt Ruby sighed. "He died, that's what happened to him. He had a heart disease."

"I'm sorry." I sucked my bottom lip, not knowing what else to say.

"He died, but not before I had a whole lot of heartache. Then I learned."

Now I was interested. "What kind of heartache? And what did you learn?"

"As much as I loved him, one day I came home early from work and saw him and my cousin, Rita Mae, hugged up on my couch." Aunt Ruby smacked her two hands together to demonstrate. "Twenty years old and hot as a firecracker. She was always a loose little thing, you know."

I opened my eyes wide. "What did you do?"

"Well, I did what any self-respecting woman could do. I fought him and her. Knocked them both out." Aunt Ruby seemed to return to her cheerful self and began to giggle. "I can laugh about it now but, I certainly wasn't laughing then."

"Wow. " I got caught up in the story.

"I was a wild thing back then, but months after I put him out, we reconciled our differences. He lived about six months after that. And one day when I came home from work, he was slumped over in his favorite chair—dead."

I squinted my eyes. "I don't mean to be disrespectful, but what's the point here?"

"The point is that life is too short to dwell on the negative. Forgive him and move on either way. Take him back or let him go, but for goodness sake, move on." Aunt Ruby used her hands to illustrate her *hit the road* signal.

"I know you're right, of course." I uncrossed my legs and slumped over in my chair. "I'm just not sure how. And I'm not sure if I'm ready."

"Time will tell, sweetie." Aunt Ruby squeezed me tight. "Listen to your heart."

I closed my eyes. "The problem is, I'm not sure if I can trust my heart."

Later in the day I left to see Justin. He was resting as well as could be expected. We didn't talk much because he was so weak. I fed him ice chips, massaged his hands and feet with shea butter, and sat with him while he slept. This mundane routine had become my life.

Before I left, Nana texted me: I'M ON BREAK. IF YOU'RE AT THE HOSPITAL I'D LIKE TO SEE YOU.

The hospital cafeteria had become our meeting spot.

Nana sipped on a large cup of coffee. "So how have you been feeling since I talked to you last?"

"Nana, I don't know how to feel anymore. In fact, I feel like maybe everyone is against me, everyone I trusted—Smooth, Tyrone, Aunt Ruby, Mama."

Nana set down her cup and tilted her head to the side. "Come on, now. What has your aunt got to do with all of this?"

I poked out my lips. "Well, she's talking to me like I should've known all along. *Smooth ain't never been no saint,* she said. I feel like such a fool."

"Don't go there." Nana put her hand up. "Trinity, this could be a blessing in disguise, the miracle we've been waiting for."

I frowned up my face. "That my husband was cheating on me when we were together—that's my miracle?"

Nana raised her eyebrows at me. "If it heals you, take it however it comes."

"It's not healing me; it's hurting me," I spat out.

Nana put her hand on top of mine. "But it may heal Justin. That's all that matters. You're beside yourself with rage right now and rightfully so. Do yourself a favor, mourn the marriage for a little while, then let it go, and move on. We don't have time to stay stuck there."

"You sound like Aunt Ruby." I sighed

"Well, if she told you the same thing, then she's right," Nana explained.

I bit my bottom lip to stop myself from snapping. "Yeah."

"I know it's hard, but Justin needs both of his parents right now, both of you. You're going to have to let this go." Nana looked straight into my eyes.

"I sure don't see how." I made the same face I used to make when I was a little girl in trouble. Nana didn't appear to be moved.

"I don't see how, either, but you will." Nana pointed upwards and smiled. "I promise you that God will make a way."

I leaned forward and whispered, "Why couldn't God have made a way when I was still married?"

"But were you willing and able to listen back then, sweetheart?" Nana kept her eyes on me as she picked up her cup of coffee.

"No, I guess I wasn't," I admitted.

She put her cup down again. "Well then, you weren't ready. Now, I'm not saying He can't fix this, but it'll be on His own terms. Not yours. The Lord is in the restoration business, but you're going to have to do your part." Nana shook her slim finger at me. "Animosity isn't going to help either way."

"Why is everyone telling me that I'm wrong? What about Smooth having a child with another woman while he was married to me? What about that?" I tapped my hand on the table and nearly knocked over my iced tea.

"Obviously, it was wrong, sweetheart, but you're not even married to the man anymore."

Nana sounded more stern than usual. "You've got to figure out what you want."

"I want Justin to be well," I said.

Nana pursed her thick lips. "And what do you want with his father?"

"I want him to be a good father to Justin, that's all." I pursed mine also.

Nana squinted her eyes at me. "Are you sure that's all you want?"

I thought about it. "Yes, I'm sure." Yet my heart was still confused.

Chapter 23

As we rode in Smooth's Mustang convertible, the top was down and my expectations were up. I needed this to go right. I was being taken to his baby's mama's house because he said this was the only way she'd see him. She wouldn't even answer his calls anymore; he had to leave a message on her voice mail if he wanted to contact her. He'd explained to me that he'd opted for the element of surprise instead. I studied his worried face, acknowledging his vulnerability. I figured he'd probably disappointed this woman time and time again, and she probably wasn't as receptive to his lies as she used to be. Could anyone blame her?

"Here we are." He backed into the uneven driveway.

I didn't respond.

The house was a small one, a shotgun house, as Mama liked to call them. You could probably make it from the front to the back in half a minute's time. I climbed out of Smooth's car and eased up to the front steps, looking around. As neighbors passed by, I wondered if they knew my husband had a baby with this woman while we were married. I closed my eyes to control my thoughts. *Help me, Lord.*

Smooth went to the door first, and rang the bell. A woman opened the door, took one look at him, then tried to close it. Smooth put his muscular arm in the door.

The woman rolled her neck. "Are you kidding me right now?"

He leaned forward and whispered a few words to the woman.

She peeped out at me. "Oh, no. I don't think so."

Smooth whispered to her again.

"I don't care. I don't want her inside my house. I don't care what you say." The woman put her hand into Smooth's face. "Don't I have a restraining order against you and her too, I believe?"

I recognized her face instantly. She was the woman I whooped the day before I went to prison.

"Come on, please. That was a long time ago." Smooth put his hands up to his mouth as though he was praying, begging.

Finally, he whispered to the woman a third time, then signaled that it was okay for me to come in. "Trinity, this is Clarisse. Clarisse, this is Trinity."

Neither of us acknowledged the other.

"Thanks." I scoffed as I passed by her, observing her tall, lean body, something I would never have. She was just as I remembered her six years ago, only I didn't realize then who she was. At that time I thought she was just a random woman. I sure didn't realize she was the mother of my husband's child.

She stood in the doorway with her arms folded, tapping her foot. "Smooth, what's this all about? And make it quick, 'cause I don't appreciate you barging in on me like this, without calling first."

"I know and I'm sorry, but I wouldn't be here if this wasn't really important. And I didn't want to chance calling and messing things up." Smooth's voice was slow and steady. He was the picture of calm, something I'd always admired about him. That's why they called him *Smooth*.

"So you call showing up at my doorstep unannounced— with some strange woman, I might add—not messing up?"

"Clarisse, I'm sorry about that. But please just close the door first." Smooth gestured for her to come and sit. "This won't take long."

Clarisse shut the door, then sat on the arm of a chair and lit a cigarette. "So now you're inviting me to sit in my own house?" She threw her head back and chuckled. "What's going on?"

I stayed close to the door in case I had to make a run for it. Prison had taught me to always look for a means of escape. I glanced around the room, looking for alternate exits, but all I noticed was that the furniture was plain and cheap. There were a few pictures hanging on the walls and one was of a little boy who seemed to look like Smooth, playing little-league football. It was too far away for me to get a good look.

Clarisse and I eyed each other. She was an inch or two shorter than me and she was slimmer in stature, very model-like. She had medium-beige-colored skin, which was much lighter than mine and she wore a long weave ponytail. I knew hair, real and synthetic. The hair looked like it was Kanekalon.

Smooth rubbed his hands together as if he was about to make a proposition. "We need to ask you something."

She raised her eyebrows. "We?"

Smooth looked over at me. "Yes, she and I."

"I remember this woman getting all in my face the last time I saw her. That's all I know."

She looked me up and down.

Smooth took a deep breath. "That was years ago, wasn't it?"

The woman folded her arms. "Yes, it was, but it wasn't long enough for me to forget."

Smooth faced me. "And she's sorry for that, aren't you?"

Anger rose up in me. "Don't be putting words in my mouth."

He shot me a look.

"Okay, okay. Yeah, I'm sorry." I folded my arms too.

"See, she's sorry." Smooth pointed to me. "Besides, she went to jail behind that incident, remember?"

She rolled her neck. "Incident? That fool jumped on me."

"Fool?" I pretended to look around, then looked at Smooth. "Is she calling me a fool?"

"Yeah, you." She stuck out her neck.

Smooth shook his head at me. "Well, that's what she's sorry about. But we're here to ask you to help our son, who is sick."

Clarisse put up her hand in a halt position. "Your son?"

"The son I had with Trinity a few months before Desmond was born," Smooth hesitantly explained.

"Oh, so let me get this straight. What are you saying to me? You've got another son with this woman?" Clarisse nodded. "No wonder I couldn't get my child-support payments."

Smooth started, "Now, just listen to me for a minute—"

"I knew you had a woman." Clarisse stood up and got in Smooth's face. "That much was clear once she came in swinging like she was crazy. But you told me it was over between you two."

I stood up too. "Uh, excuse me, but that *her*—which is *me*—was his wife at the time."

"Trinity, please," Smooth pleaded.

Clarisse stared at Smooth as she lit a cigarette, then puffed out a stream of smoke. "That's even worse. You never told me you were married to her and you certainly didn't tell me you had a kid with her."

"Welcome to Club Smooth." I poked out my lips.

Smooth gave me his mean look. "Would you please be quiet?"

I took a deep breath and decided to control my outbursts.

Smooth explained, "Look, that was long time ago. Does it really matter now?"

Clarisse plopped back down onto the couch, still facing Smooth. "Yes, but the fact of the matter is, you told me you were through with her when you got with me."

"Oh, did he now?" I sat back down and nodded.

She turned to me. "Yes, he did."

"Very interesting." I crossed my legs.

"Ladies, ladies, please," Smooth interrupted.

I rolled my eyes in disgust. "Don't even say a word to me. I refuse to go back there even for a minute. You're a liar and a cheat. Always have been and the only thing I want from you is your help saving your son."

"So let me get this straight here, you two have a son who is sick?" Clarisse inhaled, then blew out a ring of smoke. "So what exactly does that have to do with me?"

I waved the smoke from my face, then turned my whole body toward Clarisse to explain. "Our son, Justin, is very sick. He has an aggressive form of leukemia."

She took the cigarette out of her mouth. "Isn't that kind of like cancer?"

I closed my eyes and counted to three in my head before answering. "It is cancer."

Silence filled the room.

"Oh." Clarisse shot a glance at Smooth. "So?"

"Let me explain something to you." I uncrossed my legs and decided to lower my guard.

"This coming here to your house like this is not my style at all. I would never have stepped to you about this, except that your son may be the only bone-marrow donor we have left. We've already tried everyone else in our family who could possibly match. So I'm coming to you as one mother to another."

Clarisse rolled her eyes. "I still don't understand why you need my son, though."

"Because like it or not, they're brothers." I pointed to Smooth. "They both have this man's blood running through their veins and because of that, there's a good chance they just might match."

She frowned up her face and shook her head. "I don't know about all of that."

I continued, "I'm told that it's a fairly simple procedure."

"It sounds too risky for my son." She stood up and folded her arms.

"The risk is very small, but the potential benefit to my son is big." I tried to hold back my emotion. "I can't stress enough how important this is and how little time we have."

Clarisse's eyes glanced back and forth between Smooth and me. "And why should I want to help either of you?"

"Just because it would be the right thing to do," I answered.

She hunched her shoulders. "Hmph, try again."

I pointed to Smooth, who stood slumped over against the wall. "Okay, because maybe somewhere deep down you cared for this man and you don't want him to have to watch his *other* son die."

The house smelled like a combination of cigarette smoke and lemons. At the rate she was smoking, I wondered if her son would need a lung transplant someday.

She looked at Smooth again, then back at me. "I don't know about this. It sounds scary."

"It's normal to be scared. So am I." I stood up and walked over to her. "Look, the truth is if you don't help us, my kid will die."

She continued to shake her head. "I don't know. I just don't know."

"That's fine. We'll give you time to think about it." I reached into my purse for a piece of paper, then wrote down my number and handed it to her. "Call me if you decide to help. In fact, call me even if you don't."

"I'll think about it." She batted her fake eyelashes.

"Either way, I think the boys should meet." I swallowed. "After all, they're brothers."

She looked at the number, then back at me. "Why haven't you wanted them to meet until now?"

"To tell you the truth, I didn't know your son existed until yesterday. There had been rumors of Smooth's infidelity many years ago, but I kept my suspicions to myself. Next thing you know we were divorced, so it didn't seem to matter anymore, I guess."

Smooth interrupted, "I'd like to say one thing."

"No one wants to hear from you." Clarisse snapped her fingers.

"At all," I added.

Smooth interjected, "Wait a minute. Doesn't what I say matter?

"Not really, no." I directed my attention back to Clarisse.

"Nope." Clarisse turned back to me.

"Thanks for your time." I opened the door and left, without looking back.

Clarisse didn't respond.

As soon as I walked outside, the sunlight hit my face. I stood on the top step, waiting for Smooth to come out. I deliberately left the door wide open so I could hear everything.

Smooth looked nervous. "I'd like to get together with Desmond one day soon."

Clarisse paused. "I'll bet you would. You never wanted to hang out with him before."

"I'm real sorry about that. I was always trying to keep things on the down-low. Now I guess it doesn't matter," Smooth admitted.

"What about money, Smooth? Child support. I haven't had a payment in over a year," Clarisse said.

I looked behind me.

"Things have been a little slow, but I'll catch up." Smooth opened his wallet and pulled out a twenty-dollar bill.

"Catch up? Food, clothes, things he needs every single day—you can't catch up." The woman snatched the money and stuffed it into her bosom. "There's no going back. Only moving forward," Clarisse spat out.

"I'm sorry." Smooth closed his wallet.

Clarisse looked him up and down. "That's the problem. You're always sorry. I don't have time for sorry. I have a boy to support every day, not just when you feel like it. You need to get real and be a father to your boy."

Smooth looked up at a school picture on the wall. "You're right. I'd like to get to know him."

Clarisse rolled her eyes. "I don't believe that, 'cause from what I hear you don't even know your other son, either."

Smooth took a deep breath. "No, I don't but I'm trying to change that."

"I'll tell you what . . . I have to work late tomorrow, so my friend was going to pick him up from school for me." Clarisse stared at Smooth as though she was contemplating. "I'll let you pick him up instead if you promise to be there on time."

"I swear." Smooth put his hand on his heart.

I remembered when Smooth used to promise me things when we were married, looking and sounding so sincere. He'd promise to take out the garbage, promise he'd take Justin to the park, promise to be home on time, and promise that he'd always treat me with respect. Promises were a classic Smooth move. Then sometimes before the day was even over, he'd have to apologize for some discrepancy again. Life with him was always a roller-coaster ride, sometimes up, but mostly down.

"He goes to school down at Jackson Street Elementary and he gets out at two-twenty. His class lets out of the double doors by the big oak tree. If he sees you, he'll recognize you. I'll tell him tonight that you'll be coming for him." Clarisse wrote on a slip of paper, then handed it to Smooth.

"Thanks." Smooth folded the paper and shoved it into his pocket.

Clarisse rolled her eyes. "Look, this is my one and only son we're talking about. Don't mess up."

Smooth grinned, revealing his gold tooth. "I won't."

"Hmph." Clarisse peered through the doorway and our eyes met. "You'd better get back to your wife or whoever she is. She looks pretty upset to me."

I listened intently to the details of their encounter and filed it all away in my memory for later use.

When Smooth finally came out, he drove me back to Aunt Ruby's. The car ride was quiet. I was done with Smooth and I imagined he was also done with me.

"I'll keep you posted." I opened my door and climbed out of his car quickly.

"Same here," Smooth answered before he pulled off.

I nearly stumbled onto the sidewalk as I approached Ruby's Red House. I pushed through the French doors, waved to Aunt Ruby before she could stop me, and ran upstairs. Once I was in my room, I squeezed into my uniform so I could work the second shift. Greeting people with a smile wasn't easy when I knew my son was suffering. Fortunately, I was able to get through it.

Afterward, I went back to the hospital to spend the night with Justin. Nothing else mattered. Nothing. I slept by his side, waking up off and on throughout the night as the nurses checked on him. I watched them continually stick him with needles and adjust his fluids.

The next morning, instead of waking up, Justin kept going in and out of consciousness.

Sometimes he was alert and sometimes he was totally incoherent. When he opened his eyes, I told him that I loved him. And when he closed them, I prayed he'd open them again. Nana and Aunt Ruby stopped by to see Justin. So did Smooth. Tyrone kept calling and leaving messages on my voice mail and I continued to ignore them. I didn't have time to play games with yet another person.

Finally, Dr. Stanford came in. "Justin's blood count is dangerously low. He also has a slight fever. I'm afraid that without a transplant in the next couple of days, he has a slim chance of survival." Dr. Stanford took Justin's file and left the room.

The words swirled around in my head, all of them. I stared at Justin's hollow eyes and touched his shiny bald head. It felt so tender. Suddenly, the cancer was closing in on me. I needed to tell Smooth about Justin's prognosis. I looked at the clock and realized that it was 2:45. I dialed his number but it went straight to voice mail each time I tried. Then I remembered that Smooth was supposed to pick up his other son, Desmond. I wondered if he'd make it there on time or if he'd miss this opportunity. Thoughts began to race through my mind.

I wondered if I could pick up the boy instead. If I could make it to Desmond's school in time, then convince Smooth to take the child to the hospital for the blood-donor test. After all, he was the child's father. He could sign the permission forms without Clarisse. Surely, it would only take a few minutes to pull his blood. His mother wouldn't even have to know until afterwards.

Then at least we'd know if he was a match. Then I could beg, borrow, or bribe her to let her son help me. I'd do anything, anything to save my son. I had Aunt Ruby's Cadillac outside. I had to hurry if I was going to get to Desmond's school on time. So I kissed Justin's cool face and whispered good-bye. I grabbed my purse and ran out of the hospital, headed straight for the parking lot. I jumped into the driver's seat of Aunt Ruby's car and sped away.

Luckily, Aunt Ruby had a built in GPS system so I typed in Jackson Street Elementary School and the directions immediately came up. I drove as fast as the speed limit would allow, bouncing through the pothole-filled streets, grateful I had finally gotten my license again. When I arrived at the side entrance where Desmond was supposed to be waiting, I stopped to look through the crowd. Smooth was nowhere around and I wasn't sure I'd be able to recognize the boy among all the other kids. I'd only seen his picture hanging on his mother's wall once. Then I saw a boy and I knew that it was him. He looked somewhat like Justin but exactly like Smooth, even more so than my own son. There was no mistaking him at all. I took a deep breath. This was my only chance. Take the boy, head for the hospital, then tell Smooth to meet me there afterward.

I rolled down the passenger window and stopped the car. "Hey, Desmond, come here."

The boy kept walking as if he was trying to get away from me. He was probably taught, like I taught my son, not to talk to strangers.

"I'm here to pick you up," I continued.

He ignored me and continued to walk.

I moved the car up a little, following him slowly. "I'm here to pick you up for your father, *Smooth*."

The boy stopped and turned toward me.

"I know your mother, Clarisse, is working late tonight. Your father is not able to come, but I'm here for you instead. Hop in my car and we'll meet him later." I stopped the car again.

"Okay." The boy reluctantly climbed into the passenger seat.

"Don't be afraid." I smiled. "My name is Trinity and I have a son about your age."

Desmond studied my face. "How do you know how old I am? Are you a friend of my mother's?"

The words were bittersweet. "No, not at all. I'm a friend of your father's."

Desmond stared at me. "Oh, how do you know him?"

I pulled off before anyone had a chance to notice anything. "We used to be very close for many years."

"I haven't seen him in a long time." Desmond hunched his shoulders. "My mom is real upset about it. "

I kept my eyes on the road. "Well, I'm sure she is."

"She says he don't deserve to be a father." Desmond looked as if he was waiting for my reaction.

I glanced over at him quickly. "I'm sure she didn't mean that. Sometimes people are just under pressure, you know?"

"I guess so." Desmond hunched his shoulders. "Is it okay if I listen to my music?"

"Sure, go ahead." I wanted him to feel comfortable.

I couldn't believe I had just picked up Smooth's son. I was going through a range of emotions.

The boy reached into his pocket and pulled out an iPod with funny-shaped earplugs.

"Do you like music, Desmond?"

"Yep." Desmond began tapping out beats on his book bag. "I'm going to be a musician one day, like my dad."

He stuck his earplugs into his ears and I could feel the vibrations of the music. It was clearly hip-hop.

I was headed to the hospital when someone cut me off at an intersection. I swerved, then hit the brakes. As my back tires were spinning on the pavement, the phone rang.

It was Tyrone. What timing. Something made me answer it. "I'm busy." I looked at the child, who was steadily bopping his head.

"I just want a moment of your time," Tyrone pleaded.

"I don't have a moment. I'm on my way to the hospital with Smooth's son," I snapped.

Tyrone sounded frustrated. "What? Did his mother give permission for that?"

"No, but his father will as soon as I can find him," I explained. "In the meantime, he's going with me. I picked him up from school."

"Are you serious?" Tyrone actually began to stutter. "You—you've got to take him home."

"Smooth can take him home later," I shouted.

Tyrone's voice was stern. "You've got to take him back now, Trinity. I mean, this can be considered kidnapping."

"I'm not a kidnapper." I looked over at the child, who was still listening to his music.

"Take him back now," Tyrone demanded. "You could go back to prison."

"No, I won't." My eyes filled with tears.

"Yes, you will." Tyrone explained, "The police don't know you like I know you. The judge is not going to care about your son's condition. Take him back."

"I can't. Justin is dying and all I need is to check his blood to see if he's a match. That's all." I kept driving.

Tyrone sighed long and hard. "But what you're about to do is wrong. Let him go, Trinity, before it's too late. God will make another way if it's His will."

Everything had seemed so clear at first and suddenly, I was so confused. "If it's His will. *If.* You're telling me my son hangs on an *if.*"

"You're better than that. I know you are." Tyrone's voice became calmer. "Justin will have no one to fight for him if you go back to prison."

At those words, I fell apart because no one had ever believed in me before. The boy took out his earplugs and stared at me as I cried on the side of the road.

Desmond tapped me on my hand. "Lady, are you okay?"

"I'll be fine." I dried my face, then turned the car around and drove straight to Smooth's place.

Smooth cracked the door just a little. "Oh, hey."

I leaned against the door. "I'm here with Desmond. You were late."

Smooth finally opened the door to me. "Aw, man. I forgot."

I walked inside, holding Desmond's hand. "You've been smoking again."

"Just a little. It's the stress." Smooth immediately began to spray and ran to open a window. "Hey, son. How are you, man?"

"Okay, I guess." Desmond looked confused.

"Stress. Right." I let go of Desmond's hand. "Well, here's your son."

Smooth opened his arms for a hug. "Thanks, Pud—I mean, Trinity."

I ignored Smooth's gesture and looked down at the little boy. "Good-bye, Desmond." A sadness crept over me as I turned my back to them.

"Bye and thanks for the ride." Desmond tugged on my sleeve.

I looked down at him again. "You're welcome." Then I looked up at Smooth. "I'm going back to the hospital to be with *our* son." I never looked back.

Smooth met me at the door. "Trinity I—"

I put my finger up to my lips as a single tear rolled down my face. "No, don't say anything."

Chapter 24

Once again I sat in the hospital cafeteria with Nana during her break. Since it was the evening, the cafeteria wasn't as full as it was earlier. There were no tempting aromas coming from the kitchen in the back. There were a few customers scattered about, but the tables were mostly empty.

Nana took my hand and I was shaking. "Have you been praying?"

I spoke softly. "Nana, I'm all prayed out."

"Nonsense." Nana shook her head. "There's no such thing."

"I'm just tired, Nana."

Nana's face hardened. "That's understandable, but that doesn't change the need and the need is that Justin get better."

I shrugged my shoulders. "Your prayers are always so much better than mine."

"Well, James five-sixteen says 'the effectual fervent prayer of the righteous availeth much.'" Nana bent her dainty mouth into a sweet smile. "And what about that nice young man who was helping you through this?"

"You mean Tyrone? He's the one who told me about Smooth's son." I now ran the risk of becoming upset all over again.

Nana wasn't smiling. "So?"

I couldn't look her in the eyes. "So I got mad at him and accused him of not being a friend."

"And why would you do a thing like that? When he told you about another potential donor, he just did you a favor."

"I know, but it still hurts." It was like being ten years old all over again.

Nana banged her fist on the table. "Hurt or not, you shouldn't have gotten angry with him when he wasn't even the one who wronged you."

"I don't know." I stuffed down the last of my banana-nut muffin and wiped my mouth with a napkin. "It just seemed like nobody was on my side at the time."

"Girl, that's a trick of the enemy. You've got me, your Aunt Ruby, that boy's father, your uncle, your sister, and even your mama in her own way. Most of all, you've got God Almighty and I'm sure He's not pleased with how you treated that gentleman." Nana's eyebrows began to meet in the middle.

"But I really didn't mean to."

Nana's face softened. "I know, but did you tell him that?"

I looked down at the table. "No, I didn't, but he stopped me from doing something very foolish since then, so . . ."

Nana nodded her head slightly. "So now you're really embarrassed?"

I closed my eyes. "Yes, I am."

"Well, swallow your pride and call him down here." Nana pushed her chair away from the table. "You owe him an apology and a thank-you."

"You're right." I stood up and hugged her.

"My break is over, but I'll talk to you later." Nana looked into my eyes, then pointed at me. "Go handle your business."

Nana was right as usual. Before I walked through the cafeteria doors, I decided to text Tyrone: PLEASE MEET ME AT THE HOSPITAL. THANKS, TRINITY. I fretted over it a few times, then finally hit send. Before I could push through the double doors, my phone rang.

It was Alyssa, calling to check on Justin's condition.

"Hi, Alyssa." I was glad to hear from my sister.

"Hi, how are you holding up?" Alyssa's voice was scratchy, as if she'd been talking too much. "How's Justin?"

"Right now he's stable, but his blood count is very low." I paused, remembering Nana's words about faith. "The doctor says he doesn't have much time, but I don't believe that."

Alyssa sighed. "Of course you don't. So what's next?"

I wasn't in the mood to hear Alyssa's mouth, but she had to know sooner or later.

"There's nothing next. We've exhausted all of our resources, except . . ."

"Except what?" Alyssa waited.

I knew there would be an outburst. "Except that Smooth has a son."

"He has a what?" Alyssa began to mumble under her breath. "When did this happen?"

"Apparently while he was married to me," I explained.

Alyssa yelled into the phone. "Oh no, he did not. I knew that no-good—"

"Look, I don't have time to talk about Smooth's escapades right now. I just found out about it myself, but I'm grateful." I closed my eyes as the enormity of the situation hit me.

"Nana and I have been praying for a miracle. I need the boy's mother to agree to test her son."

"Of course. She has to," Alyssa snapped.

"But she doesn't have to. She doesn't know or care for me. In fact, I once fought the lady years ago," I told her.

Alyssa sounded disappointed. "You fought her?"

"Yeah, I'd come to hook up with Smooth and found her at his apartment. It was right before I went away." I wasn't proud of what I'd done. "It's a long story, though."

Alyssa continued, "So, what does that have to do with anything? That was then and this is now. My nephew needs her help, so she's got to help."

I chuckled. "Well, thanks for that, Ms. Attorney. I wish you were here to convince *her* of that."

"I've got a heavy caseload, but I can fly in this coming weekend," Alyssa responded.

"Thanks." I looked around at all of the medical staff walking through the halls. "I'll let you know, but according to his doctor, that may be too late. We're praying for a miracle *now*."

Alyssa pretended to be choking. "Excuse me. Since when do you pray?"

Suddenly I realized that I hadn't really talked to my sister since she'd left. "Since I've had an encounter with God. Since I've had nothing else."

Alyssa's voice dripped with sarcasm. "Really?"

"Things are back to how they should be now, back to how they used to be," I explained.

"What are you talking about?"

I had to explain. "Do you remember when we were little and Nana used to take us all to church all the time?"

Alyssa paused. "Yeah."

"Well, things were good then and they're good again now. Good between me and God, that is." I walked back and forth, holding the phone close to my ear. "My visions don't even scare me anymore."

"Are you still having those?"

I continued to walk, looking down at my feet. "Of course, I am. I've always had them."

"Oh, I didn't know that." Alyssa was silent.

When I looked up, I saw Tyrone walking toward me. "Uh, yeah—but Alyssa, I'll call you back later. A friend of mine is here." Without even waiting for her response, I ended the call.

"That's good to hear." Tyrone grinned. "I wasn't sure I was still your friend."

Startled, my mouth opened wide but it took a minute for the words to come out. "I just sent out the text. How did you get here so fast?"

"Actually, I was already on my way down here, hoping that you'd be here and that you'd see me." Tyrone sat down in one of the waiting-room chairs.

Thanks for coming." I tried to force my lips into a smile, but I was unsuccessful.

"No problem." Tyrone leaned back in his seat.

I finally got the courage to look into his eyes. "I need to apologize for my behavior the other day. I didn't mean to—"

Tyrone waved his hands in front of him. "It's okay. No need to explain. I dropped a bomb on you and you reacted well . . . normally."

"Yeah, whatever normal is." I sighed.

"I'm sorry I didn't tell you sooner." Tyrone looked down. "I'm so ashamed."

"It's not your fault I didn't know." I shook my head. "I don't really blame you. I was just angry."

Tyrone looked sincere. "Now that I'm a different person, I'm ashamed to have been a part of it."

"Don't worry. It wasn't you committing the adultery." I couldn't look him in the eyes, so I looked around the room.

"No, but I knew about it, laughed about it. Even covered for him. I thought Smooth was cool back then. Didn't know any better, I guess."

I looked down to avoid eye contact. "I know how men are."

Tyrone's expression became more serious. "No, that's not how *all* men are. And I'm not *that man* anymore."

I finally focused in on his face. "It's okay, I forgive you. You don't have to convince me about who you are. I can see with my own heart that you're not the same man you were."

"Well, that's a good thing." Tyrone smiled and I noticed that he had trimmed his mustache.

"You're a good thing." I grabbed his hand. "Thanks for helping me and for being my friend this whole time, even when I've been so difficult."

"You haven't been so bad." Tyrone squeezed my hand, then separated his from mine. "You're just going through a lot all at once."

"Come on, you saved me from catching a kidnapping charge." I shook my head and curled my lips. "That's all I need."

"Okay, so you were a little irrational, but you have a good heart." Tyrone put both hands on his heart. "God judges the heart."

"I sure hope so." I looked away from him.

"I know so." Tyrone reached across the chairs and hugged me.

I felt a warmth I wasn't used to, but it sure felt nice. "Anyway, I'd better get back to Justin."

"I'd like to go with you to say hello." Tyrone's eyes lit up. "I've missed that kid."

I put my hand up to my face, trying to contain my emotions. "Yeah, I'm sure he's missed you too."

We both stood up and faced the direction of Justin's room.

Tyrone put his arm around my shoulders as we walked. "Everything is going to be all right."

"Because God is in control." I smiled.

"Yes," Tyrone agreed.

Suddenly we heard a familiar voice say, "You've got a lot of nerve, bruh."

I spun around on my heels and it was Smooth. "Smooth, don't even think about making a scene now."

Tyrone shook his head and stepped back. "Here we go again."

Smooth stepped up to Tyrone. "Are you kidding me?" Then he looked at me. "Is this who you want now?"

I walked right up to him. "I've already told you who I want or don't want is none of your concern. The only thing I want right now is for our son to recover."

A middle-aged nurse with brown and blond hair came up to us and spoke with a Caribbean accent. "May I suggest that you all lower your voices or we're going to have security escort you all out."

"I'm so sorry, ma'am." I shot a glance at Smooth. "Everything is under control, I promise."

Smooth threw up his hands. "Sorry, I don't want any trouble. I'm just here to see my boy. And to bring good news."

"I'm watching you." The nurse looked Smooth up and down, then walked away.

I stood in front of Smooth. "What good news?"

Smooth turned around and pointed toward the elevators. There was Clarisse and Desmond. "She agreed to at least let the boys meet."

I clapped my hands together and ran over to her. "Oh, thank you, thank you, thank you for coming."

She immediately put her hands out when she saw me coming. "I ain't promising nothing, except that they can meet each other. It's not the kids' fault who their trifling daddy is." She cut her eyes at Smooth.

She and her son were given the appropriate protective gear, mask and all, then they were led by a nurse to Justin's room. I followed behind them.

I was skeptical about leaving Tyrone and Smooth alone together, but I prayed that they would be able to settle their differences as mature adults. I knew Tyrone would not be the problem. Smooth, I wasn't too sure about.

We entered the room quietly and I walked over to my son's bed, leaving Clarisse and Desmond behind me. Looking from one boy to the other, I realized they could have almost been twins, except for that little part of Justin that marked him as my son, like the one dimple in his left cheek and my big eyes. Yes, he had my eyes and Mama had always teased him about it.

Other than those two features, he was his father's child, a little replica of him.

"Justin, baby, Mommy is here with someone I want you to meet." I rubbed his hand. "Do you remember when I told you about Desmond the other day? Your dad's Desmond?"

Justin was so weak he could only blink, but I knew he understood. I almost broke down right at that moment. *Lord, help me hold it together.*

"Well, Desmond and his mother are here to see you." I pulled up two chairs next to Justin's bed and motioned for Desmond to come. Then I sat down.

Desmond sat down next to me. "Hey, man. What's up?"

Justin nodded slightly. Desmond looked around the room.

"You can keep talking to him, honey, and he'll answer the best way he can. He's very weak." I couldn't take my eyes off of them.

"Okay," Desmond turned back to Justin. "So I hear that we're brothers. And that's cool, 'cause I always wanted a brother." Desmond looked up at his mother.

She didn't move or say a word.

"Anyway, I know you're very sick, but I just wanted to meet you. Maybe when you get better we can play together sometimes." Desmond looked directly at Justin. "Do you like football?"

Justin blinked his eyes twice, then moved his hand toward Desmond.

Desmond reached out to touch him and Justin wrapped his thin fingers around Desmond's. A tear slid down Justin's face.

An even bigger one slid down mine. "He loves football."

Then Justin closed his eyes and drifted off to sleep.

"He's asleep now, Desmond. It's the medicine in his IV." I pointed to the IV pole. "It makes him sleep through the pain."

"Okay, okay, I'll do it." Clarisse put her hands up to her eyes.

"Excuse me?" I looked up at her.

"I'll let Desmond test to see if your son can use his blood." Clarisse continued to smack her gum. "I don't hate Smooth that much. And that boy of yours hasn't done anything wrong."

"Thank you. Thank you so much." I grabbed her and hugged her.

She looked as if she was cringing under my touch, but I didn't care. In fact, I couldn't even remember when I stopped saying *thank you*, because it went on outside of Justin's room, all the way to the examination room and probably a good period after that. Then Smooth and I waited for Desmond's test to be over.

Tyrone had gone down to the cafeteria where he could wait and yet not be in the way. I thought that was very sweet of him. Nana stopped in as she was doing her rounds on Justin's floor. Aunt Ruby called to see if I needed anything. Even Mama called and left a message on my voice mail, although I couldn't answer her call. Everyone around me spoke love and everything around me spoke faith. I couldn't take the chance that a phone call from Mama would mess up the flow.

Smooth looked over at me after twiddling his big thumbs. "I'm sorry 'bout everything."

I looked straight ahead. "None of it matters anymore."

"It doesn't?" Smooth slid closer to me.

I smiled briefly. "No, I forgive you."

Smooth squinted his dark eyes. "You do?"

I closed my eyes and saw angels carrying me. "Yeah, 'cause I've been forgiven."

Smooth rummaged through his pockets until he found a piece of gum. "What in the world are you talking about, woman?"

"Something you're just not going to understand right now." I lifted my hands in a praying motion. "Nothing else matters except love and I've finally accepted that."

"So you do still love me?" Smooth stuffed the wad of gum into his mouth all at once.

"No, no, not at all." I giggled at his arrogance.

Smooth frowned up. "Then you love that Bingo dude?"

I waved my hands. "No, no. And his name is Tyrone, for the record."

Smooth stared at me. "So you love him, then?"

His ignorance was getting on my nerves. "I knew you wouldn't understand. I'm not talking about loving a man. I'm talking about the love of God, the kind of love that makes me love you, despite what you've done to me, or even love your baby's mama, Clarisse—everybody, anybody."

Smooth's already wide nose began to spread. "Your mama was right. Those visions have finally driven you crazy."

"Not at all. I have a sound mind. In fact, it's better than ever before. Back when I was locked up in that teeny-weeny cell, that's when I was losing my mind, waiting for every day to be my last day. Now, that's torture. And I didn't deserve that, but I've forgiven even that old lady who lied on me, who stole six years from me. I've got to love her too." I began to feel a spirit of joy come over me.

I remembered the day my court-appointed attorney came to visit me. He told me that a woman had confessed to the crime I'd been accused of. I was surprised and overwhelmed to hear that my sentence could be overturned. She was a middle-aged, dark-skinned, African American woman with a long curly weave that looked like mine and a height and weight similar to mine. She'd come into the diner that evening, ready to kill the Hartford family because of what they'd done to her daughter. As it turns out, the Hartfords had fired her daughter, with no explanation, six months earlier. Apparently, this unemployment happened at a critical time in the young lady's life, causing her to drop out of college. Then shortly afterward, she committed suicide. The real killer, a heartbroken mother, had snapped at the death of her only child, and set her mind on a killing spree of the ones she deemed responsible. Unfortunately, that evening, the real killer had looked very much like me. Same build, same hair, same complexion. That was how the police got an eyewitness account from a bifocal-wearing, Caucasian senior citizen, who perhaps thought that all blacks looked alike anyway.

"Yep, you've really lost it," Smooth confirmed.

"Nope. Actually, I used to be lost, but now I'm found. " I giggled at the thought of all I'd overcome.

When Desmond and his mother emerged, Smooth offered to take them home. I waved good-bye as I watched them all pile into the elevator.

I remembered that Tyrone was still in the cafeteria, so I sent him a text, asking him to bring me up a coffee. He brought up a coffee and a turkey-and-cheese sandwich.

"Thanks." I was so hungry that I gobbled it down.

"This time I'd like to see Justin, if you don't mind," Tyrone asked, before I went in to see Justin again. This time Tyrone came with me and sat while I watched Justin sleep. He prayed for Justin, then for me, and this time I didn't feel awkward. As I felt myself feeling tired, Tyrone said good-bye and slipped out quietly.

Somewhere in the middle of the night, Justin came down with a high fever, but I remained calm. As I saw his doctor and the nurses scrambling to get him stabilized, I closed my eyes and saw Justin playing with his brother. The image gave me comfort until morning.

When I opened my eyes, Dr. Stanford was standing over me. "What is it?"

"We've finally found a match for Justin: Desmond McGee. We'll need to get him in as soon as possible," Dr. Stanford said.

"Only by the grace of God." I allowed tears to run freely down my face.

With Dr. Stanford's words, the wheels were set in motion. I called Smooth and told him the news so that he could relay the message to Clarisse. Immediately, they transferred Justin to the bone-marrow transplant unit, then assigned to us a pre-transplant coordinator, Mrs. Conley. Mrs. Conley gave us the details concerning the series of tests that were done on him: a bone-marrow biopsy and aspirate, pulmonary function tests, echocardiogram, additional cardiac or stress tests, electrocardiogram, CAT scan, PET scan, bone survey, blood and urine tests, infectious-disease tests, psychosocial evaluation, and dental evaluation. Desmond also had his share of tests: blood work, chest X-ray, EKG, and a physical examination and health history.

Then Dr, Stanford spoke to Smooth and me. "You two have some papers to sign. I do want you to be aware of possible complications after the transplant, which include anemia, cataracts, damage to the kidneys, liver, lungs, and heart, bleeding in the lungs, intestines, brain, and other areas of the body, inflammation and sores in the mouth, throat, esophagus, and stomach—called mucositis— pain, stomach problems, including diarrhea, nausea, and vomiting, even delayed growth in children. Infections can also be very serious."

"Sounds a little rough," Smooth concluded.I remained silent as I prayed to myself.

"There is a possibility of graft failure, which means that the new cells do not settle into the body and start producing stem cells." Dr. Stanford looked over his papers. "Then there's also graft-versus-host disease."

I wanted to know everything."What's that?"

Dr. Stanford explained, "It's a condition in which the donor cells attack your own body."

I bit my bottom lip. "Oh, I see."

"Those are a lot of things to worry about." Smooth ran his hand across his head.

Dr. Stanford smiled for the first time."The risks are many, but the potential reward outweighs the risks."

I looked into his green eyes. "So the cancer should be gone?"

"If all goes well, then yes," Dr. Stanford confirmed.

I continued, "So what's next, Doctor?"

"We'll be monitoring his blood count and vital signs closely." Dr. Stanford pushed his glasses up on his nose. "He will continue to be fed by IV until he's better. He'll also be given antibiotics, antifungals, and antiviral drugs to prevent or treat infections, along with other medications."

I nodded. "Okay." It was done as far as I was concerned. I had to believe that it was done.

Dr. Stanford didn't look up from his clipboard. "He may need quite a few blood transfusions as well. It's just a part of the procedure."

"All right." I was ready.

Smooth didn't respond.

"He'll undergo a few days of chemotherapy or radiation, which will destroy bone marrow and cancerous cells and makes room for the new bone marrow. We call this the conditioning or preparative regimen. Then we'll put a flexible tube called a catheter into a large vein in his chest right above the heart."

I was a little shaky about that. "The heart?"

"Yes, this will help him get the fluids he'll need to receive without us running an IV through his hands." Dr. Stanford set his clipboard down on the table. "That's where we'll begin."

Smooth interrupted Dr. Stanford. "What about the surgery?"

"Well, there's actually no surgery involved for Justin. We'll perform the whole procedure right in Justin's room. Desmond, however, will endure a surgical procedure." Smooth stared at the doctor.

"What will happen to Desmond?"

It hurt me to see the love Smooth had for his other son, although I understood it.

"Since Desmond will be the donor in a bone-marrow harvest, that's done in the operating room. He'll be under general anesthesia. One needle will be inserted into the hip bone through the rear cavity. Unfortunately, he will experience several punctures to the skin on each hip and several punctures to the bone. I've already explained this to his mother."

"That sounds horrible," Smooth said.

Seeing Smooth's fear mixed with my own, I held back tears.

Dr. Stanford ignored Smooth's comment. "However, there are no stitches or incisions involved. Now, we need signed consents from both sets of parents before we can proceed with apheresis and transplant." He handed Smooth the papers and a pen.

Smooth signed, then passed them to me. I signed also. I stood up. "Thank you, Doctor."

"Thanks, man." Smooth also extended his hand to the doctor as he stood up.

Dr. Stanford shook Smooth's hand, then patted me on the shoulder. "At least we have a donor."

I shot a look at Smooth and he looked away. "Right."

"Doesn't Desmond's mom have to sign also?"

"Actually, she already has." Dr. Stanford held up the papers with her signature on it.

It was a miracle that she had agreed to the donor harvesting at all. *Thank you, Lord.*

By the time Dr. Stanford left and I'd turned around, Smooth was right in my face.

He was so close I could feel his breath. "What is it?"

"I miss what we had." Smooth reached out for my hand.

I slipped it away from him. "Yeah, it was good at first. A really long time ago."

Smooth began to lick his full lips, which was something I'd always responded to. "We can have it all again, baby."

I took a giant step sideways. "You don't understand. I have it all now."

Smooth shook his head. "What?"

"I've got everything I want. I was named Trinity for a reason. I've got the Father, the Son, and the Holy Ghost."

Smooth made his eyebrows touch. "You're crazier than I thought,"

"Maybe. But if that's the case, being crazy sure feels good." I smiled at my freedom. "Better than it's ever felt."

Chapter 25

Rosalee couldn't believe what she was hearing. She had been excited when she heard that her grandson had a donor. She hadn't bothered to ask the details, because it wasn't important at the time. Yet, it had been a month since Justin's transplant and there had been complication after complication, causing him to have multiple blood transfusions and stopping him from being discharged. Ruby Jean had called to give her an update on Justin's post-transplant condition and it was then that she'd found out the unthinkable. She just couldn't believe that it was true.

Rosalee raised her voice. "What do you mean that rascal has another son?"

"Yesiree, and the son was a perfect match for Justin," Ruby Jean said.

Rosalee could hardly believe what she was hearing. "Has he lost his mind, disrespecting Trinity like that?"

Ruby sighed at her sister's response. "I don't know about all that. I didn't call to make no trouble. Besides, that's in the past."

"No, that's in the right here and now as far as I'm concerned." Rosalee lifted herself off of the couch and began to pace the living room floor, something she did quite often.

Ruby decided she would defuse the situation. "Now, Rosalee, don't go putting your nose in where it doesn't belong."

"I'll put my nose anywhere I want and you sure can't stop me." Rosalee circled the couch, mumbling to herself.

"Rosalee, are you still there?"

Rosalee was seething with rage. "Of course I'm here. Where else would I be?"

"Anyway, I just wanted you to know what's going on with the child." Ruby hoped she could get out of this without more arguing.

"Oh, come on. Don't tell me you didn't call to cause no trouble." Rosalee sucked her teeth long and hard. "Trouble always follows you."

Ruby started, "Now look here, Rosalee Crawford—"

"I ain't no Crawford no more, either, so stop calling me that. I ain't married to *that* man no more now that he's six feet under."

"You're so morbid," Ruby Jean snapped. "Don't you have any respect at all for the dead?"

"Not when the dead don't have no respect for me." Rosalee stretched the phone cord as far as it could go. "Don't you worry about who I respect."

Ruby made her final plea. "Look, Justin has taken a turn for the worse. He's very sick, clinging to life. The doctors don't expect him to make it. Please keep that in mind."

"Well, what can I do about that now?"

"Rosalee, you're impossible." Ruby Jean sighed into the phone.

"Anyway, I've had enough of this conversation and definitely enough of you." Rosalee slammed the phone down, still mumbling to herself.

Rosalee didn't know what to make of the situation, except that it was scandalous, just scandalous. She knew that her daughter finding and marrying *that man* in *that city* was a bad idea. Why couldn't she have listened to her for once?

Rosalee thought about it for a moment as she shuffled back and forth; her nerves were a confused mess. She couldn't wrap her mind around the fact that Smooth McGee had made a fool of her daughter and disgraced the family name. He was probably at the hospital laughing at them all right now, she imagined. Not only that, but her mother-in-law, Pauline Crawford, was probably there too, poisoning Trinity's mind against her own mother. She'd be there at the hospital too, minding Trinity's business, no doubt. If Rosalee went to New Orleans and discreetly got rid of them both, no one would be the wiser. Besides, the world would be a better place without them, she decided.

Chapter 26

The family waiting area was so quiet at times that you could hear a pin drop and yet at other times you could hear the wailing of distraught family members as they lost a loved one.

Either way, the atmosphere was tense. The room seemed to be void of color and smells and life, just pale blue walls and soft-backed chairs. Doctors, nurses, and other medical staff moved about with delicate precision, wearing soft-soled shoes for comfort. Were they really comfortable, I wondered, or did they really feel their patients' pain?

Once again, Smooth and I sat and waited together at the hospital, except this time Clarisse, Aunt Ruby, and Nana sat with us. The allogeneic stem-cell transplant had been completed four weeks ago. It was now June and Justin's body still wasn't responding well to treatment. Dr. Stanford had ordered a round of antibiotics to detoxify his body from infection, but Justin continued to lie limp and unresponsive.

Smooth and I had taken turns going in and out of Justin's room, almost mechanically. We were weary and the stress had begun to show on each of our faces, although we didn't discuss it.

We simply held onto each other at certain moments as if we were feeding off of each other's strength.

Alyssa showed up while we were all talking in the waiting area.

I ran up to her as soon as I saw her. "Alyssa, what are you doing here?"

"I had to come and see my nephew." Alyssa readjusted her designer handbag. "I told you I might fly in."

Aunt Ruby interjected, "But we could've picked you up—"

Alyssa shrugged. "I took a cab straight from the airport. It was a last-minute flight, you know?"

Nana was the second person to greet her with a hug.

Alyssa looked into Nana's eyes and sighed. "I'm sorry about the last time, Nana. I—"

"Say no more about it. All has been forgotten." Nana patted Alyssa on the back, then returned to her seat.

Aunt Ruby fussed, "Well, you still could've called. I would've brought you a plate or something."

"That's all right, I'm not here for me. I'm here for Justin, remember?" Alyssa rolled her eyes at Smooth, then sat down beside Aunt Ruby. "How is he?"

"He's had everything from nausea, vomiting, diarrhea, and fever over the past few weeks and he's very weak, but he's alive," I explained.

"That's the truth." Nana threw up her right hand. "Glory."

"Alyssa, this is Desmond's mother, Clarisse." I looked from Alyssa to Clarisse and back again. "Desmond is the donor."

"Nice to meet you." Alyssa glanced back at me.

"Hi." Clarisse smacked her gum.

"Desmond is our little hero." I tried to hide the solemn mood I was in.

Alyssa turned back to Clarisse. "So how is your son?"

"He's doing fine," Smooth answered.

"Clearly, I was talking to her," Alyssa snapped. "Not to you."

"You always did have a big mouth," Smooth snapped back.

Alyssa frowned up her entire face. "And you were always scandalous."

"Alyssa, please." I jumped into the conversation just in time.

"All right, I'm sorry." Alyssa did her speak-to-the-hand stance. "It's just that when I look at him, he makes me sick."

"I'm not too happy seeing you either," Smooth taunted.

"Stop it, both of you. This is the last time I'm warning you or you'll both have to leave," I warned.

"The two of you are acting like children." Nana shook her finger at both of them. "This is a time to pray. Not fight."

"I got it," Alyssa confirmed.

"She's got a point there." Aunt Ruby shook her head so violently that her wig became crooked. "I don't see this much excitement except when I'm watching my reality shows."

Clarisse yawned. "To answer your question, Desmond is doing okay. His procedure was an outpatient one."

"Apheresis," Alyssa corrected. "I did some research."

Clarisse responded, "Yeah, that's it."

"So we've been waiting for Justin's blood counts to return to safe levels. It has been an uphill battle." I closed my eyes briefly as I pushed out the words. "Then he had a relapse and ended up with an infection. His visitors are limited, you know?"

"I know." Alyssa squirmed in her seat as if the chair didn't suit her. "I came to support you, mostly."

Clarisse quietly waved good-bye to everyone and left to go to work. Alyssa and I sat huddled together, arm in arm, until Dr. Stanford came out.

Dr. Stanford glanced at his clipboard before settling his eyes on me. "The parents may go in now, but just for a few minutes."

I waited to hear if there would be more words of hope or of encouragement, but there were none. "Okay."

"He needs his rest." Dr. Stanford walked away.

Then Smooth and I held each other as we started off to see our son. We slipped into our protective gear, then went in to see Justin. The grip of Smooth's hands was intense and the heat of his warm body felt comforting as he held onto me. As soon as we entered the room, I sensed that Justin was ready to give up.

I pulled myself away from Smooth and walked toward my son. "Justin, Jesus does love you, but that doesn't mean you're ready to go now." Everything in me wanted to collapse, but I had to hold it together. His pupils appeared to be dilated, yet they didn't follow me as I moved.

He didn't even acknowledge that we were in the room. I touched his forehead and his body felt cool to my touch. I knew that death was in the room to steal my son. I could feel it. With the dry, cold air in the room, I could taste it. I dropped to my knees beside Justin's bed and began to pray.

"Father, God, only you know the outcome of this situation. Only you know what we need. May your will be done in my son's life and mine. And may I be able to accept whatever the outcome may be. In your precious name, Jesus. Amen."

When I looked up I saw that Smooth had bowed his head. I smiled through the tears that were building up behind my eyelids. Then I closed my eyes to calm myself and pray. I began to recite the 23rd Psalm, then the 27th. The words comforted me: *Yea, though I walk through the valley of the shadow of death, I will fear no evil . . .*

I watched the monitors and the slow drip of the IV. I talked to him as much as I cried out to God, but Justin was no longer responding. I could tell that his breathing and pulse were faint. Would he even live through the day?

My heart ached at the notion that I could lose my only child. Yet, at that moment, I was willing to let him go. He had been through so much pain. How could I selfishly want him to endure anymore? I'd been on my knees praying and kissing Justin's limp hand, when suddenly, I saw a flash of light.

I closed my eyes and there Justin was sitting upright, looking healthy, and at that moment I knew that Justin would be all right. I didn't know how or when he would begin to get better, but I knew he would live. Immediately there was a peace that covered me while I was in Justin's room. Smooth came up from behind me and grabbed my hands, trying to comfort me. I felt sorry for him because I knew he was the one who needed comforting. I placed my head on Smooth's shoulder as I watched Justin struggle to breathe.

"I can't stand to see him like this." I placed my head on Smooth's shoulder as I watched Justin struggle to breathe. "I want this to be over."

Just as I had spoken, Justin's machine beeped. His heart rate had decreased to almost nothing. "Get some help. My baby is flatlining," I ran out to the hallway and shouted.

The emergency staff came in and ushered us both out as they went about their duties, trying to get his heart to beat again. This all looked too familiar. I remembered the first day in the ambulance and how I'd prayed. We'd come so far since then, almost full circle. I knew God wouldn't leave me.

Nana grabbed me. "What happened, child?"

"I think Justin may be going into cardiac arrest. At least, that's what I heard one of the nurses say," I explained.

"It's going to be all right," Nana said.

I nodded. "I know it is, Nana. This time I know that it's going to be just fine."

As Nana began to pray for Justin, I heard shuffled footsteps. The rhythm of them was familiar. So I turned on my heels and saw Mama.

Mama was right up on Smooth as though she was going to hit him with a bottle.

"Smooth, watch out." I pointed to Mama.

Smooth ducked and Mama ended up swinging against the air. Thankfully, Nana caught the bottle before it smashed into a thousand pieces.

"See, Trinity, you do still love him," Mama spat out.

I shook my head. "What's wrong with you, Mama?"

Aunt Ruby and Alyssa grabbed Mama by the arms and restrained her.

Alyssa shook her head. "Is this what you came to New Orleans for?"

"I came to get him because of what he's done and I came to get my daughters back."

Mama squirmed against her restraints.

Smooth looked down in shame and didn't say a word.

"Well, I can't blame you for wanting to hurt Mr. Smooth McGee. We all do." Alyssa looked at him and rolled her eyes. "But your daughters were never gone. We were just angry because you did us wrong." Alyssa spoke firmly. "You should've let us have our father."

"I'm sorry. I was wrong." Mama's arms became limp. "I guess I though he wouldn't be that important to you if I kept him out of your lives like I did."

Nana spoke up. "Why did you hate me and my son so much after all these years?"

Mama stood up tall to face Nana. "I was tired of your son 'cause of the life we had together."

Nana didn't back down "But is it fair to have blamed him for everything, Rosalee?"

"Maybe. Maybe not. Truth is, I was afraid of you," Mama said.

Nana pointed to herself. "Afraid of me? Why would you be?"

"Something about you was beautiful and powerful and I was kind of jealous of ya."

Mama hung her head down. "Seemed like you had so much and I had nothing. Seemed like you loved him and my kids so much."

Nana stood right in front of Mama. "Yes, and what's wrong with that?"

"I ain't never had nobody love me like that. Not your son. Not even my own mama. Nobody." Tears began to run from Mama's light eyes.

"That's not true. All of us here love ya, Rosalee." Aunt Ruby threw her arms around Mama.

Despite the vision I had earlier, I was shaking. "Quiet down, please. My son is busy fighting for his life." I was in a daze.

Mama looked at my red, swollen eyes, then realized something was wrong. "What's happening with Justin?"

Silence filled the room. Smooth closed his eyes. Alyssa cast her eyes downward. Aunt Ruby grabbed my hand and Nana put her hands up against her lips in a praying form.

Then Dr. Stanford came out of Justin's room and said, "I'm sorry." And everything went black.

Epilogue

It was a beautiful August day. The sun shone brightly over Ruby's Red House. The smell of fresh Louisiana iris wafted through the air. It had been two months since Justin's transplant and one month since the day Justin's heart stopped beating. Miraculously, just as the doctors had given up on him and were about to pronounce him dead, his heart began to beat again. Knowing that my son was alive and recovering made mine begin to beat again too.

All was finally right with my world now that things were right with my Creator. I'd not just gone to prison, but I'd been a prisoner of my own mind. I smiled to myself at how foolish I was to believe I could ever live without the Lord. I shook my head as I thought of all the time I'd wasted. *Thank you, Lord, for your patience, mercy, and grace.* There was that word again, except this time I knew for sure I'd experienced it. Even in my lowest hours, I'd experienced it.

Glory to your name, Lord.

Suddenly, there was a knock at my room door.

"Come in," I shouted.

To my surprise, it was Tyrone. He walked over to me. "Leaving so soon?"

"I'm trying." I barely looked up. When I did, my eyes caught his and I stopped packing.

I sat down on the love seat and he sat beside me, leaving enough space for us to face each other comfortably.

He was dressed simply in blue denim jeans and a plain white T-shirt. It was nothing extravagant, but that was just his way. His smile was enough to light up the whole room, though. I knew that I'd miss him once I was gone.

I crossed my legs. "What brings you by here so early?"

"Are you kidding me? Did you think I wouldn't stop by to say good-bye?"

I hunched my shoulders. "I don't know. I figured you might be busy."

"Not that busy." Tyrone was staring at my face. "I've got a surprise for you."

"Oh, I love surprises." I peeked at the wall clock. "What is it? 'Cause I've got to hustle."

"I see." Tyrone looked up at the clock also. "But haven't you been hustling all your life?"

Tyrone was right about that. Ever since I could remember, I'd had to hustle for something or another.

"It's time to relax and enjoy life a little," Tyrone said.

I closed my eyes, then let out a long breath. "That sounds nice, but I've got to take care of my son."

"But who is taking care of you?"

I didn't answer. "Yeah, me and Justin have got to get back to Baton Rouge. We've got to leave now that Justin has been released. Ruby's Red House is no place to raise a little boy, especially not one recovering from leukemia." I stood up and continued folding clothes.

"Besides, he's already missed enough school for the year and they say he won't be able to return to real school for another four months. I've got to make special arrangements for him to be homeschooled."

"Homeschooled?"

"Yeah, there are some online programs and stuff. I'm sure I qualify for some assistance too." I plopped back down, sighing. "Yeah, I've got to transfer his medical records, set up at home care, then get him registered—"

Tyrone interrupted, "Well, that takes care of Justin, but what are you going to do when you get there?"

"Hopefully, I can get my job at the gas station back while I go to beauty school and look for a better job. My attorney promised that I'll receive a big settlement at some point, but who knows when that'll be." I shook my head. "Everything is tied up in litigation right now."

"What if you don't have to go back to Baton Rouge?" Tyrone pointed to the door.

"What are you talking about?" I peeped over at the door as if I was really expecting to see Baton Rouge. "Justin has missed enough school this year. It's time for him to get back to his school and friends."

"What if you could live here? Couldn't Justin meet new friends?"

"I guess so, but what reason would I have to stay? My search is over and thanks to you I got more than I bargained for." I shrugged. "It's all good, though."

Tyrone looked embarrassed. "Again, I'm really sorry that things didn't work out between you and Smooth, but I think meeting Desmond was a good thing."

"Yes, it was definitely a good thing." I nodded. "My son being asleep in the next room proves that."

Tyrone stood up and walked over to me. "But what about you?"

I pointed to myself and mouthed the words, "What *about* me?"

"What about what you want?"

I shook my head. "I don't know if I have a right to want anything else. God has been so good to me already."

Tyrone reached into his pockets and pulled out a business card, then handed it to me. "What if I told you that I talked to a friend of mine who owns Benny's Barbershop on Water Street and convinced him that he needs to get a hair stylist in to help him with female cuts and maybe even braids?"

"Are you kidding me?"

"No, I told him it's about time he got a partner to help him bring variety to the shop. You know you could help him make it into a unisex salon. I mean, he's always complaining about females asking him to cut their hair." Tyrone threw his head back and laughed. "It's really not his specialty."

My mouth dropped wide open. "I don't know. I don't have my license yet or anything. I'd have to finish school first."

"Well, I've got that covered too," Tyrone added.

"What do you mean?"

"I did some research and as long as you don't do perms or deal with any chemicals, you don't have to have a cosmetology license just yet. In the meantime, your work can actually be considered an apprenticeship."

"Really?" I squinted at him. "How did you know that?"

"Well, I've got another friend of mine who owns an African braid shop in New York and she's never been to cosmetology school." Tyrone started slapping his hands together. "She's doing good, making money, and it's all legit."

I shook my head, in awe of his resourcefulness. "Wow, you've got a lot of friends, huh?"

Tyrone threw up his hands. "I'm a friendly guy."

"I see." I couldn't stop smiling. "It would take time to get customers, to build my clientele. I don't know. How would I be able to pay rent while I do my cosmetology course?"

Tyrone didn't seem to entertain my doubts. "And Benny has a cute little apartment over his shop that he's willing to rent out to you for half price if you work for him."

Then I started to dream for a minute. "Maybe Aunt Ruby would let me work here part-time until business picks up."

"Yep." Tyrone gave me the thumbs-up signal.

"I'm impressed. You seem to have everything all figured out." I sat back down in a daze, then looked up at him. "Why do you care what happens to me?"

"Because I was told to love my neighbor as myself." Tyrone chuckled.

I gave him the eye.

Tyrone's face became serious. "Especially when that neighbor is as beautiful as you."

Nodding, I began to get the idea. "Are you sure Benny won't mind a woman working in his shop?"

"Nah, Benny is almost an old man. And he has no family, either. My guess is he'll be needing someone who can take over the shop totally in a few years. He won't be able to handle the business on his own much longer," Tyrone explained.

I jumped out of my seat. "When can I meet Mr. Benny?"

"As soon as you're ready," Tyrone answered.

I reached for Tyrone's hand and shook it. "And how can I ever thank you?"

Tyrone grasped my hand in his and pulled me toward him. "How about you let me take you out?"

I looked into his dark brown eyes. "You've already taken me *out*."

Tyrone explained, "No, I mean *out* on an official date."

I thought about it for a moment, then fluttered my eyes at him. "Okay, it's a deal."

"I just have one more question." Tyrone fiddled with his mustache.

I put my hands on my hips. "What is it?"

He looked directly into my eyes. "What about Smooth?"

"Those days are over, including all of the other mess I carried around in me." I demonstrated the stop signal with my hands. "No more. The only thing I'm carrying now is peace."

Tyrone seemed to breathe a sigh of relief. Then he gave me a quick but gentle hug before backing away. "I like the way you talk, Ms. Trinity."

"Me too, Ty." I could feel myself blushing. "Me too."

For the first time I was not ashamed of my name. It suited me just fine. No more fears or doubts. Just living the life God gave me, knowing it would all fit together for His glory. By the grace of God, it would all fit together for *when kingdom comes.*

About the Author

Ashea S. Goldson, originally from Brooklyn, New York, and now residing in a Metro Atlanta suburb, is a graduate of Fordham University who is honored to call herself a *kingdom writer*. She is a down to earth author, freelance writer, and entrepreneur who loves her family, friends, students, and ministry. After spending over twenty years as an educator and co-owner of a Christian school, she now spends her days indulging her creativity as a full time writer and screenwriter.

As a Black Expressions bestselling author and award winning poet, with an insatiable passion for the written word, she continues to write books, songs, poetry, plays, and screenplays. She is currently working on her eighth Christian fiction novel, along with a number of creative projects, including the launch of a film production company.

An avid reader and a continual supporter of literacy, she also tutors students in reading and writing. In addition to this she hosts a blogtalkradio show called WordThirst Authors & Gospel Showcase which highlights the work of other like-minded visionaries. Feel free to contact her at asheagold@yahoo.com. or log onto www.asheagoldson.com.

DISCUSSION QUESTIONS

1. What did you think about Trinity's mother's abrasive behavior?
2. Why do you think Trinity's mother kept her father's death a secret?
3. Why do you think Trinity's mother was so negative about Trinity returning to New Orleans?
4. Did you think that Trinity made the right decision when she went back to New Orleans?
5. What did you think about Smooth McGee? What did you think about Trinity and Smooth's relationship?
6. How did Nana help Trinity come to terms with her gift of prophesy?
7. Do you think that Trinity did all she could for her son?
8. Do you think that Tyrone really helped Trinity? If so, how?
9. Do you think that Trinity and Smooth will be reunited? Why or why not?
10. Do you think that Tyrone and Trinity will become more than friends? Why or why not?
11. Did you think that Justin might die?
12. Did you think that Trinity would find a donor for her son? What did you think of Clarisse? What did you think of Smooth and Clarisse's relationship? What about Smooth and Desmond's relationship?
13. Do you think Aunt Ruby was a help or a hindrance?
14. What do you think finally turned Trinity's heart toward God?